LAST MÉTRO TO
BLEECKER STREET

A NOVEL BY

PETER EMANUEL GOLDMAN

This is a work of fiction. Names, characters, businesses, places, events and incidents are either the products of the author's imagination or used in a fictitious manner. Any resemblance to actual persons, living or dead, or actual events is purely coincidental.

Cover photo and all interior photos by Peter Emanuel Goldman, except the photo on page 113.

Also by Peter Emanuel Goldman

FILMS

Echoes of Silence

Wheel of Ashes

The Sensualists

Pestilent City

Night Crawlers

NBC in Lebanon: A Study of Media Misrepresentation

BOOKS

The Media's War Against Israel
(Co-Editor)

The Arab-Israel Conflict
(In Danish)

The Other Refugee Problem: Jews From Arab Lands
(In Danish)

For Glenna and Stasia

From the beginning it was never anything but chaos; it was a fluid which enveloped me, which I breathed in through the gills. In the substrata where the moon shone steady and opaque, it was smooth and fecundating; above it was a jangle and a discord. In everything I quickly saw the opposite, the contradiction, and between the real and the unreal the irony, the paradox.

Henry Miller, Tropic of Capricorn

A chassidic rebbe was once asked: "If you could save one thing from your burning nume, what would it be?" "The fire," ansered the Rebbe, "because it is the 'brenn' [the fire, the passion] which makes life worth living." Indeed, without an inner fire burning in the soul of man, there is no real life. Life becomes meaningful when man "burns from within" for his ideals and his determination in life.

Rabbi Dr. Nathan Lopes Cardozo

The body is called a "small city." Just as two kings wage war over a town, which each wishes to capture and rule … so do the two souls—the Divine and the vitalizing animal soul that comes from the kelipah [shell of impurity and evil]—wage war against each other over the body and all its limbs.

Rabbi Schneur Zalman of Liadi, the Tanya

And just before I turn to stone, I catch one kindling eye, that signals "You are not alone," for all must sin who die.

Josef Attilla (Hungarian poet).

Preface

The eternal conflict between religion and sex, the spirit and the demands of the body, this life versus reward and punishment in the world-to-come, have always been major themes in my life and in the lives of many of my friends. So, too, for the characters in *Last Métro to Bleecker Street* who spend much of their time desperately longing and searching for experience and sex in the Greenwich Village and Paris of the 1960's. Yet, these despairing and sensitive souls, who haunt the streets and cafes, are also searching for meaning and, eventually, for God.

Belgian writer, Maurice Maeterlinck, expressed it well: "We think we have discovered a horde of wonderful treasure trove, and yet when we emerge again into the light of day we see that all we have brought back with us is false stones and chips of glass. But for all this, the treasure goes on glimmering in the darkness, unchanged."

While there have been many books about the Sixties, most of them are either political (Vietnam, Kennedys, Mississippi) or icon-cultural (Woodstock, Beatles, Rolling Stones), or a kind of upbeat artistic memories. I spent the Sixties shuttling mostly between Paris and Greenwich

Village with a little time in Denmark, Providence, R.I. and P-Town and knew many of the main players. Yet for me and the friends I knew, the Sixties was personal, mostly desperation and despair, the torn lining of the gleaming coat. We were lost souls. It was neither rock nor politics. It was cafes and cafe conversation, folk music, poetry, sexual hunger, irreconcilable conflicts, despair, aimlessness and chaos.

Our main literary influences were Henry Miller, Jack Kerouac, Camus, Hesse and Dostoevsky. Other writers we read avidly included John Dos Passos and anything by Thomas Mann, Kafka, Musil, Remarque, Tolstoy, Orwell, Waugh and Nathanael West. We were also fascinated by the mystical writings of Gurdjieff, Ouspensky and Tibetan mysticism such as the Tibetan Book of the Dead.

In poetry there was Blake and his mysticism and Rimbaud for his youthful despair. Of course, we read the beat poets, Allen Ginsberg and Gregory Corso. But Blake and Rimbaud were closer to our souls. We were also fascinated by T.S. Eliot. Each of his lines seemed to contain so many hidden meanings.

In France there was Céline, his writing filled with a vicious cynicism and hatred for everything bourgeois. I also liked reading the more stylized work of Mauriac and Maurois, and who could forget Francoise Sagan's *Bonjour Tristesse* and Simenon's Inspector Maigret.

Our favorite haunts were the Figaro, Rienzi and the Cedar Tavern. Later it was the Improv, filled with theatre people after work. In Paris it was the Café Monaco at the Place de l'Odéon.

Our musicians were first and foremost the folk, bluegrass, and blues musicians: Leadbelly, Mississippi John Hurt, the Carter Family, Pete Seeger, Joan Baez, Woody Guthrie, the Stanley Brothers, Scruggs and Flatt, Bob Dylan, The Mamas and the Papas, The Kingston Trio, Bob Gibson, The Weavers.

Occasionally I played in Washington Square Park, on Paris streets and my guitar accompanied me everywhere. I believed that as long as I could sing, my despair would never totally destroy me. Now that I'm in my 80s, I've stopped singing and I wish I knew how to begin again.

I did a fair amount of street singing before it became popular and in 1975 I made an LP record in Denmark... my own music and songs, but influenced by American country, bluegrass, blues and folk music.

I knew many of the famous painters and posed for some of them including both Soyer brothers. My favorite was Larry Rivers. Those large incomplete canvases he worked on in his West Village loft seemed to contain hidden, unspoken meanings. I was 19 when I first met him, and he seemed to represent all that mysterious, bohemian experience I craved. Of course, I didn't know he was sleeping with my girlfriend at the time.

The filmmakers who fascinated us were Godard, Truffaut, Antonioni, Shirley Clarke, Cassavetes, Bergman, Agnes Varda (*Cléo de 5á7*), though my favorite film was by the little-known French director, Alain Jessua, *Life Upside Down*.

And, of course, there was sex. Sex filled the vacuum in our lives — at times it was nearly all-consuming — but as we veered towards insanity, all that remained was chaos, until some of us found God. This caused a different kind of chaos and confusion. Many others became intellectuals or artists or became insane.

Now, 60 years later I worry about illness, money, my children, religion, death, a world spinning out of control, the next world. Too many fears. Sex now seems relatively unimportant, but it was important to us when we were young. At times, it was all consuming.

During this period I became rather well known as an "Underground" filmmaker. My first full-length film, *Echoes of Silence,* became a classic of the New American or "Underground" cinema. Later films, including the short, *Pestilent City*, and the feature, *Wheel of Ashes*, (shot in Paris after Jean-Luc Godard arranged a scholarship for me) won critical acclaim. Later, when I became politically aware after the slaughter of the Israeli athletes at the Munich Olympics in 1972, I had my first awakening as a Jew.

I also did a "B" film, *The Sensualists,* which played on every 42nd Street in the United States. In between films I did some still photography. During my travels the negatives became lost, but 50 years later they arrived in a package sent from Paris to Miami. This has led to three exhibitions and a book of my photos. Despite this creative activity, inner turmoil drove me almost to suicide. The same can be said for many of the people I knew. I think drugs, especially LSD, contributed to the mental weakness. Two fools from Harvard, Alpert and Leary, were telling us how wonderful LSD was. They helped destroy a good part of a generation.

The founder of the Hasidic movement, the Ba'al Shem Tov, said that there were 42 stages in a person's life, equivalent to the 42 journeys taken by the children of Israel in the desert after leaving Egypt. This book covers part of the journey.

The poems in the chapters about Kelly are written by "Kelly." Kelly's poems have never been published, yet I still think that she is one of the greatest American poets. The people I cared about had haunted eyes, needs, passion, sensitivity, with lonely footsteps echoing on silent streets. Seekers. This book is for them.

Kindling Eyes

DAVID, 1960

My philosophy paper on suicide is due tomorrow, and if I don't turn it in I won't graduate—yet more powerful than the mind and logic—more powerful than Wittgenstein, Berdyaev, Heidegger, Kierkegaard and Nietzsche is emotion... and the most powerful emotion is sex... and sex incarnate is lying naked on my bed, her Brobdingnagian breasts and scared brown eyes pointing at the ceiling.

I think of the Yankees to ease the intense desire. Clothes strewn on the floor, I lie next to her and caress her huge breasts. She doesn't move or react. Nothing.

I can't wait anymore and I move on top of her cataleptic body, spread her legs a little with my hand and push my way into her. She is dry, tight, unmoving. As I come, the first thought to enter my mind is a quote from Camus, "There is but one truly serious philosophical problem, and that is suicide."

A year ago, I almost committed suicide after months of deep despair and helpless depression. Suicide is not just a philosophical problem. It lurks within me. The possibility is always there.

Susan is still lying on her back, her eyes staring at the ceiling, not at me. I don't know what her problem is. Fear? Frigidity? Dislike? So many American women have sexual problems... men, too. We are all confused.

I take my guitar, sit on a chair, the instrument covering my nakedness, and start strumming some blues. Finally, Susan stirs and sits up.

"I'm not used to this," she says.

"Neither am I."

"I'll bet…"

I want to say something nice to her to make her feel better, but I don't know what to say. I was never any good at mouthing polite banalities. I usually remain silent.

Even though the sex was not good, I feel relaxed, the need satisfied. It's the idea of possessing a sexy woman, which is the most important thing, not the act itself. After a few days, the need will return, controlling me, or, at least, a good part of me.

Outside, twilight—soft campus sounds. In three weeks, I will be on my way to Europe. I am nervous... the unknown, vast, frightening.

Two days later I am sitting in a windowsill in the main building at Bennington watching all the gentle, longhaired, artsy girls walk by. It is too much for me. I have gotten shy and self-conscious. With so many girls to choose from, it becomes too obvious. I withdraw into myself and cannot approach anyone... only stare. The girls like my long hair, bohemian, poetic look. At least many of them do. Some of them are frightened, since all the other young men have short, neat hair or crew cuts.

A pencil-thin girl with a haunted look approaches me and says, "You're a Gemini, aren't you?" She's right, and it makes me wonder if there isn't some truth in astrology. I sense that she's picking me up, but I'm not interested in her, so I only smile and nod.

Outside, Bennington is trees, flowers, grass, woods, missed opportunities and unrequited or un-acted-upon longings.

In Boston, walking the familiar streets the night before graduation, I try to make sense of who I am and why I am. I agree with Heidegger who places human existence before an essence—God—that may or may not exist. Without God there is only a human ethic and everything is possible. I have total freedom, but this freedom means constant indecision, fear, chaos. I can go left or I can go right.

I have no direction; I do not know who I am. I have my music, my books, my smile, my fears. Why can't I be like Camus' Meursault and overcome my fears by realizing that everything is absurd... that "nothing has the least importance." That's how I would like to be, but I am not. I *do* care what happens to me, yet I don't know why.

* * *

It should be paradise but it really seems more like the opposite. Seth and I and 200 high school girls aboard the *S.S. Orania* on the way to Europe. Every one of them seems to be in love with me and I don't know whom to choose. There's never any place to go, anyway, and most of them are virgins… afraid. If I was frustrated before the trip, it's worse now. There *is* a god and his name is irony.

Early morning… awake in the dock. Sounds of voices with strong cockney accents. Feeling strange, alone, frightened. What am I doing here? Where do we go from here? Leaving the ship, this high school girl hands me a 95- page love letter.

"David, I have found your name is David through my Chapel Hill friend who found it out from your Chapel Hill friend. I am standing at the side of the ship now, looking at the black water and thinking of you. I think, David, that I am falling in love with you, though I know only a little bit about you. But would you believe how much I have thought about that little? I will tell you, David, what I know about you and why I love it.

"David, the first time I saw you I loved you! This doesn't happen often, but it is even more of a miracle, because before I saw you I was sure, with old-world weariness, that I would *never* love anybody again, after all my terrible affairs, which it is better to announce than to hint at, since you, David, lovely David, have dispelled their gloom!

"I adore you. I am sitting here in my top bunk hugging myself, and scribbling with adoration for you, you darling, you joy. But why do we have to have spaghetti? And why am I so fat. *Now* you think I'm a fat, nervous, awkward, little, hair-ribboned Chapel Hill girl. Oh, what merriment! David, every time I meet your eyes I feel like jumping across the table and dancing around in circles with you in wild glee. This is the effect you have on poor girls; they drop in your path, *darling*. What a boy! What a boy!

"Oh, but David, my David, you don't know, you think I am this stupid little girl with a crush on you, when really I am a *goddess*. Oh, how I love you.

"Gail"

I am flattered, but don't know what to say. She is plain ... Not my type… But this is the way it always is. Why can't she be another?

England is rain. Seth and I have rented a Deux Chevaux Citroen and drive to Oxford after spending the night in a London youth hostel. Most of our spare time in England is spent in pubs learning to play darts. When they hear we are Americans, they talk politics. Pub politics seem to agree that Eisenhower is an old man who has been conquered by events, and that the U.S. needs a young energetic president.

Two hundred girls in love with me on a ship and I never got laid once. I am horny. Pain, passion and chaotic poetry give me a haunted look like a Dostoevsky character.

In Holland the sun is shining, which is a relief after so many days of rain in England. The country is beautiful and the women are sexy. They all seem to have muscular legs, like athletes. But I am feeling shy as Seth and I sit in a restaurant in Rotterdam, where I open my phrase book and try to learn a few words in Dutch…

Seth is driving as I look out of the window at the flat, but lovely, country. The sand dunes on the beach are the country's highest mountains. There are not too many cars; almost everyone rides bikes, or motorbikes. A few thinly-planted trees are scattered here and there with small egg-shaped haystacks rising in rows from the earth. Field upon field stretches out in the distance containing vegetables, red-roofed houses and, of course, windmills.

As we pass through the towns we notice the traditional Dutch costumes still being worn by the older generation, but not by the younger generation, of course. Their favorite music is American rock and roll.

Vlissingen, a small resort town on the coast. We park the Deux Chevaux, called "Ugly Duckling" in Dutch, near the center. There is a carnival in town and we wander over. Everyone is busy putting up the rides and the stands. I become friendly with the family that runs the carnival. They have a young daughter, blonde, blue eyes, teenager... very shy. When she hears we are Americans she produces a guitar and tells me she loves rock and roll. I take the guitar and start playing—not rock and roll—but folk and bluegrass music. Soon a crowd of Dutch kids has gathered—light-haired, lively, expressive, beautiful kids. They appreciate my music. I look up. A beautiful girl with reddish hair is looking at me. I smile at her and receive a warm smile back.

Annika is an athlete, a javelin thrower, yet she is thin and lithe. We are walking to my hotel, my arm around her shoulder. I need her badly, but, as we mount the stairs, the owner of the hotel blocks our path. She spreads her five fingers across her face indicating jail. Annika does not look more than her 17 years. We leave. We cannot go to her place since she lives with her parents. I'll find a place, I say, but it is now becoming sordid and she is getting nervous and has to go home. I have lost her. My depression increases, spoiling the beauty of the day and the beauty of the country.

Outside Hamburg we pick up two German girls hitchhiking. They are young, (18, 19)... One of them is sexy... I'm the first Jew they've ever met, a novelty, an exhibit in a sideshow. I had wanted to avoid Germany and its memory of concentration camps, and here we are with two German girls. Both Seth and I trying to make one of them. The uglier one wants me, while the prettier one seems to have erected a barrier. However, she invites us to spend the night at her parents' home.

The mother is retiring, mousy; the father, however, likes to talk. A former soldier, he survived the Russian front. He is as peaceful and friendly as anyone I have ever met. "German history I like not. Too much war... Too much violence." Confusing. The lovely daughter goes to bed. I hope she will come into my room during the night. She does not. Perhaps she was hoping the same, but I felt too awkward and unsure.

I assume Copenhagen is an attractive city, but all I can think of is the women. Sometimes I wish I could just be an observer, calmly, objectively, dispassionately watching the passing scene, instead of being a passionate participant. English seems to be the main language in Copenhagen. American tourists and G.I.'s everywhere. Dancing with a hard, sexy Danish girl who refuses to believe I'm an American. She wanders off to find a G.I. while I wander back to my room alone.

We will go to Stockholm to visit MajBritt who spent a year as an exchange high school student in the States. She was too wild and loose, and kept getting shuttled from family to family. A plain girl with round firm breasts, she...

> Dear David
>
> I am already much too dependent on you. I am
> afraid I will suffocate you with my love. You do not
> feel tied down—just now, but if you come back, don't
> ever tell what you did. No tears, no... but black emptiness. I would like to touch your warm body with my
> lips now and hold out my hand for you to kiss and
> give me strength. I need you desperately.

I am so sorry you could not come down from Boston. I felt lonely and despairing. I did not know where I would be the next day—Maybe at 74th Street, but just as well in Detroit. As usual I felt lost—this time not in the big city but in a huge impersonal organization. I needed someone terribly. To come in close contact with... someone to feel that I was human. I need someone to be with all the time... not just glorious moments and then a big, black nothing till the next flash of holiness. Because I am a woman I must have you here to give me warmth and kindness, too, in return for force and lyrics, for a woman can never go beyond and above herself. I would not care if you were together with other girls, or if you, like Dean, ran away to Los Angeles or Mexico… Only if I was so sure of my strength that I could wait…and make you return… But I am not.

MajBritt

Stockholm is the most beautiful city I have ever seen. It is built on the water in a series of connecting islands and peninsulas. Its physical plant is breathtaking. Everywhere there are public parks, concerts, urinals, baths.

As usual we are homeless. I am tired of this homelessness. In some ways, Stockholm is much like the United States—from hamburgers and hot dogs to Parker pens, Chevrolets, American nightclubs, American music.

The works of Carl Miles, the sculptor, adorn the city. Parks with nude statues spitting water, churches with black pointed wooden domes.

The old town and the palace are situated on a small island with narrow streets and squares from medieval times.

The youth hostel is located on a big frigate, a four master, which lies in the harbor. In a nearby park is the public bath, while next to the park is the Tetley Tea House where foreign students and other youngsters gather. There are always several French art students doing pastel drawings in the streets. It seems the most copied artists are Franz Marc and Marc Chagall.

MajBritt is not home when we get there. She is in Germany. Her parents are very welcoming and we spend a day with them. But I am restless. It is time to go to Paris and prepare for the year. Seth takes the car and heads towards Russia, while I take the train.

European train travel is exciting. It is multi-lingual and multi-border. Customs officials entering the cars, asking for passports. There is something very lonely and incomprehensible about train stations. It reflects my own loneliness and apprehensions. In my compartment there is a girl from Belgium with an English boyfriend; a Swedish boy going to Paris for vacation; a French lady returning home; a German girl on the way to school in Lubeck (pretty)... She gets off at Copenhagen. A mother and a daughter from Hamburg. Our second-class compartment seats eight comfortably.

You can tell what country you are in by the shape of the haystacks. In Germany they come to a point, in Scandinavia there are many peaks, while in Belgium they are rounder and taller than in Germany.

As the train speeds by towns and villages, I see the lights in the homes. There are homes with fathers, mothers, children, warmth, comfort, evening meals, stability. Everything I lack. I am driven by things I do not understand, and as I see the lights, curtains, families, I feel an outcast, alone. I have my parents at home, loving parents, yet they can never understand what tortures me... They can hold me, sympathize, occasionally give me money ... but they can never give me peace.

Stockholm, Nykoping, Helsingborg, Helisingor, Copenhagen, Hamburg, Lubeck, Bremen, Dusseldorf, Köln, Aachen, Liege, PARIS.

It is impossible to find a room in Paris except in hotels. An empty apartment or room simply does not exist. They are bequeathed from friend to friend like precious family jewels. My French is abominable, which makes me terribly shy and afraid to talk. I register for courses in French at the Alliance Française and plan to remain there until October when the Sorbonne begins. It is August and most of the French have deserted the city. The Quartier Latin is filled with foreign students learning the language. I spend hours staring at a map of Paris, not knowing where to begin. There is so much. My first impressions of the city have all come from wandering the dark streets of the Quartier Latin which is now very quiet and empty with the students on vacation. The amazing thing about Paris is that you *feel* its history. The city still looks ancient; one can imagine the barricades in the streets. I walk over to the Panthéon along deserted streets, passing the Facultés of the university before returning to my hotel on the Rue des Écoles.

I run into three girls from college. One of them is with an Algerian boy who suggests that I move into his hotel in the *cinquième*, the Hotel des Alliés on Rue Berthollet. I now have an address and a telephone number—GOBelins 47-52, a large double bed with rolled pillow in the French fashion. The room costs 8,000 francs a month, which comes to 37 dollars. A shower costs 110 francs. If I shower twice a week, this will be nine showers a month or 990 francs, an additional $2, or $39 in all.

The Rue Berthollet is on the outskirts of the Latin Quarter, a quiet residential area, 15-20 minutes from the Alliance Française, 10 minutes from the Sorbonne. I am moving my belongings from the Rue des Écoles when a man in a small truck beckons to me to hop aboard. His name is Michel and he runs a modest hotel-restaurant, as run-down and dirty as the ones in Mexico. He rounds up students and feeds them, but only if they are "comrades" and not *capitalistes*. Since I'm sloppily dressed and a student, I qualify as a "comrade."

I am given a huge meal and I promise to come back the next night. Michel says he will feed me any time for 200 francs (40 cents). I return the next day with my guitar and play for the half dozen or so people who are gathered there. Nobody listens, but everybody applauds. There are some Germans there. Most of the friends I make seem to be German. The younger generation of Germans is the most "sympathique" people in Europe, and I seem to have more in common with the young Germans than with anyone else. They love American folk music and they play it all the time.

I am crying... real tears... lying on my bed staring at the cracks in the ceiling. I am thinking of the last two years of my life ... at college... in the Village. A combination of intense frustration and beauty stemming from the incomprehensibility of it all. There is something intangible which I cannot understand. When I think of my friends, my actions, my conflicts, I begin to cry. It is somehow irrevocably tied up with folk music, which is the age-old bond of tears. I am afraid to leave my past. I am afraid of Paris. I don't want to go any further...

> Dear David,
>
> I have such curiosity to see you again! Wonder whether/how much you've changed? I have. People never change, I suppose, only "come out" differently.

Maya no longer has ass-length hair. I cut it! Now I look like this...

Was just becoming a real "pro" model in N.Y.C. when I left. I'll be back though. It's my home and my love. Everyone asks, now and then, about that beautiful handsome boy (name—David). Gleefully, proudly exclaim "In Paris." Modeled for a man named Reisman and as I gazed at the walls there was a picture; it really surprised me. Of you.

It is you.

Do write, my Dot. Think of thin cold Vermont air. Think of Spaghetti searches. Think of 42nd St. Think of San Remo's and me.

Love

Maya

I think of Maya. Backstage at a Pete Seeger Concert at the Cooper Union. ... I am 19, desperate with desire and trying not to stare too hard at this tall, wild-looking redhead, who is talking to Seeger. Seeger brings me over to meet Woody Guthrie who is sitting in a chair ill from Parkinson's disease. In the presence of such greatness it is hard to know what to say... The redhead approaches me, "Do you know Julie Carmody?" she asks. "No," I say. "You look like her," she says, and smiles. She takes me back to her loft on University Place not far from the Cedar Bar and the Living Theatre. She has big breasts and a round ass, nice thighs. We make love. It is my first time. At last, at last, at last. After so many years of longing, of masturbation, of shyness.

I split my time between Maya's place and my parents'. At a party a week later, I meet a tall, bohemian girl with nice legs and a plain face. We make love, and as I walk home to my parents at 5 in the morning with that special spring coolness/warmth in the air, I feel ecstatic... I have been unfaithful to my mistress.

Maya is a model and I begin modeling, too, at the Art Students League, the Henry Street Settlement, and for various artists. We hang out at the Cedar Bar with the abstract expressionists. I make my living from the realists, but socialize with the expressionists.

Three months earlier I had been at college on the verge of suicide, filled with desire, leading a life which seemed meaningless. Melvin and I read Camus, *L'étranger*, and decide to do away with ourselves. We turn on the gas but do not complete the act. As the gas fills the room, I strum on my guitar "If I could live on a Foggy Mountain Top, I'd sail away to the West. I'd sail all around this whole wide world to the girl that I love best..."

According to Camus, there is no God, no purpose... so why live? We turn off the gas. We live.

I cannot do my work. My father calls a psychiatrist. He asks me what I intend to do. "Be a film director and marry a Swedish Princess," I say. The psychiatrist tells my father I am out of touch with reality and recommends my hospitalization. Instead, I leave school.

I am walking downtown on Madison Avenue looking at corporate American types with their short-clipped, clean-cut hair, the girls in their tight skirts and their empty faces. I can never be a part of this. I am different... I do not want to be a part of it, but I do not know where to go, who I am. I cannot compromise... I cannot conform and be like them, but I have no other direction. Thus I have fear—fear of the future, fear of aging, fear of insanity, fear of sickness, death. My hair is long... My eyes see different things. Sometimes I have gone through the motions and tried to get jobs in offices but it has always failed. Instead, I get jobs as a dishwasher, art model, truck loader.

I do not belong in the world of Middle America, but I do not seem to belong anywhere else. I am not a writer, painter, filmmaker; I am a poet who does not write poetry. Perhaps there is a fear of failure if I were to try to get my feelings on paper. I enter an office building on Park Avenue, one of those tall glass buildings where they shuffle paper from one basket to another. I stare at the people and look at the women. They glance at me and look away. We have nothing in common. I walk over to 5th Avenue and head to the Village. Below 14th Street I feel more at ease. I pass the Provincetown Playhouse. I would like to be part of the acting world, but I am not an actor, nor a stagehand, nor a scene designer.

Outside of the Figaro, on the corner of Bleecker and MacDougal, I stand and watch the passing people. I start talking to a girl I've met a couple of times, but she does not attract me. Soon she leaves and Michael comes along... We chat monosyllabically, while our eyes, as if under their own power, scan the streets for women. Michael is dark, lean, and hungry... like me.

We walk up Bleecker. He has a friend in what is now becoming the East Village who has some pot, and he invites me along. I have nothing better to do so I join him. The pad is nearly barren, a couple of mattresses, some pillows, a chair, a wobbly table. His friend and another guy and two unattractive bohemian girls are lying around smoking. I take a joint and after a few puffs feel high.

Soon I will get hungry and then tired, but Michael and I will continue walking around looking for something... our eyes searching every face, every building, every store, but not really seeing. We think we want a woman, but perhaps it is something else. Michael is a painter, at least he has that. I have only this ability to relate to people, to be accepted, to empathize with those down, different, crazy, unattached wanderers.

I also have this nature, which is restless, and wants to experience every-thing, yet which seems to know mostly suffering.

Dear David

If yours was a letter written after many months of thinking and choosing words and thoughts, mine is one written after five minutes of no thought and am happy/glad from reading what you wrote; and an eagerness to hear from you again so I am writing immediately. Yes, yes, you are infinitely welcome, with guitar and friends of all sexes; we will contrive all the food you want, a younger (but not too younger) sister, or a small brother if that is the way your taste runs, and Dina (the same sister mentioned) says she can find you the text of the 'Pallet on the Floor' you so earnestly requested. Don't forget your guitar, because I am teaching myself to play the mandolin and we can have much fun singing and playing.

Finished Murphy, think it is fantastic and recom-mend it to any and all fans of Beckett. It is in some respects, I think, a key to Waiting for G. and Fin de Partie.

My hair is long; I am hideously desperate for someone to talk to. When you come I shall probably fall on you like the Assyrian swept down like a wolf on the fold in my eagerness for the sight of someone or something resembling people. Come at once, just call before you do, and I shall compose odes in your honor...

Do you know Ibsen's Nora? 'The most wonderful
thing in the world is going to happen soon.' That's
how I feel. I am so self-supporting. I am going to
write. I am going to sing. I am going to be an artist...

much, much, much love

Donna

Melvin is also in New York. He is doing some work for a family and tells me that their daughter is a knockout. Nelly is a tall, voluptuous high school girl and we have an immediate attraction. We walk to the Cedar Tavern and Nelly tells me she is not a virgin. She leans close to me and whispers in my ear that she is wet with desire for me. Maya is away for the day so we go to our apartment on University Place and make love.

I am fascinated by her. She is sexy, wild, passionate, creative and crazy about me.

One night I return to the loft on University Place and it is filled with about 15 of the dirtiest, seediest people I have ever seen, sitting, lying down, smoking hash or shooting up; "friends" of Maya. I leave. Our romance is over. But our ties are not over. She has gotten pregnant and returns home to Indianapolis to have an abortion.

Nickey is in town with his banjo and we give a street concert at Place St. Michel in front of a large audience. People seem to like our music and a lot of coins are thrown into the cigar box. We sing until my voice is gone.

Paris is unbelievably fascinating. There is so much life, movement and artistry here. The whole city is a museum. The booksellers along the Seine—thousands of sidewalk cafés crowded with interesting people. My best friend in Paris is the Algerian boy, Khier, who showed me to my hotel. He works in the Post Office and I will eat with him in the canteen there tonight. After that we are going to St. Michel to meet two French girls, who are both dancers and had listened to me playing the night before. After so many foreigners, they will be the first young French people I will have met. Khier and I sit in the café, but the girls do not arrive.

A girl with a great body is standing at a bus stop. I want her but I am too timid, too sensitive... I am possessed with too much self-awareness and an overly conscious mind, which results in paralysis of action. I would like to live a life where nothing matters, yet to me everything matters. It is all too serious.

I walk slowly past the bus stop, pretend to look in a window... I am aching with desire. Her face is cold, insensitive, bourgeois, vacuous... Most people are like that... The mass of men and women are empty inside. They do not see. I am outside, alone. I search for a kindling eye... a spark... there is none.

And just before I turn to stone
I catch one kindling eye
It signals, "You are not alone,
For all must sin who die."

Attila Joszef, the Hungarian poet, wrote those lines.

I wander, feeling the rhythm of the streets. Beautiful girls pass, indifferent to my longing... Indifferent to everything. I suffer, for I am alive. They are hollow and dead. A group of young people—beatniks—are sitting near the entrance to the Odéon Metro stop. They are laughing at an old lady, a hunchback, who can hardly walk. They are insensitive. They laugh at suffering. Nothing matters to them... But they seem happy...

Maybe I should be like them, living only for the moment. But my mind is filled with too many thoughts and conflicts and that self-awareness that prevents enjoyment.

I am walking on the Right Bank now... The Tuileries, the Champs Elysées, past Notre Dame to the île St. Louis. The Louvre is filled with Americans. I cannot interest myself in the paintings. I continue—Place de la Concorde, Rue de Rivoli... and soon I have reached the Bastille where a Fête is being held. It is run by the newspaper, *L'Humanité*, the Communist paper in Paris... a gigantic sprawling affair, attended by hundreds of thousands of people ("Une foule immense" to quote *L'Humanité*).

The main attraction is the appearance of the Negro-American singer Paul Robeson. Robeson sings "Old Man River" and "Joe Hill" and follows with a rousing speech in praise of the French Communist Party, the Soviet Union, Stalingrad (he quotes FDR). When Robeson finishes talking about "our fight," the entertainment ends with a strong rendition of "L'Internationale" ("L'Internationale sera le genre humain.") Crazy hats are everywhere... most of them shaped like Russian hats, colored red with white stars. The size of the crowd is a bit scary. But they say that Communism in France is different from Communism in Russia. Less ideological, less rigid, less militant, less homogenous.

It is now night and I wander back to the Seine. I pass the Défense d'Afficher signs, the cafés, the shops. Every street in Paris is packed with small shops... One need never leave one's block to buy anything. The Communists will never be a match for the small shopkeepers. The woman guarding the caisse, checking every centime, will control France. The buildings along the Seine are lit up in spectacular display... But I am lonely... and I feel the women. I am walking up Rue Saint-Denis with the prostitutes standing inside doorways showing off their bodies...

Dark shadows creep by... lonely men... men consumed with lust... their souls and beings worth nothing... enveloped by lust. I am one of them, though I pretend not to be... I have walked the gamut... I avoid Rue Saint-Denis on the way back to the hotel... I cannot find peace.

My misunderstood friend,

After I wrote my mother a magical letter, I thought of you and of the beauty and power which is inhibiting your screwed up little self. A beauty that is sleeping and I hope will break forth one day. Your inner beauty will not become a dominant part of you because you are not whole yet. I do not want to smash your ego, but you are still a boy. I would like to see you as a man. You are not whole in the sense that you wish to think yourself "sick." You are not metaphysically sick and you cannot attain that beat "sickness" because you have no cause. You have nothing to fight for... I have seen so many "beat," sick people and they are lost— and you are not lost. You live and you are vibrant, but your vibrancy is not whole. These sick people believe they suffer, but they do not. They believe they live life, but they do not. For living is not just a momentary thing—it is always present. It is a standing up straight in order to fight the nothingness. To know that life is absurd. Then to affirm the nothingness by the development of oneself and also to commit oneself. You can do neither as of now because you are not aware of the nothingness of life and you cannot commit yourself.

This is shown by your desire to experience everything at the same time.

You must learn to give to people or you cannot receive from them. You cannot ask them for help in any of your problems because you cannot give to them. Tell us all your problems and we listen. I cannot help you now or ever because you do not really give. You look into my eyes and see yourself reflected. Thus, you could never love because you cannot see the soul of the other. Fine souls they are. You are so tied up in knots that you enjoy yourself this way. You really make no attempt to untie these knots. And it is up to you to do this. You must work out your own salvation.

Behind the facade of indifference, beatness, and other characteristics, there is sensitivity, compassion and greatness. But the theories about David cover them all up... smother them. I look at Laurie, Joanie and Karen and many others and I become scared. They are lost in their own individual ways. But you are not, and this is why I have hope for you. There is so much more I can say, but I am afraid to because it will scare you away.

Loveness, Linda

I find the letter from Linda in my cubbyhole at the hotel desk. There is also a letter from my parents. Linda and I had made love the day before graduation. Just the one time... then she fled to Pennsylvania and I fled to France. I fled in search of and in fear of. She?

My parents are at the Cape—sand, sandals, salt water, the beer hall, the Colony near the Wharf, Fisher Road, New York artists, white-capped and loud-shirted tourists emerging from the Boston Belle—midget sailboats rocked in the wake of the Belle—the Provincetown Playhouse—Dennis, Hyannis... Commercial Street with its continual traffic of cars and people along its narrow way—Bradford Street leading to the Dunes. The dunes along the beach and the Portuguese fishermen who watch the summer transformation... Hans Hoffman... high dunes near Truro... walking along the beach past the semi-nude bodies. One extraordinary body on the beach and I am talking to her, but she is unresponsive and I walk away... Wellfleet and Holiday House... Sitting often in the same bar watching the bearded man in sandals sketch portraits...

Maureen is a high school girl... sandals, bohemian, firm legs, innocent... I have my guitar, she her art. We become a pair but do not make love... I meet Sally in the Holiday House. Here is no innocence, just a look that says "sex." I can feel that she is mine, that I will be an "experience" for her. I promise to pick her up at her place at 8, and when I arrive the headlights of my car illumine her naked body on the road doing a lascivious dance. She has the biggest and firmest ass I have ever seen... I take her back to the cabin I am sharing on the beach and we make love... I feel I have attained something... I have found something, and for one or two days there is peace, but then there is nothing except loneliness, restlessness, yearning, comfort in music and the never-ending need for a new experience.

I wandered and I watched the people on Commercial Street in the same way I am now walking and staring at the faces in Paris. And I observe every look, every gesture. But I am apart...

I do not want to go to my empty room, so I knock on Khier's door. He is one of several Algerians living in the hotel. When he was 16, he worked 14 hours a day washing dishes and made 60NF (12 dollars) a month. This was supposed to support a family of six. Usually, he had only bread to eat. He joined the FLN at 17, was caught by the French, tortured, and thrown into prison. He has had a brain concussion since his beatings four years ago. The French let him out of jail to join the French Army to fight against his friends. He says that if an Arab does well, the French get jealous and will fire all successful Algerians.

Khier invites me in, offers me tea and we discuss our loneliness.

Night... I am on the Rue de la Huchette... I enter a bar, have a beer. Boring faces; I pay, leave. Next door is a dance *cave*. I hesitate, walk past it. I do not like dancing, or the people one finds there... but my loneliness leads me down the stairs. I pay the 5 francs, enter and watch the dancers. I cannot communicate... There are several sexy girls but I am too depressed to mouth the necessary banalities. Then I notice a girl with reddish brown hair. She is staring at me. Our eyes meet... She looks away, but I have seen enough. She wants me to speak to her. I smile. She smiles back. Her name is Tatyana... She is German—from Wuppertal. She is working as an au pair for a family of writers in Montmartre. She is fairly attractive but not really my type... Our souls communicate, but my body is not all afire. I sense the tragedy to come.

When we make love that night, I do not experience the fulfillment or joy I need... but she is someone special, someone to get close to. But I am not ready or able to get close to anybody. Yet, later, after I have hurt her, her letter to me with its moving German to English constructions brings her closer to me.

Dear David,
    When I saw you the first time in this *cave*, I was
surprised. This was my first reaction. I had been in

this *cave* one time before. I went there without expectation. I had only given the promise to my friend to show her a Parisian Jazz *cave*. I was surprised because there was in this place full of demi-degenerated boring men a human being who was different.

I watched you with increasing interest. I noticed your sensuality, which had absolutely nothing in common with the affected perversity of the Frenchmen, but which arose out of the deepest depth of your being so naturally that it nearly had something pure. Then you noticed me. I was irritated at first as I was unable to continue watching you quietly. But as you know there is only a step from curiosity to the wish of possession, and urge of conquest is the logical consequence. Then after you had gone but returned after some minutes, I suddenly was so frightened that I began to tremble like a little girl who falls in love for the first time in her life. And exactly at this moment something strange happened to me. I was no longer myself. I was so afraid of you. I did not want to sleep with you... However, I knew exactly that I would do it, and I was embarrassed about myself. I knew, like you, that sensuality is never a basis on which a man and a woman can live together.

If you hadn't played the guitar I would have gone, but music is one of those elements which exercises the greatest force on me. So I listened and then I saw your hands. They are so sensitive, so *sensible*, and if ever hands may express the character of a man your hands told me that you never could be in the position of hurting anybody. When I had been with you Friday I left nearly happy as I noticed that you felt good in my presence, that you liked me. I knew exactly that you did not love me and that I still did not love you, for love in my opinion, is something which cannot exist within three days, which is something so fragile, needing so much care, patience and time to grow.

Well, now you know just a little bit. Oh, yes, you wanted to know something about the men in my life. Eh bien, there is in Germany a boy whom I don't love, but whom I appreciate very much. I never slept with him, but only the knowledge that he exists will help me over this. My love for him is like the admiration of a little girl for her big brother. I know that he will be someday a great scientist. He is belonging to those men whose intelligence, like yours, is superior to the usual way. But his intelligence is based on logical reasons, while yours, I believe, arises from intuition, sensibility and above all of this enormous mobility of the spirit which is the privilege of the Jews. From my Russian ancestors I have inherited a melancholy, which is a dominant part of my being. I don't know if you want to see me again, (but nevertheless I will be at the Lion Thursday 11 h and it would be fine if you would, too). But finally I should like to tell you that you will be among those men who will leave traces in

my soul, but even if they hurt I know that I shall grow
from them, and for this I thank you.

Tatyana

Tatyana's letter is sweet and painful at the same time. Sweet because it is so flattering and painful because I have hurt someone I like... and because I cannot love her or desire her enough, we both must suffer. I am walking down Boulevard St. Michel. Every sexy girl that passes me is like a blow in the stomach. I must possess her, and when I don't, I suffer. A blonde with a full, but slender, body passes and gives me a quick glance. I stop, hesitate, and this time I follow her. She slows up as she glances into a café, and fearfully I speak...

"Bonjour"

She glances at me, smiles "Bonjour" and keeps walking. My French is still terrible and so I switch to English.

"Where are you from?"

"Sweden"

"I was there this summer."

"Did you like it?"

Et cetera.

She agrees to sit for a few minutes in a café filled with students, tourists and others. Her name is Katerina, from a small town, Vesterås, in the north of Sweden. Katerina likes to talk. She is intelligent and beautiful as well. I want her desperately... She agrees to see me tonight. We will meet in her hotel room... I am supposed to meet Tatyana, but I will call her and change the day.

Dear David,

The short meeting of two human children... I met you David, a couple of hours in Paris and I feel intensely that you were a kindred soul. To me you were just as unreal as I myself. You entered my world naturally without anything being changed or destroyed. You could speak and understand my 'language,' perhaps you could see what I saw, hear the swelling from the cosmic music of the stars...

I live in my world of dreams. I am often a stranger in Reality.—I love the sky. The sea is my god. The storm is my father. The tree is my mother. Longing and melancholy are my share of inheritance. I need the sun, music and beauty. This is me. Often I feel old as if I have lived for centuries. Sometimes people feel that and get almost afraid.

We will meet again and everything will be much easier. But until that time let us meet in the thoughts. Write to me. I need letters. I have spoken to the silence.

Your Katerina

Everything is fear. My mind is constantly dwelling in the dark regions of the soul. Fear of dying, fear of disease, fear of loneliness, fear of indecision... A pain in my stomach is cancer. I am obsessed... for days I can think of nothing else.

Sleeping with women brings little joy. There is the continual longing, the nervousness... the apartness... the fear of venereal disease. I desire women and fear them. I hate my desire, which sometimes is all-consuming,.. Yet I do not want to show my desire, admit to it. It is a source of shame, of anguish. Usually I sleep with women I do not desire. They want me and I need someone, but there is mostly emptiness. There is confusion. I do not know who I am, where I am going, what I am doing. My wanderings have an aimlessness. I observe everything: the shops, windows, the cafés, but my essence demands experience.

I talk to people, but I do not feel like a real person. I have no direction, therefore no definition, no being. This is chaos. This is the border of insanity. I go out on the street and I walk, but I cannot communicate, because I am all multi-split thought and no action, no being... like a ghost. Today I walked into a café at the Odéon. It was filled with bohemians in animated conversation. I stood there watching, shy, wanting to join a group. No one spoke to me and I spoke to no one. I watch; I want to break the barrier of apartness, but finally I leave.

In some ways I am so alive, but in some ways I am near dying. The city conquers me. I can only become its master when I have found a place to live, a job and a woman... otherwise it spits me out, defeated, squashed.

I shall spend the rest of my life torn by indecision. I have never been able to decide and probably never will decide what I am going to do for a vocation or a way of life. I cannot even be a vagabond, for my roots are too strong. I want all, and, thus, I get nothing. I want to be everywhere and, thus, I go nowhere. I do not want to be limited by having a profession and being something concrete like a teacher, lawyer, etc. I want to be me, and the me that I am is too diversified to become anything concrete.

Each morning I decide how I shall live. Shall I go to work, shall I take off in a boat and never see my parents again; shall I write, shall I lay on the floor in filth without moving, shall I be intense and hateful without compromise, shall I compromise and get women and play the game and try to be happy. One day this, one day that. I am told I am out of touch with reality. I know the only reality: Chaos.

Cool Was Kelly

KELLY 1961

Cool
was Kelly;
what with the
hanging hair over
green-shadowed
eyes
stretch-black tights
holed in one knee,
and the Bopping French-fringed
skirt

Cool,
she was a-
slinging her
wooden tray from
dusk to dusty dawn
in "Cafe
What for,"
carrying strange named
coffee and,
turning pale eyes
on Tourist Cats for
gift-bread;
and hard
was her tray when
she crashed it

to home over
some grabbin' hand's
head.

Cool
was Kelly,
sitting watchful in
Folk music's balm,
digging the
Feelings of knowing words helping
Inside Burnings,
and digging
a sometimes helping
Friend-Squeeze in
the dark.

And the streets was cold and we was all looking around, looking for ways to make bread so we could pay for food. The only warm place was Rienzi's and those that had no pad sat around brown tables hoping the waitress would let them stay.

Fred had gone to see if some cat was around who promised us a free meal—He didn't dig him, but he was hungry. Eileen was cursing because she was scared he wouldn't come back and she'd be left on the streets alone.

Barbara and Joey was holding hands quiet-like, and John was saying he should have died.

I was lonely for something; the lights didn't help and hands touching my shoulders "hello" in passing made me sad.

Cool, so Cool
after work
when
the folk music

> sent her drifting down
> MacDougal Street -
> Straight shouldered and
> walking easy,
> eyes looking for
> the Feeling
> in a
> What or Who;
> feet tired, wanting to
> stop, but heart hoping to
> have hope.

We gave up on Frank, so we shared a Rienzi's hamburger and Eileen left to go take a shower in my room.

People was feeling bad; mouths were saying, "Hey man, how are you," but eyes was saying "fuck it."

I was tired; tired of running from drinking to splintered floors because somebody I loved was not loving me, and I was worn out with being cool. I was hating cats that reached for me because they wasn't him, and I was cursing myself for not having money to get rid of the cough and maybe look pretty.

The coffee houses were calling us to our jobs—we all went down the same street to work for maybe-tips and $2 pay.

Old "Four Winds" was lit up with candles and Phil the kitchen boy was saying, "This place is wet and fucked up like me."

Folk singers tuned guitars and a drunk spade yelled pain-poetry from the stage.

Tourists started wandering in and it was bad. I didn't look at them, just stood sprattle-footed and waited. Sometimes I had to talk about the

Menu and my mouth was troubled with moving. Sometimes they gave me quarters for tips, but once I had to kick a man and hit another with my tray. He was quiet afterwards, because I swung it hard and took all the bitter feeling out on his head and grabbing hand. Only I shook and shook afterwards.

Barbara and Joey came in with some wine, and as I passed by with my orders, they'd give me swallows. It was red and hot and I wished it were all mine.

They sat, and Joey played with her hair, and they had no bread but there was wine and loving. I couldn't watch.

Eileen came running and hadn't found Fred; she couldn't sneak back to my room and was angry. I found a place for her in the shack out back of the Winds because I didn't want to share my bed and talk tonight about it all. I was sort of mad inside because the other night she had loved Fred in my room and I had sat in the dark trying to make like I couldn't hear. I went to hide in the bathroom, but the sounds was all over the hall and the manager winked at me the next day.

> Cool,
> when she thought
> she found it once
> on
> a pallet with a
> Village Cat;
> Even Cool
> when she woke gasping
> shaking off
> false-loving hands
> turned sweaty in

> dawn's bitter Knowing
> to run ragged to
> Street Sounds healing
> sutures.

Lyle came up and borrowed $1; he was hungry. The folksinger yelled and the "drag" out front was cold and people was wandering too much. I am writing this in the Winds on a notebook I carry around to get it out on. There are no customers now. The music is still floating, but soon the sun will come up and we can leave for the streets or a bed somewhere.

I will go to my room and try not to think. I hope I pass out. That's all I want now because wanting much don't help.

> Yeah, Kelly was
> Going Home
> on the Morning Train,
> but to
> make it realer
> she shot Cocaine;
> Cocaine loved her
> and loved her
> good,
> like no damn
> Folk Singer
> ever could;
> She shot it deep
> till it reached
> her soul, then
> rolled down her

sleeve till
the Peace
took hold.

I am not conscious of anything but pain and the need to run to the streets to escape death. For I will cut and there will be no mistake this time.

I want to stop the pain—I want so desperately to *want* to live, to hope, to feel, so I hunt the streets.

There is only an incredible loneliness. In the coffee house, people pass and speak words I've heard before, and I want to go to sleep forever.

> Cool
> was Kelly, Waiting Kelly
> but slant was her eyes
> when self-made saviors would
> rap about their
> healing arms and warm pads.

> Cool
> was Kelly when the
> baby died a
> Un-wed baby's death in
> a bloody split room,
> but hot
> were her eyes and
> wet was her hair.

A fairly new boy in the Village who can still laugh is sitting beside me. His name is Bob. I crawl up on his lap because I am drowning. I want to feel loved. The pain is hard, so I draw my feet up in a knot and hang on to Bob's shirt. My guts hurt.

Bob pats me on the back. He is holding me like a child and is not thinking of me as a woman, thank God, because I am not a woman now—I am an inside screaming, afraid and fighting to live.

> Cool;
> always Watching and
> Waiting
> and if there was
> torn inside—tears
> her writin' pen
> scribbled the wet
> on paper to read
> when that
> Morning Train
> come rolling in
> and Split was her smile
> as she walked to the
> lights, digging
> Alone.

Philip comes in and joins us. Philip and I met in the hospital waiting room, a place where you go when you don't have much money. I couldn't stop coughing, and he had the clap. He was horrified when he discovered the doctor was also a nun. We are friends, and since that day we have always laughed together, but now I cannot even speak. There is dust in my mouth.

Philip and Bob talk and joke; no one mentions me curled up, as if it were natural. I feel somewhat safer now, and I am able to sit up enough to smoke.

Philip has to wait for a phone call at home, but Bob has to drag for another hour. Philip says "come with me old buddy and we'll get a head start." He does not think of me as a woman either, and I am glad and feel safe.

Suddenly I have to get off the streets—they are suffocating me. We grab a cab—the pad is in the Bowery. But the place is clean and large, and I forget the roaches and cracked lives of the Village Plaza Hotel where I stay.

> Cool,
> was Kelly;
> until the Tired
> came and
> Cocaine
> couldn't help the
> Waiting;
> the tray shook off
> coffee cups and dreams
> and tourist eyes
> laughed
> too deep;
>
> Cooly
> screamed the voice inside that said
> "There is no more

than candles"
But
sad was the look as clean hair and pointed shoes
walked safely by on
the arm of a watchful man;
and Ragged
flew Kelly's hair
on the way to
the pad; pushed by
voice's sharp fingers;

I feel more and more at ease—dizzy from the pill, so better—We sit on a mattress on the floor (of course) and pass the wine bottle. I tell him I feel dizzier and want to pass out. He laughs and hits me with a pillow. We are laughing, laughing, children playing a game we remember.

Suddenly we stop, look at the room, the candle and the mattress on the floor. "My God," says Philip, "We're beatniks." We are very still. We are going nowhere and have no energy to go, anyway. There is a soft sadness and the wine makes me want to scream.

We are afraid to think more, so we hit with the pillows again. One flies to a corner and Philip tickles me. Then he kisses me hard and I draw up into a knot. I want to be held close, but want no sex—he has noticed that "old buddy" is a girl, and I damn everything. I blab something about Niko, trying to make it sound as if he loves me madly, but he only says "you need something so bad." I know there is nothing I can have and my arm shakes.

Cool
was Kelly

> except for the shaking hands when
> she shot an empty needle
> deep.
> Wondering was her going look,
> and Cool was
> the cop
> who found another
> beatnik junkie chick
> sprawled frozen
> on a crying floor

Philip is pulling me and saying, "easy, easy, I won't hurt you." But I am pushing away. I am afraid of sex with him, but am more afraid of being alone and not being held tight to ease the pain. I think of being held tight, so tight and safe. I go limp. My head is dizzy. It doesn't matter anyway. So what.

Afterwards I feel a deep loss; maybe loss of respect—oh, funny word for me. I am a beatnik chick who was balled in a pad. And it doesn't matter in the long run (and God knows it's a long run), so that makes it hurt more.

I want to leave because of the awful loneliness of not being alone, the terrible spoof of love is hurting hideously, but the fear is still there. I have to hang on to something or someone. Bob and Melanie come in. There is more wine, some talk, and I relax a little. It's over and he will not want me again.

Bob is looking at me with half closed eyes and cursing Melanie behind her back, because he has to sleep with her tonight. Philip is suddenly running around naked. I am sick of naked men.

Melanie and Bob undress and crawl to one of the mattresses. I'm quite dizzy now, so I just flop down on the pallet in the next room. I hate to have to fight to keep breathing and live, and I feel ridiculous because I have loved and learned my love doesn't matter. No one's love matters. I feel at ease with these people because they seem to know nothing matters, either.

Melanie leaves the room and Bob and Philip and I talk about getting a pad together. We say we won't sleep together, so we won't have problems and get hung up. I like the idea of having them around—we could laugh together and when the Death came and I had to fight, fight, I wouldn't be alone. There would be life beside me. We plan to look for a place tomorrow. I hope they will take care of me.

Melanie returns. The light goes out and Philip sits beside me. I think he is going to hug me goodnight so I reach upwards. But he pulls me up and pulls my dress off. He takes me again and hurts my body. But I am grateful because this night I did not die.

I did not cut.

I live.

> (Yeah
> Kelly took that
> Morning Train;
> last golden words was
> "Screw Cocaine.")
> Cool is the Scene she left behind;
>
> Cool
> are the bards
> tourists and bread, the

wanderings, searching
songs, the
streets glowing footsteps.

Cool
is the coffee house
crew, knowing
Where It's At
at all times;
God so cool

But sad are the eyes,
maybe looking down there;
And
long is the hair of rain
falling on
Washington Square.

Silent Echoes

DAVID 1961

I am wandering the gray cobbled Paris streets as I head toward the quay and cross the Pont Neuf. Ricardo is there, doing a large sidewalk portrait of a woman. I kneel down and we speak. Ricardo is short, dark, good looking, dressed in a black turtleneck and black pants... We do not speak of much. My eyes watch the passersby... He draws.

Ricardo is from Chile and always dresses in black. De Pina, another painter with a ponytail, is from Argentina and always dresses in white. He has stopped on the bridge and is chatting with us. I know them both, yet I do not really know them. They have not revealed themselves to me. Perhaps, as Linda wrote, I see only my reflection in their eyes.

I leave... walk up to the Rue de Buçi, Rue de Seine. There is a store selling religious articles, Buddhas, Hindu pieces, crosses, etc. There is a small wooden Buddha in the window. I go in and ask the price. It is cheap... I buy it and start walking towards the Boulevard St. Michel. A stunning blonde with an approachable face is sitting in a café. I am buoyed by my talk with Ricardo and De Pina and so I walk right up to her and hold out the Buddha.

"Would you like to rub the Buddha's stomach?"

"What did you say?" she says seriously.

"I asked if you'd like to rub a Buddha's stomach... Here, watch."

I sit down next to her and show her how to rub the Buddha's stomach. The girl has a fantastic figure and I feel a surge of overwhelming desire.

"What do you do?" she says. Her accent is German.

"I'm a flying carpet salesman," I tell her.

"A flying carpet salesman?"

Her name is Marlene, from Stuttgart, in Paris for a holiday. We walk together to my hotel in the *cinquième*, my arm around her. Upstairs I take my guitar and begin playing. Her face is aglow. I put the guitar down, rub my hand on her thigh and slowly push her down on the bed. She has large firm breasts and as my hand goes under her sweater she starts breathing heavily, almost gasping. She is excited, but not as excited as I am. I can hardly believe my luck. However, as my hand reaches under her skirt, she grabs it and yells "nein" and sits up. I don't believe it.

I am crazy with desire, burning with desire, consumed by it and she is saying "no." We stare at each other. I reach towards her.

"I'm afraid."

"Afraid of what?"

"I don't know..."

I pick up the guitar and desultorily play chords... Marlene looks anguished. She is a virgin; she is saving herself for love. She wants me terribly, she says, but she can't do "it."

She is now standing by the door... I want to jump her, rape her, but I stare immobilized at her beautiful departing form.

> Dear David,
>
> I don't believe that I am frigid, but it is correct if you think. I try to avoid sex although it is yet so basic to me. My lovely sister says the same. I did never believe you are a saint. Horrible! I dislike dispassionate humans (with exceptions). But it is impossible for me (as I told you) to be united with a man only physically. It is very important to communicate in every respect, with spirit, mind, etc. *Reine Geschlechtstiere sind mir widerlich!* I think it would be the best for me to meet a man who is much older than me, who satisfies my tenderness necessity, who appears as a father, and who did not undertake a general attack of my virginity (hi hi)...
>
> Die Luft is ein turkisher Teppich,
>
> Auf dem sick hinter die Schwermut Reisen last.
>
> Your Marlene

The air does not cure my "schwermut", my melancholy, however.

Days of buckling French bureaucracy trying to get my Carte de Séjour so I can register at the Sorbonne.

I read *L'Enfer* by Henri Barbusse, which helps me with my French vocabulary. I get my Carte de Séjour and a student restaurant card so that I can get a meal for 20 cents. The lines are long, however, and the food not particularly good, but I soon learn to peel an apple in one strip without breaking it. My major accomplishment so far in Paris.

Tatyana tells me of her experiences at the end of the war. For months and months Goebbels and Co. had been broadcasting stories of American atrocities, and telling everyone that the American army would butcher everybody if it conquered Germany. Tatyana said she hid in her cellar and remembers when the first American soldiers arrived. They came to the house all bloody and looking horrible because they had been fighting at the front. As they opened the door, she stood there waiting to be killed. Instead of killing her, however, the soldiers gave her chocolate. She says she will never forget that.

I take Tatyana to a movie, *Les Etoiles*. It is a German-Bulgarian production by Kurt Wolf. The subject matter is Jews in a concentration camp in Bulgaria waiting to be shipped to Auschwitz in Poland, and a young German officer, an artist, who falls in love with one of the Jewish girls. It is a story of his discovery of his human (anti-Nazi) ideas and his attempt to put them into practice by helping the Jews get medicine and the underground get arms. The film is fantastic, realistic and painful...

In one week, Tatyana is going home to Germany. She wants me to come with her. I agree. It will be good to get away from Paris. I cannot stand the French (nor for that matter can anyone else). The air here is dirty. I have little desire to learn the language. French youth seem cruel. They dislike foreigners, and foreigners dislike the French... All my friends are foreigners.

There are too many "students" in Paris. I am constantly forced to stand in lines stretching far in the distance. And half the time I'm not sure what I'm standing in line for. This milling, massive student world around the Sorbonne is incomprehensible. There are hundreds of student agencies, bureaus, houses, restaurants all requiring some type of card. In Paris, one is "carteified" not identified. The number of bookstores in the Quartier is overwhelming. Everyone else seems to know what he is doing... which books to buy, which courses to take. I can't figure it out. I finally get registered at the Faculté des Lettres to study contemporary history, but I know my French is not really good enough.

I eat one meal a day in the student canteen and the rest of the time I have soup, bread, cheese, milk and oranges in my room. My parents send me a little money and words from another world. Speaking of other worlds, I saw *Mon Oncle*, the Jacques Tati film.

There's a big, bloody right wing rally at the Arc de Triomphe in favor of keeping Algeria French (I think it will become independent). I miss the rally, but read the newspaper accounts which say that anywhere from three to nine people were killed, depending, as always, on which paper you read. For example, *Paris Jour* had big headlines that read 45 wounded, nine killed, etc. *Le Figaro* reported the rally on page six as occurring without any grave incidents.

Tatyana is reading *Exodus*. The Holocaust has created, it seems, a strange link between Germans and Jews. A link of repentance? A link of fascination? A link of enemies? A link of... Most of my friends in Paris are German, as if the new generation is repudiating the old. But do the archetypes of a nation ever really change? The Jews, filled with guilt and suffering, the French with poetic decadence, and the Germans with a mystical paganism, which becomes first lyrical and then godless and cruel.

The bookstores have opened and hundreds of students crowd into them. I walk down the Rue de la Huchette and lean against a building. An interesting-looking oriental boy approaches me with a box. He extends the box towards me and says, "I present you with the head of St. John the Baptist." This is Carlos.

Two days later I see Carlos in a café on Boulevard St. Germain. I join him. He tells me of all his love affairs with men, his poetry, his decadence. He is totally alive, different and interesting.

Carlos is a writer, political columnist, exotic dancer. He shows me a letter from T.S. Eliot calling him the savior of American letters. Carlos went to Columbia graduate school at 14 with Mark Van Doren, Lionel Trilling, etc., and he reawakens my interest in the intellect, which has been dormant these past months. I'd started to consider all intellectual endeavors meaningless. Two weeks ago I was on the Métro reading a critique of Pasternak's work and had decided that all intellectual matters were stupid, worthless, pointless, and that only the emotional and physical aspects of a person should be considered.

Carlos is living in a tiny room on the Rue de l'Ancienne Comédie. I bring him some of my writings and he tells me that I'm a genius and the profoundest person he has ever met... He also tells me that he is in love with me because I am gentle, beautiful and a creative genius. I feel none of these, but he has reawakened my confidence in myself.

> Mon cher Davidus,
>
> I write this on a bench beside the poplar-lined road that leads from the little chateau of my friends to the national road here in Versailles. The wind roars in my ears like some gigantic and icy demon. My hands are almost frozen and to keep myself warm I drink

from a bottle of Cognac that I pilfered from the cellar of my hosts. I have not slept all night. I keep thinking of you.

I wrote you yesterday and I slipped the letter inside your room earlier this evening when I dropped in at your hotel to find out if you were around. You were not in—I do not know if you ever felt that strange sensation of falling down an abyss which I felt tonight, which I now feel upon learning that you were, you are, somewhere else.

I wrote you and said that I am, I was, trying to learn to disdain you. To forget your name—to erase totally in my mind the lineaments of your smile, the glow of your eyes, the beautiful contours of your being! These things are easier said than done.

Oh, David, David, if only there were a way to ensnare in a net of words the great feeling I have for you—if only there were a way to ask the stubborn letters formed by my pen to shine forth with the love, the light that gnaws my spirit at this moment now, and ever since I met you. Perhaps, then, you will not think my love is that absurd. Perhaps, then, you will learn to pity me—and learn perhaps, to stretch your hand to me—in the darkness, in the forest of sorrows.

Come to me like the stag in the legend, the gentle doe, and lick the wound of my soul. Lick, lick the wound of my soul. Kiss my mangled spirit—enfold me.

I love you

C

The irony of Carlos' beautiful and heart-felt letter makes me sad. This beautiful soul loves me and desires me, but my body needs and desires women. Why this incessant need for women? I am a poet; I observe and see and understand the inner working of people's souls when I have time to look... Why does this magic and magnetic attraction of man and woman overshadow everything else, make everything else seem less important? Politics, the beauty of nature, the phenomenal architecture in Paris, the interesting faces, power, money, religion, philosophy, sports, literature... all become secondary to the glance in the street or in the café. Why? Carlos is a genius, a poet of the first order, a searcher, a soft, sensitive soul, yet because of his desires he plunges down into the depths of despair, so that all other aspects of the person and the soul seem not to matter. It's been said that the sex urge and religious yearning are the opposite sides of the same coin, but since I do not believe, I cannot reverse the coin.

Tomorrow I will be leaving for Germany with Tatyana, so I wander over to L'Odéon... An interesting girl is sitting on the terrace of the Relais Odéon, and I find an empty table next to her. I watch her shaking hand as she finishes her third cup of coffee. She is drunk, but there is a spirit in her drunkenness, a spirit that shows in her smile in such contrast to the cold, empty faces of the others. I sense a madness in the girl, and it is this madness that attracts me.

Because you are different and because you suffer you are inextricably linked to me... I understand you with your shaking hands and unsteady gaze. You have traversed the barrier that separates the understanding from the imbeciles.

Shall we talk? Shall we meet? Why is it so difficult for two human beings to talk? But now you are part of me because your image and your soul are on this piece of paper.

I go home without talking to her. My footsteps echo in the night streets, and as I pass the café on the corner of Rue Berthollet a lovely blonde face peers out through the café window. I sigh deeply and walk on.

The road—hitchhiking from Paris via Reims, Luxembourg, Trier... It is cold wintry weather, but I am glad for the clear air at long last. I can breathe again. In Paris everyone coughs, and, because the air is so sickly, I always have pains in my chest. In the Ardennes in northern France, Tatyana and I run into the first snow of the year. The northern French are much nicer than the Parisian French, and it feels good to get away from the sensuous city. Luxembourg is a beautiful city set on two or three different levels. It resembles the fairy-tale cities that we often read about.

Tatyana's parents don't know what to make of me. They are fairly elderly and believe that their daughter is still an innocent virgin whom they must protect. They don't know that she's had two abortions already. I also eat bread and water with my meals, which apparently is very unusual in Germany.

In Germany it is potatoes, potatoes and potatoes. I go upstairs and begin to read. A few moments later Tatyana comes in. "Quickly, we have only a few minutes." We hurriedly take off some of our clothes and I am inside her and we both come immediately. It is exciting, the most exciting fuck we've had. The spice of the forbidden—her parents downstairs—has made the moment. Tatyana has become my closest friend... perhaps the closest friend I have ever had in my life. We are so much alike in our thinking, and we know each other so well in mind and body that it is a new experience for me. I don't love her, but it is always hard for me to live through the winters. Tatyana made the winter and my life bearable.

Back in Paris, I have nowhere to live since I have given up my hotel room due to poverty. There are several letters from my parents, which Khier gives me. I feel like crying when I read them. They are so nice and warm and I know that there is always a home to come back to.

I stay with friends, until I am offered a room near l'Opéra for six dollars a month... I need somehow to keep busy, and hope to have enough male and female friends to combat the loneliness. I don't know what to do with myself. The 10-year-old son of the family where Tatyana stays thinks I should become an actor.

> Dear David,
>
> I am here in Paris with my friends Karen and Astrid. I wrote a long letter to you on the train but I don't have enough English words to translate the letter. I am too stupid. I met an artist and he says he likes me very much. He has a fantastic face, but all day I wanted you. Excuse me, I am too stupid. To live is stupid. Pourquoi vive-je? Ça, je ne sais pas. I beg you to write.
>
> Marlene

I don't want to see Marlene; she drives me crazy. She is madly in love with me, yet won't sleep with me. I go to the Caméleon... Eduardo is there, talking to René, a black American photographer from the West Indies. René lived in the Village for many years and has the exaggerated movements of an artistic homosexual. He is very interesting and I like him. Once when we were eating in a restaurant he showed me how he could get every morsel from a chicken using only his knife and fork. René is one of those people who seems to just drift in and out of cafés, in and out of my life. I sit with them and decide to eat... I order a cheese sandwich and a *demi*. The beer is awful... A beautiful tall blonde, obviously a dancer, walks in and sits down at the table next to us. My eyes are all over her... René is talking, but I am hardly listening. I say something to the blonde, but she ignores it or doesn't hear me. I sigh, turn around, tear up a napkin and then turn again to the blonde and ask her if she'll join us. She says she is waiting for someone. "Until he comes," I say. She shrugs and takes a seat at our table. She is German, a dancer, a Blue Bell girl, the most famous chorus line in Europe. She is perfect... face, body, bust, thighs, legs, and very natural as if unaware of her beauty. When I ask her if she'll meet me, unbelievably she says "yes," and we make a date for the next day.

Her body is perfect, yet somehow it doesn't excite me as we lie in bed together. There is something sexless about Vibeke. But for the next couple of weeks Vibeke becomes my girlfriend.

I have moved into a small hotel on Rue de l'Ancienne Comédie with Carlos, who sleeps on the floor. One night Carlos tries to seduce me and almost succeeds. We spend a lot of time together. He has found a straw wig of long blonde hair, and sitting in the Monaco I put it on. As Carlos makes graceful hand motions, people stare at us, and Åsa, who is sitting with us, feels a bit embarrassed. A friend of Åsa's from Sweden—Kerstin—joins us. She is a student at the Beaux Arts, not very attractive, but sexy in a way, because she is so feminine... She looks at me from under her long, unkempt blonde hair. Carlos is jealous, but I need someone. It seems I always do... For one night Kerstin and I become lovers but I do not show up for our next date.

I have started itching in my genital area, an incredible all-consuming itch. Nothing seems to help it. The mystery is solved when Tatyana, now back in Paris, tells me she has crabs... Stupidly, I shave my pubic hair and apply some cream that does no good at all, and now I am itching twice as much.

My thoughts drift back to college. I picture myself running under arches with a guitar in my hand, my hair long, and feeling that if I can sing, everything will be OK. Books were the bright spot of college and high school—Books and sports, shining lights in the mire of frustration of life amongst the bourgeois, virginal and restrictive. When I was 12, I read Dostoevsky's Crime and Punishment and identified with Raskolnikov for years. In college, some girls called me "Alyosha" after the saintly brother in the Brothers Karamazov... There must be that aspect in me, but at times it seems so distant or so buried. Oh yes, there is Alyosha, but there is also Dmitri and Ivan.

The book that probably had the greatest influence on my life was Dos Passos' *USA*. It awakened my interest in history, especially contemporary revolutionary history in Europe and the between-the-wars period of the United States. The workingman's struggle for better conditions, brought to life in Union songs, was inspiring. Set to beautiful hymns, songs like "Farther along, we'll get our fair wages"—always awoke something in me.

Faulkner, Hemingway, Melville, Mann, Hardy, Eliot, Tolstoy, Orwell, Stendhal, Balzac, Shakespeare, Marlowe, Isherwood, Mauriac, Cocteau, Malraux—all spoke to me.

Evenings in a rented co-operative apartment, I sing, while worshipful, long-haired, semi-sexless party girls sit at my feet—folk songs, bluegrass music, union songs, etc.

Courses in philosophy, reformation history, literature, discussions, late night and all night study... Important last year, it seems almost irrelevant now. Something else is churning inside me, yet I don't know what it is.

Now in Paris, I read Henry Miller—still banned in the U.S.—and Céline. Miller's people are all deformed but all alive. Every word is an ode to life, and I wish I could capture his verve, his *joie de vivre*. I wonder if it is all real. Once he wrote that the first person to write a truly honest account of himself would revolutionize the world—the implication being that his stories are not totally honest, that there is much held back. Céline's people are deformed, disgusting, crooked, but fascinating. Anything that rejects and reacts against the stultified bourgeois and narrow society has a fascination for me...

Sports also fascinate me. I was always faster than almost everyone I played with—a faster runner and faster reflexes. I love team sports. When I read a newspaper I turn to the sports pages first. If I have the luxury of living in a hotel with a hall toilet with a seat, I will take *France Soir* or *L'Equipe* and read the sports news. I have even become interested in bicycle riding, and names like Anquetil—meaningless in the States— hold my interest here.

Sports are a great escape... a neutral area of the mind where it can come to rest... Images that are interesting but not painful. Crossword puzzles also have the effect of using the mind, but not using it. Passing time with full concentration on something of no importance outside of the self. Almost like meditation. But the escape of the sports pages and crossword puzzles cannot go on forever. There is the return to reality, the return to choice, the return to the streets, the return to my mind.

The gnawing fear in the stomach from not knowing what to do, where to go. It is as if one needs some definite action to be defined, and when one is not defined one is in chaos and panic, and enmeshed in a sense of unreality. I wander over to Le Mistral to help pass the time, to read a book, perhaps to have a conversation or find a woman.

Joel, another classmate from college, has invited me to Munich for *Karnival* and I decide to go. I take the night train and spend the following night on the floor of some American friend of Joel's. The itching is growing unbearable and I am wandering around a strange city with a strange language trying to find a doctor. The offices are always closed and I feel scared and lonely and cut off. I finally get to see a doctor who says the crab eggs are still there and gives me a cream, but it, too, doesn't help.

I am sleeping on someone's floor, without occupation, tortured by the itch, lonely without a woman... and when I think I have reached the nadir of my misery, for the first time in my life I am overwhelmed with a feeling of inner peace.

In a *bierstube* called the Weinbauer, where a lot of students gather, I meet Sean. He is a sculptor—American—at the Kunstakademie. Sean is joyful, manic and I need his energy to pick me up.

The itching has taken over my life... I have just finished painting myself with a medicine which is supposed to kill crab eggs, leaving my skin dirty and yellow. The medicine stains everything and it is very embarrassing. Walking is uncomfortable; I am practically forced to sit still. I go to another doctor who gives me a different cream...

My inner peace has disappeared... Frustration, bitterness and hatred have replaced it.

I remember now that the trip started with exhaustion when the alarm clock rang and I turned it off. Sean did not move, and Susan who was with him did not move. So back to bed until eight thirty when "Wake up, Sean, it's eight thirty. We were supposed to be on the road an hour ago."

"Ah, fuck," and he turned to Susan with an erection and entered her pumping up and down under the towel, while I stood and watched.

And he jumped out of bed still naked, his penis hanging down, while Susan asked what time it was because she had to model at the Akademie. And the place was a mess and we laughed at what the owner would say when he saw it.

It started off also in frustration, my frustration. It had been a long time since I had been with a woman and I hated Susan because she used people... not because she had come to my bed once and refused to sleep with me, and here she was in bed with Sean. But I hated her and I lay there most of the night embroiled in my frustrations thinking I could stab her with a knife in the morning. I imagined all sorts of scenes, especially with guns—getting revenge and what to do with the body. The sensualist in me had finally conquered any vestiges of morality that remained, and if I had a gun I know I would have killed her and ended my life at the same time. But, no, perhaps the act of killing her would bring some relief. I didn't kill her. I seethed inside but remained calm, hating her.

And Sean, happy to have fucked goodbye to Munich slipped into his lederhosen, ate the coffee and rolls, and then with my guitar and valise we went downstairs and Sean—still drunk from the night before—as he had been drunk every night for a month —entered the gas station and asked them how to get to the Autobahn to Stuttgart.

We are walking. I am silent. Sean is noisy, yelling in German and English to passersby. It is in my silence that all is explained; it is the silence of not wanting to live but doing so anyway, of going through the motions of living.

Life begins to return; Sean brings it out. He is on a rampage through the streets of Munich; the city is his, while I am its slave. Munich passes by the tram. It rolls, while our baggage fills a corner of the tram. Munich, fascinating Munich, in its ambiguity, with its love/hate images. Munich, the home of the Nazi movement in its terror and cruelty, now filled with smiling, friendly Bavarians. How hard it is to explain. I have realized that at the base of every man lies the irrational, the sensual, which at one time or another assumes complete control of each of us.

THE ROAD—The road is a strange place. One is so near so many people, yet one is alone. Last night I dreamt of the road from Paris to Munich. It was called the "Munchener Road," and it was dark, with only the faint starlight providing a weak illumination. It was a tree-lined road and a lonely couple walked on it. There were no cars; bicycles were parked against the trees. It was a beautiful dream. I seemed to be happy to have made the discovery of this mysterious road.

The real road, however, bears little resemblance to my dream fantasy. From Munich to Kiel on the German border, and to Strasbourg on the French, it is the fast, powerful impersonal Autobahn. We stand on the curved entrances holding signs. We have one which says "USA" for American soldiers, but these soldiers never stop.

Sean standing in the Weinbauer half drunk, barking at a dog, yelling at the waitress, "He bites, he bites," while everyone laughs. This same Sean now on the road watching the cars go by: "I'll tell you now, I'm going back to Munich." But before he does, we are picked up. A hundred kilometers further and again standing on the road, the almost unused entrance to the powerful Autobahn.

We sit. Sean is now morose, while I, freed from the cruel stimulus of the city, rest in the sunshine playing my guitar and singing to a world I despise, but singing just the same. No cars stop. Finally, overburdened with baggage, we deposit our valises in a *gästhaus* and abandon them. We roam through the *gästhaus* speaking to people and asking for a lift. But no lifts until—MIRACLE—two friends from Schwabing, Inger and

Carrie, leap out of a car with Frankfurt plates and we are off again, this time as far as Stuttgart.

But that night we get no further and we stand in the cold waiting, waiting. At seven o'clock we quit to look for a room for the night. It is a world apart, the world of hitchhiking. It is a world where you feel free and yet helpless, where you become completely dependent on others... And seeing all the cars pass you going in your direction, big cars with empty back seats. But they do not stop. Hitchhiking is frustration. Paris plates—A Mercedes from Baden-Baden. "Nach Karlsruhe," I yell, but the car with the Karlsruhe plates rolls by.

A cold double room in a pension. After dinner, Sean, exhausted from the night before, goes to bed immediately. There is a wedding going on beneath our room. It is difficult to sleep as the oom pah pah German music rattles the floor and the walls.

Heidi Heido heida
Heidi heido heida
Heidi, heido, heidaaaaaaaaaaaaaaaaaaaaaaaaaah

Whirling couples on the dance floor, all very ordinary, bourgeois-looking, lacking personality. A heavy-set blonde waitress speaking English she learned from the G.I.'s—But nothing there for me, so after a beer, I, too, go to bed and scratch my body, which itches, itches, itches.

The next day began with the cold and ended with Marianne. Hitchhiking had never been so bad, and finally at ten o'clock at night in a town only sixty kilometers from Strasbourg we gave up and decided to take the train to Paris. We entered the waiting room and sat down at a table, but not until Sean had banged the table of a French girl who, surrounded by soldiers, was concentrating on her newspaper. She seemed afraid to look at the vultures that hovered nearby. Nor did she look at Sean; I, too, pass unnoticed.

Hours of waiting—fatigue... falling into a light sleep. Sean wants to sculpt the girl because she is not wearing a brassiere.

It is midnight and the train arrives. There are no seats. The train is filled with soldiers on leave. Sean and I stand in the aisle; the girl is there with us. She is not beautiful, but attractive. I stare at her; she does not return the gaze. Sean stretches out on the floor. Finally, after a long and torturous hesitation, I speak to her. I show her a little wooden teddy bear that Ingeborg passed on to me through Sean. Ah, Ingeborg, how I remember. We returned together to my room on Baaderstrasse, my face which was death and her beautiful face, and her beautiful—but for me—sexless body. Her face could bring no light into my life, hélas, it couldn't. Her softness, her understanding couldn't help, for that day I had seen a magnificent sensual creature whom I desired so badly that my body shook and shook—only this girl's body could help...

We get undressed, my Ingeborg. I feel nothing. We lie side by side petting a little and stop. I am not excited. I bring the image of *that* girl into my mind. I shut my eyes; I want her so badly. I am hot as I think of her sitting on the bus... I begin to enter Ingeborg, and as I enter her vagina, where the pleasure should be most intense, she lets forth a cry of pain ejecting my penis which comes all over the outer lips of her organ. And we lie there in the silence saying nothing... motionless... doomed.

And I looked at her, at Ingeborg, at this wonderful understanding person who had given herself to me and who lay next to me trying to understand my unhappiness and to help me, and I hated her. Yes, suddenly I was filled with hatred for her. Why must she be next to me and not the sensual girl on the bus? Ah, how irrational hatred is—how irrational and basic to every man. And then I could not stand it any longer. I twisted and turned on the bed, banging my head with my hands, the image of the *other* girl in my mind. And I didn't have her. I had Ingeborg, beautiful, sweet Ingeborg, whom I did not want... Ingeborg... Ingeborg...

And I show your wooden bear to the girl. She looks at it, smiles, hands it back and continues reading. I leave and then come back. We talk. She answers my questions mechanically, looking out of the window. I join Sean on the floor for a half hour, being kicked and trod upon by all the passing people. We lean against each other and try to sleep, but I cannot. Sean walks to the other side of the car, stretches out on the floor and falls asleep. I again speak to the girl, searching for the right things to say with my incomplete French. Long silences follow each phrase and she answers mechanically. She is still cold. She teaches Greek and Latin in the Sorbonne. She has adopted the name Marilus.

I tell her mine is Danius.

I lie down on the floor and try to sleep, but am jostled at every stop by people entering and leaving their compartments. Again back to Marilus and again the same coldness, the same silences, the same staring out the window. Back to the floor; but it is no use. Sean is sleeping. I lie silently... I look at the girl. I approach her again, and this time when I speak to her, her hand goes into mine and she lowers her face close to my lips.

That night Danius and Marilus bared their bodies to each other in the twilight and culminated their desire under an open window that let in the Paris sky.

Paris. Warm, sunny day, nowhere to live, and then to discover that beneath so much beauty lies emptiness.

It was too early to visit anyone, and so we sat down at the Relais Odéon on the terrace, while I held my guitar and Sean tried to sketch...

And I was dirty, unshaven, hungry, tired, but it was a new life opening up, for it is life and I had stopped dying. Death had been left momentarily behind. And it stayed behind for a week until it caught up with me suddenly and overpowered me one night. Two sexy but stupid German girls had frustrated me and I refused to talk to them because they were so empty and insensitive. And I was again the truthful man. So I walked. I couldn't go to my room because I ached and desired and hated too much, so I walked along St. Germain until death caught me and I could go no further, and so collapsed against a tree not being able to move another step, having nowhere to go, having no hope and I stayed leaning against this tree watching a girl waiting for someone to come out of the Metro entrance... But I stopped standing and instead sat against the wall of a building on the Boulevard and stared at all the people walking by and they stared at me but they turned their faces away when they saw me.

And the week when I lived it was orgasms, orgasms, orgasms and little more. And I was buoyant in sex, though most of it turned out to be promise and not fulfillment... But I was young; I was youth. Sean and I walked along St. Michel, and when we would smile at a girl she would smile back, and I would chase her and speak to her, make a date for the next day with one, the day after with another.

And then Sean would see a Negress and I would approach her and tell her how much Sean loved her and that he couldn't speak French, and you could see that she was flattered and she smiled. Sean took her hand and held it for a while until she realized what she was doing and withdrew it.

It was a day of continuing ecstasy which ended with one of the girls I had picked up, a French girl who agreed to sleep with me, but when she took off her clothes, I did not like her flabby flat-chested body and so fell asleep unable and unwilling to get an erection.

For four days it continued like that. I could pick up a girl anywhere and everywhere: the street, a café, the Métro. I felt powerful, powerful. But then Sean became morose and wanted to leave Paris, and I needed Sean to help me as he needed me to help him, and so it ended and death began again to creep up on me, minute-by-minute, incident by incident. And not only death but truth came along, too. And with truth I could not fight any more... and with the coming of truth goes happiness, flees youthfulness. Truth destroys these... truth destroys beauty, joy. Ah, truth, how I am thy slave and how I hate thee.

Carlos was not back; he was visiting Rimbaud's home in Charleville. But finally he returns and I visit him, and there is Carlos in bed with some Frenchman with smelly feet and an idiotic grin on his face. And Carlos touches the man's chest, and the Frenchman closes his eyes with pleasure and grabs Carlos, while Carlos tries to stretch his hand out to me and rid himself of this disgusting creature with whom he has fucked all night.

Carlos, Carlos, whose small oriental body and imaginative mind has become the lure and goal of the rich men's sons in Asia, Europe and America. This twentieth century courtesan says he still loves me and smiles at his own degeneracy, which he blames on me because I destroyed his religion and made him desire.

But the Frenchman refuses to leave, and so I go out to get something in the café at the corner of Rue de Buci, Rue Mazarine and Rue de l'Ancienne Comédie and Rue St. André des Arts and then return to Carlos's room. The Frenchman has arisen, short, mustached, typical looking, smirking, too insensitive to realize that he is not wanted by either of us.

Where did Carlos find him? "On the street. He's insane; he had at least nine ejaculations."

"Quoi? Qu'est-ce-que tu dis?" he asks Carlos.

"Rien, ma cherie," replies Carlos, and then to me, "Where can we lose him?"

Lose him we do, and we wander off together. Carlos is talkative while I say nothing. He talks of Rimbaud in whose room he has lived and shows me the book he is writing on Rimbaud... But I feel the spring, and with the spring I feel the women and Carlos who loves me cannot help. I cannot remain. Carlos takes my hand and kisses me on the cheek, but I withdraw it. We can find no happiness together, for the women with their beautiful legs stand between us.

And I got up from the bench in the park where we are sitting and started to walk in the hot sun, and this sun reflected off the silver cross lying on top of the firm full breasts of a young girl. I breathe deeply and sadly and walked faster.

Hot sun on the quay by the Seine in front of Notre Dame. Carlos dancing oriental dances to my guitar music. Madness... madness, let us snub them all. For I have reached up to Heaven and pulled down a jelly-fish and squeezed it... and hiding our faces and laughing hysterically we cross over to Place St. Michel. Today we will play pederasts, tomorrow tourists, the next day gods—"And we will end it all by copulating under a bridge," says Carlos, and I give him a nasty look.

Carlos and I roam together. Why am I so silent with him? It is because I feel the spring and feel the women. Carlos talks about Rimbaud. We are young and, like him, we are wandering in our season in Hell, in our madness, without knowing why. We are him; he is us.

"One evening I seated beauty on my knee and I found her bitter, and cursed her," wrote Rimbaud. "I continued to purge my mind of all hope and all joy, to strangle it... I think I am in hell, therefore I am in hell. I saw the hell of a woman back there, and I shall be free to possess truths in my soul and body... and the spring brought me the idiot's frightful laughter."

I saw the spring coming towards me in the form of two beautiful girls. I decided this time to smile at spring, and all I received for my effort was two empty looks from two painted faces.

Today I wrote to Tatyana telling her that I have discovered the ironical paradox of life, and that it is so ironic and ambiguous in its nature that it cannot be expressed in words or understood by others.

I am haunted by two images. The Café Mabillon on Boulevard St. Germain... A certain group of youths sits there every day, all day. I do not know if they are girls or boys or mixed, but I know that when I see them, this strange group, that the world is mad, that insanity is the rule, that anarchy and the irrational are the basic truths of man, and that so-called sane people of the world are really sick. They are deceived, living in a self-deception multiplied so many times that it is now impossible to find the core.

And there is a second image. She comes often into the Mabillon. She is the most beautiful, stunning creature I have ever seen—tall, beautiful large breasts, tight cord skirt above the knees, molding unbelievable curves and exposing the bottoms of sensual thighs and full calves. Her hair is reddish blonde and done in Brigitte Bardot style... and on her breast she wears a large golden cross. She walks with her head up, looking neither right nor left... proud and mighty... all conquering. And yet I know that underneath it all there will be found a sickness, a misery, an insanity. This is the lot of man. I know it. I know it. I know it.

Southern Rape

KELLY 1961

My first mistake was to think that Alabama had changed. From the look in my Daddy's eyes, a look that said "slut," and a glance at my terrified mother, afraid to ever contradict the tyrant, I knew I'd made a mistake coming home.

"Girls down here don't dress like that," she said, eying my torn khakis. "Here, you dress like a lady."

She didn't think I was much of a lady last time I was here, since they stuck me in a mental hospital, had me declared incompetent and took away my kids.

"I want to see my children," I said hopefully.

"They're not your children," my father said. "They're ours."

"Well, I'm still the natural mother and I think I should see them."

"We'll think about it," was all my father had to say.

They invite me into the kitchen, these two strangers who are my parents. They are wary. After all, I've been living in Greenwich Village in New York and they don't know what kind of creature I am. They're also afraid that maybe I'll commit suicide, which would cause them all kinds

67

of problems—you know... police, hospitals, funeral, gossip, expenses. They'd be happier for me to do it up north.

I know I shouldn't have come, but I want to see my kids and I want to get away from the streets. Maybe I fooled myself into thinking that my mother would hold me and be a mother. But I can see she really hates me. I turned out wrong.

It must have been my fault that Billy Joe went out drinking every night and came home and beat the shit out of me. If I'd behaved myself, a nice upstanding southern gentleman like Billy Joe Lewis would never do such a thing. Well, they didn't know that Billy Joe Lewis was a son of a bitch with a mean streak and more emotional problems than anybody I ever met. He was a sadist and I was his victim. On our marriage night he got drunk and beat me. And yet I stuck it out for three years, living in terror... gave him two children, whom he didn't care for, went crazy, smashed the house, slashed my wrists, didn't die, but ended up being declared insane and losing my children.

The silence at the table is heavy. It is finally broken by my father.

"So Kelly, what ya been doing up there in New York?"

"Not much... writing, working as a waitress."

"A waitress... that pay well?"

"Not too well, but enough to get by on."

I'd probably better not tell them about the cafe Four Winds and all the weirdoes who come in there and the drugs, the loneliness, the streets, the filthy pads, the whole Village scene. But I have no other home. This is not home.

We eat in silence. The faint smell of flowers from the outside comes through the window. There is a lazy beauty about the rural south, but there is also viciousness.

We make small talk, avoiding the subject of my/their children.

"Where are Sally and Billy," I finally get the nerve to ask.

"At your aunt's," says my mother.

"I see."

"Look Kelly," my father says in his official voice, "I don't know if it's a good idea for you to see them. It might just confuse them."

The silence is deadly. Now the truth is on the table. I'm not to see my children. Any illusions I had of getting them back, of them loving me, of me loving them... are gone.

I don't say a word. I've got to get out of here. There's a bus back tomorrow, so I've got to make it through the night.

"Where are you going?" asks my mother.

"Out," I say.

"When will you be back?"

"I don't know."

"We'll leave the key under the mat."

I'm crying inside and tears are forming. I'm trapped and there's no exit. "Hell is other people," wrote Sartre. He was half right. If I didn't need love and comfort and a shoulder or something I could take all the crap... But I need. I needed a man so I married a sadist like Billy Joe. I need my kids and I lost them. I need to escape so I drink or take dope... and now I need to talk to somebody. Anybody.

It's about a mile to town and I wonder if Ray's luncheonette is still there. This used to be the local hangout. Probably run into somebody I know. Maybe I can meet a man who will help me get through the night. It is starting to scream in my gut like I want to bend over and just lie on the ground. I can't do it; I force myself to go on.

Ray's is still there and the denizens are still there too. Blue jeans and cowboy boots give me a leer as I walk in. I ignore him and go to a table in the corner.

"Well, well, if it isn't Kelly back from Greenwich Village." I look up. It's Danny who works in the gas station, a friend of Billy Joe's.

"Hey guys, come on over and meet a real beatnik," yells Danny. I hadn't noticed the others, but four more guys, two of whom I vaguely recognize walk over to my table smiling.

"Mind if we sit down," says one of them.

I nod. I guess even this company is better than none at all. These guys almost make the Village characters look decent. Danny makes introductions. Frank, Bobby, Darnell and Sam.

The faces are a blur.

"Now why's a sophisticated northern girl like you returning back to poor old Alabama to do some slumming?" asks Danny, warming up to his role. Danny's going to be the comedian and I'm the straight man.

Sam leans towards me... He's short, stocky, not very pleasant looking. I smell whisky on his breath. "What is it like?" he says. "Is it really free love?"

"Yeah," adds Darnell... "does everybody fuck everybody else like it says in the magazines?"

"No, it's just like anywhere else... People eat, dress, go to the bathroom."

"But they take dope and have orgies..."

These guys have been reading magazine articles about the beat generation and here I am, a veritable, authentic representative. I don't know what gets into me but I decide to play along.

"Everybody smokes dope in New York. Then after we're high we kind of pair off... you know... take a guitar and go to someone's pad, and have a little orgy. With all the orgies and all the pot there's not much time for anything else..."

Their eyes are widening. I think I've gone too far. This is southern man; southern ladies don't talk like that. They are looking at each other almost embarrassed. Danny breaks the silence. "We're going to have a little party... why don't you come with us."

I'm frightened. I know that when a southern gentleman starts to drink he becomes a southern beast. Yet I'm so lonely and the thought of going back to my mommy and daddy's is frightening. Maybe I could sit in the luncheonette, but it's going to close. Maybe one of them will be nice; we can talk; I can be held. Frank has been the quietest. He seems shy, almost pleasant. I wouldn't mind snuggling up to him... just to be held...

We go outside. Danny has a pickup truck and I get in the cab with Danny and Frank. Darnell, Bobby and Sam go in the back. Danny takes a fifth of bourbon and hands it to Sam. I look at Frank. He looks away.

"I haven't seen you before," I say.

"My folks moved out here a few years ago. Dad works for the Tanolin Company."

He seems almost afraid to look at me.

"You really live in Greenwich Village?" he says.

I give him my nicest smile and I can sense his warming. I look outside. There are no lights.

"Where are we going?" I ask Danny.

"I know a nice place where we can have a party, undisturbed."

"But there are no other girls," I say. "What kind of party is this?"

"You just come down from New York. You're our guest of honor."

"Wouldn't want to share you with any other girls."

"Your hospitality's a bit too generous for me. I think I'd like to get out," I say.

"Hell you'd never find your way back from here, Kelly honey."

Now I'm really frightened.

"What are we going to do at this party?"

"Hell, you're just gonna tell us country boys about the big city and all the beatniks you know. Just talk," says Danny, "That's all."

I turn to Frankie. "Tell him to take me home."

"Don't worry, Kelly, everything will be all right."

In the back, the boys are passing around the bottle as the truck enters a wooded area. It is very dark. Danny drives for about five more minutes and stops in an opening surrounded by trees on one side, the river on the other.

"Everybody out," he says.

"Where are we?"

"This is where the party is... get out."

I climb out of the cab. The three boys have hopped to the ground from the back of the truck.

They're trying to get up the nerve to rape me. There is only silence.

Darnell breaks the silence. "Tell us about the guys you fucked in New York," he says.

I don't reply.

They stand close to me. Danny puts his hands on my breasts. I brush it off.

"We're just trying to be friendly, Kelly. You can be friendly to all them New York beatniks, then you can be friendly to us."

"Leave me alone please," I say. "I got all kinds of diseases in New York."

They look at each other and hesitate. Suddenly Sam lunges at me and pushes me to the ground. "You whore," he yells.

They are on top of me. I scream but a hand smacks me on the mouth and I taste blood. I can't move. At least two of them are holding me while the others are ripping off my clothes.

"Wow look at those tits."

"Who goes first?"

I stop struggling. I pull inside myself. I am not there. One of them enters me and it hurts, so I scream again, but the hands are holding me down and I am helpless.

I shut my eyes and try to remove my mind from what's going on, but there are hands all over me and I'm hurting in my vagina. They're not going to let me live after this; they're going to kill me. I don't want to die in a backwoods in Alabama. I never had a chance. I've tried, God, I've tried... but I never had a chance.

I try to find a comfort zone, but there is none. I think of that handsome boy, Niko, who spent a night with me, but that brings pain. I think of my children, but that's also pain. The Village, the cafes, the streets, everything is pain. There is nowhere peaceful to rest my mind. Finally, I think of the flowers outside my parents' home. As a kid, I loved the smell. While one of the animals enters me I think of flowers... I smell the flowers. I see the little girl who was me. Whatever they are doing to my body I am no longer there.

When it's over I lie there and wonder if they are going to kill me. Instead I am pulled to my feet and I hear Danny's voice... "Don't tell anybody, Kelly. No one will believe you. They'll just think you're a slut from Greenwich Village who got what she deserved."

Another voice: "We can't leave her here. We gotta take her somewhere."

Danny's voice, "We'll take you home to your Daddy..."

I am put in the front seat of the truck and we drive in the night. They let me off near my parent's home. The key is under the mat. I turn on the water in the bathtub and ease my body in. It feels comforting. I cannot even cry.

City of Light, City of Darkness

DAVID 1961

I have been plagued by a terrible chest cold all winter, but it is finally clearing up and I can begin singing again. In the hot sun we sit on the quays of the Seine joined by some English and American Friends. I play folk songs, sad, yet beautiful music, the tragic stories of unrequited love, death, loneliness, injustice, etc. It harmonizes with my mood. I feel the songs, and though I don't sing well, I communicate something to those listening. Later Nickey comes by with his banjo and we decide to play for some money on Boulevard St. Michel. We gather a large and appreciative crowd, but soon two men who have been listening ask us to come with them. Policemen! As they are walking me towards their waiting car, a girl who had been listening slips a note into my pocket.

The policeman asks me for my identity card. I had left it at the hotel, so we drive there and I go up to my room to fetch it. The policeman looks at it wordlessly and tells me to come with him to the station. At the station he sits me down and begins firing questions in a neutral/unfriendly way. Sources of income, what I do, where I'm from, etc. He tells me it's illegal to play for money in the streets and they may keep me in prison. I start to feel frightened. He signals for a uniformed policeman to find me a cell. This is no joke. Just then another detective comes into the room and asks my interrogator what is going on. By the deferential way my interrogator replies it is apparent that the second detective is the boss.

When he discovers that I am being held for playing guitar in the street he tells my interrogator to let me go. He walks me outside, shakes my hand, invites me for a drink at the café. I thank him and decline.

I take the girl's note out of my pocket.

> I hope you haven't got any trouble for this arrest.
> I hate that kind of things in France, and they are so rude.
> If you are free before 11 pm, you can phone me, just to tell me that you are all right because I feel very sad knowing you are by the police station.
> My number is DAU 74-25.
> My name Corinne. The girl with black raincoat from Paris.
>
> My best thoughts,
> Amicalement, Corinne

She has put a telephone *jeton* in the envelope.

I call her and we agree to meet the next day. When she arrives at the Caméleon, she is looking very attractive. Corrine tells me she is married and can only meet me in the afternoon. Her husband is a worker, poorly paid, and they live in run-down housing on the outskirts of Paris. Usually, his salary lasts only half the month, and for 15 days they eat bread and soup. We go back to my hotel and make love. She is small but firm, shapely and very passionate.

But Corinne is trouble. We meet a few more times, but her husband, suspicious, has her followed. Two tough looking guys stop me outside the hotel and tell me if I see her again they will have me killed. We are supposed to meet the next day. I tell her about the threat, but she says she has to see me at least once more and will be at my room at two. At 2:30 no Corinne. I leave.

> "Je viens d'arriver. Il est 3 heures moins vingt-huit. Je comprend que tu te sois impatienté. Je ne peux retourner chez moi. Mon train est à neuf heures ce soir. Quelle barbe. Je serai au café tabac du coin, dans l'arriè-salle. Ce café-tabac au bout de la rue Bertholet. A droite en sortant de l'hôtel. Viens me chercher si tu... C

Corinne has given me back my confidence. Now with my improved French I am feeling much more at home in Paris and I even pick up a French girl in the Métro named Maryvonne. She is a secretary and lives in a small *chambre de bonne* in the 19th. Climbing the seven flights of stairs is exhausting, yet I am glad for her warmth and comfort. However, she is not one of the beauties I see passing in the street, so I know I will not see her again. She has a passionate *sympathique* face, but her body does not excite me. I am drawn to people who like me, who are attracted to me. It is hard to say no—one needs to be loved and one does not want to hurt them, yet I always end up hurting them... and hurting myself. The next day there is a letter in my box.

> I'd opened my door to you without knowing who you were. From now on it will stay open so that you can come whenever you want, anytime you desire.
>
> To say goodnight, I am sending you this short poem by Robert Desnos called, 'Conte de Fées.'
>
> Il était un grand nombre de fois un homme qui aimait une femme.
>
> Il était un grand nombre de fois une femme qui aimait un homme.
>
> Il était un grand nombre de fois un homme et une femme qui n'aimaient pas celle et celui qui les aimaient.
>
> Il était une fois peut-être un homme et une femme qui s'aimaient.
>
> Affecteusement
Maryvonne

With Maryvonne's letter in my pocket I go to my French class at the Institute Catholique but cannot concentrate, so I sit and stare at a Dutch girl who is so sexy that my body gets weak.

I leave the school and see an old woman on a bench near the bus stop. She tells me her problems... Children who ignore her, insufficient social security... a gangrenous leg. She tells me about her visits to the hospital and all her miseries. I reply, I question, I lend a needed ear, yet my mind is on my own troubles... I have pain in my chest... Could it be my heart? For days I can think of nothing else.

Back in the Latin Quarter, I buy a book of poems by Jacques Prévert and André Verdet—

"Pauvre Joueur de bilboquets

A quoi penses-tu?

Je pense aux filles aux milles bouquets

Je pense aux filles aux milles beaux culs."

Mais le plus beau cul de tous is walking up the Boulevard St. Michel. Erect, beautiful, firm, she wiggles her ass like an invitation. One man after another tries to pick her up, but she ignores them. Her sex appeal is incredible... heads turn, gasp. I follow her and watch the show. Just before reaching the Luxembourg gardens I pass her, turn around and laugh at her.

"What a show," I say in French, "Every man on the street is after you."

"What did you say?" she replies in English.

She is an American—this sexiest girl in Paris—living in Montparnasse and... I keep talking, my stomach in a knot... A real prize. And she becomes mine... sort of... We go up to my room, I and this woman whose body and walk has implanted itself on every male mind in the Quarter. We undress, and then she tells me she is afraid. She is a virgin. She lies stiff, unmoving while I stroke her. I get an erection and I force my way in and come immediately. She has not reacted. We have made "love." My first virgin. Another chalk mark... I walk her home, say goodbye. We are alone.

A letter from Marlene.

Dear David

Coming very late to my house today I found your letter. Since two hours I try to write something down on this paper clearly enough to be understood. The last five weeks I live like a delusion. First, I spent 9 days in a sanitarium because I am very anemic. After, I was obliged to take a course of medical treatment. And when I returned I lost a hundred marks and now have no money.

David I tried to push away thoughts about you in the back of my mind ("Oh, Dr. Freud" as you sing...) with an outermost moderate success. (What a sentence) I see you in my mind's eye, sitting like a graceful young cat on the bed playing guitar. I've never seen before a man so good looking as you are. But more than your beauty I like your good head and your intelligence. You must absolutely send me a new picture. In my next letter I will enclose a photograph of mine if I can find one.

Our last meeting was a great disappointment for you, and you didn't try to conceal it. As I heard you on the phone speaking to Tatyana about your problems and referring to me, I was hurt. Then I went to Mrs. Ostreicher telling her about us. She likes you very much but she believes you only desire my body and are trying to sleep with me until I do it. First I thought this is a solution. But then I feel ashamed.

I would be very glad to come visit you but I cannot promise it. 100 marks are at the moment very much for me and I can't borrow them from my mother because it is impossible to let her know that Marlene goes to Paris to sleep with a man.

Please cheri, write me so soon as possible. I feel so unhappy and alone. The only thing is to work and to learn. I learn French and Swedish now, for I want to have my next holidays in France or in Scandinavia. Parce que je t'aime, je t'embrasse.

Ta Marlene

With Tatyana in Germany, the family she stays with has offered me her position as *au pair*. It is an interesting family. Their close friends are Sartre and Ionesco. I would take the job, but I am not sure I want to stay in Paris. Friends have invited me to visit them in Germany and in Yugoslavia, and I would like to visit Israel. Paris is beautiful and sunny, but I want to travel. I feel freer and happier than I have before, but that moment of inner peace that I experienced in Munich has not returned. It is also time to think about returning to the States. I have been accepted at Berkeley graduate school to study history, so I ship my trunk with most of my things in it to my parents' house.

There are two boats leaving for the States in August—a Holland American Line student ship from Rotterdam or the French Line from Le Havre. The Holland American line is $35 cheaper ($185) than the French line... but do I want a student atmosphere or do I want privacy?

I meet a French girl sitting in the Monaco. She has sad eyes, a plain face. Her name is Nanouche. She tells me she is pregnant and is going to a "Bonne Femme" to have a "filthy operation" and undoubtedly be maimed for life. I ask her why she doesn't go to a doctor, but she says she needs 40,000 francs (85 dollars) for the operation, and she doesn't have the money. I lend her the money, though I know I will never see it, or her, again...

I have been asked to contribute to a literary magazine that some friends are starting. I have no intention of writing a novel or a traditional-style short story. This is the style of the past. As Ralph Waldo Emerson said, these novels will disappear and be replaced by diaries and autobiographies in which the author chooses what is important from experience and is able to record the *truth*!

I write to Marlene and tell her I am leaving on a trip to Israel. I will be stopping in Berlin and Munich. Does she want to meet me? "Yes," she answers, "in Munich."

Wandering through East Berlin. It seems like the war has just ended. Most of the buildings are still bombed out, unlike West Berlin where the rubble has been changed to newly constructed apartment buildings.

There is one long, wide avenue, Stalinallé, newly built with a strange, white, almost Georgian architecture that resembles a stage set. As I walk, the first Russian soldiers I have ever seen emerge from this white, dreamlike architecture. I stare at them, fascinated.

I go to a jazz club in the West (The Germans are jazz crazy) but am feeling withdrawn, shy, lonely. Back in the hotel I read *Studs Lonigan*. I have read *Lolita, Catcher in the Rye* and *The Web and the Rock* in three days.

The weather is gray and overcast, like my mood.

Munich again. Scenes of defeats. A friend finds me a room in an abandoned building on Karlsbachstrasse, and I walk around the town looking at the architecture and the students.

When Marlene arrives, it is cold and rainy. There is hardly any heat in the flat and she stands shivering in her sweater. Marlene walks around the apartment, chattering, trying to avoid the moment she has come for. Her first time! She is torn between desire and fear. And I am also torn, between lust and dislike. I realize that I don't like Marlene. She writes poetic letters, but her soul is not a poet's soul. There is coldness in her soul. Her father was killed during the war, and her relations with her mother were never too good. She needs affection from a man, but there is a lack of a spark or warmth in the interior of her soul. There is an acute intelligence and a literary sense, but without real understanding. I sense all this instinctively. My feelings for her are purely physical. I need her body, but I do not need her.

As usual I have nothing in the house to offer, and so we get undressed, my Marlene; she lies naked under the covers not moving, frightened. I undress, join her, and caress her, and I become excited, touching her sexy body. But she does not move... she lies frigid, like a steel rod. It is almost like being with a corpse except for the eyes which open and close. I am erect; I touch her in her vaginal area, her clitoris, her breasts, but there is little response. When I try to enter her there is resistance... I press and press, but she is frigid... stone cold... a barrier of steel. And I end up coming on her thigh, and we both lay there, a universe apart, united only by depression.

She is crying soft tears. "I cannot, I cannot... I'm sorry, so sorry..." She tries to caress my face, but I lie on my back staring at the ceiling, which is now shadowed by the approaching dusk, and I ask "WHY?"

A letter from Marianne (Marilus) at American Express, Munich, along with a letter from Colette.

Dear David,

"Genevieve brought me the money last Saturday and Monday I gave it to your friend, Nanouche, who came to see me, strange, beautiful—you must love her. I gave her the 40,000 francs, follement, without knowing her. I liked her. Don't worry if she doesn't give it back to you. I will make it good.

The streets of Paris are soft, soft as tears. I left for Brittany. There were gold cliffs, strange violet flowers, a too-beautiful music, as well as extraordinary friends who I could die with. I dove into icy water and dried my hair in the sun. I stretched out on red rocks, filled with a joy which could bring tears...

Here in Paris, I miss your guitar and your piercing eyes. Many kisses on your face...

Marianne

I had met Colette on the quay, playing my guitar. A small, blonde, French girl, she had studied in the States. As I played, there were sparks between us, but later, she proved to be ephemeral as a ghost. She floated, she weaved; she was here, there, fascinating, long straight hair, but crazy, untouchable. I wanted to see her, to grasp her essence, to enter her and perhaps penetrate that mystery. I wrote to her, and told her my itinerary.

Dear, Dear David,

Your letter is beautiful because I read it after having run in the wind while going crazy.

I cannot kill my childhood because it is part of me still, and because I am afraid of love and of life and especially of viellesse and maturité...

So, I continue to search for the white sun and the cold wind. You sound as if you are lost and alone, but you, too, will find joy that only children can know.

Tu sais l'ennivrement de la ville et le froid qui te rends très fort.

I am working, and I read Tagore and write on my walls with a magic marker—but I want to go away (India)—will you come?

And as I said, your letter is soft like a smile that wants to cry and is trembling—but that is the fever caught in the cities, and you and I are sick and lost—but it is beautiful, and one day there will be peace and eternity and a lonely winter beach—the guitar will cry and we will smile.

Until then
Colette

In Vienna I meet Jean-Pierre and we haunt the cafés together. I like the atmosphere in Vienna. The people are extremely friendly to foreigners. Last night I was buying some bread and cheese from a stand and when the woman found out I was a foreign student she gave it to me free.

I play guitar in the middle of town for an hour, and everybody who passes drops a shilling into the hat. I split the money with Jean-Pierre who is broke. I am glad to have him around because we speak French together and my French is starting to flow. For the first time, I am comfortable in the language.

Vienna is not at all bohemian, and it has almost a small-town naiveté that is certainly pleasant after the cruel sophistication of Paris.

The culture here is half oriented towards Western Europe and half towards Eastern Europe. There are many Slavic types. Here, I can go into the most expensive establishments and feel reasonably at ease, which I could never do in New York or Paris.

Sitting with Jean-Pierre in the café, the hunger for women returns. It ends in bed with a girl who has one of the most beautiful bodies I have ever seen. She wears a large cross around her neck and is so firm and shapely as to be unbelievable. I, apparently, didn't make her too happy as she doesn't show up the next day for our date, which leaves me depressed but not despondent... It is time to leave Vienna. Jean-Pierre is going to return to Paris, while I head south to Graz.

Playing guitar and singing in the central station in Graz with people filling up my hat with schillings until the police stop me. The next day I leave for Yugoslavia with a picture of me playing the guitar in the local newspaper.

Hitchhiking goes well, though there are hardly any cars in Yugoslavia. The countryside is beautiful and the people friendly. Kids stand on the side of the road and wave. In the fields the farmers drive teams of two oxen. I have yet to see a tractor. I get a lift with a truck driver who lets me off on the outskirts of Zagreb. As I stand in the middle of an almost empty road, some students approach me and ask me to come with them. We speak German (German is the second language here.) They are art students and they are laughing at something that I don't understand. I follow them into a large building and up onto a stage... There is little light and perhaps 50-60 students sitting in chairs in the auditorium. It turns out that I am being auctioned off. I am won by an attractive blonde girl who gives me her address. I look for the address later but do not find it. Neither of us gets our prize.

In Zagreb I stay with a friend, Vlatko, whom I know from Paris. In the evening the whole city goes outside and strolls up and down the streets. Back and forth, back and forth... It's peaceful... secure. A friend of Vlatko's teaches me a song in the Slovenian language about a father who has two beautiful, white horses. The catchy tune stays with me and I sing it wherever I go.

Reading D.H. Lawrence on the train to Sarajevo where world wars are started and East meets West in littered streets. Sarajevo is in Bosnia, which is predominantly Moslem as opposed to Zagreb, which is in Catholic Croatia. Few Yugoslavs feel like Yugoslavs, but rather like Slovenes, Croats, Serbs, Bosnians, Macedonians, etc. The Sarajevo station is very modern, but outside the station a group of gypsies camp out.

Everywhere in Yugoslavia one finds American movies, comic strips, rock and roll. It's hard to tell one is in a Communist state except for the fact that the banks and tourist offices are all state-run and there is no opposition party.

The countryside is filled with kids walking home from school, playing soccer bare-footed in the fields. There are peasant girls in red dresses, and the oxen-drawn carts are everywhere. The policemen wear red stars on their caps, and in the cities people jump on and off crowded trams going full speed. There are two official alphabets, Latin for the Croatian language and Cyrillic for the Serbian. All the street signs are in both alphabets.

In Sarajevo I am the pied piper walking through the streets followed by a flock of kids for whom I play and sing. The Yugoslav kids are wonderful; they are inquisitive, friendly and uncorrupted.

The train ride from Sarajevo to Dubrovnik cuts through a series of tunnels, some of them five miles long. From Sarajevo to the coast there is a special train built on narrow gauge tracks and pulled by a coal engine. The whole train trip, with a top speed of 20 miles an hour, passes through the mountains where Tito and the partisans fought the Germans in World War II.

Every time one enters a tunnel the soot from the engine fills all the cars, making breathing uncomfortable. At every station we leave the cars and walk to pumps to drink water... Nobody cares if the train leaves or not, for it never goes faster than a man can run, and most Yugoslavs board trains after they have started.

I play my guitar for the passengers, a couple of whom speak English. One, a boy in the Air Force stationed at Zagreb, is returning to Dubrovnik to visit his family for the first time in a year-and-a-half.

The sights are beautiful... The most fantastic being the actual approach to Dubrovnik and the sea. The train, chugging along like the first steam engines, winds down the mountainside over-looking the Adriatic, which is always a blue-green color. Lambs and some type of a mountain goat herded by a lonely shepherd watch the train. White houses with red roofs occasionally dot the mountainside. Finally, one arrives at the station and is greeted by a horde of taxi drivers, hotel own-ers and ancient, ugly prostitutes. A ten minute trolley ride to the city and, lo, there is no city, but instead a Medieval wall. This is Dubrovnik... it is the same wall that has stood for ten centuries. People in modern dress seem ludicrous. The city should be empty. It is a museum, a beauti-ful anachronism.

Mon Cher Davidus,

I received your Dubrovnik postcard today.

I write this inside the Caméléon on the first step of the stone staircase leading down to the dance cellar.

Did you know that in all the times I have been to the

Caméléon I have never not even once seen the looks of its 'cave' nor do I intend to; let it be—for me one of those little mysteries—like those countries I have never been to and certain beautiful creatures whose faces I have momentarily worshipped, but whose personalities were denied me; it is less painful that way—not as fraught with despair as having known and loved another whom one never hopes to see again.

Dear David,

Your loneliness is something I share, but someday you shall move farther and farther away from me, and I do not mean just in the physical sense, either. The chasms that can separate two hearts are even more immeasurable (and far more terrible) than spatial distance.

I shall lie to you if I say that I think of you often. I ceased to think of you even before our final farewell—instead you have become an eradicable part of my existence that, though not naming you, I evoke you in my least conscious gesture. Even from the very first moment I saw you, your entire being has been stamped like an indelible seal on mine.

But so much for my feelings. I protest them too much. I should learn the ultimate eloquence of pure silence.

Love
Carlos

The trip by boat from Dubrovnik to Piraeus lasts two days aboard the Yugoslavian ship "Orebic." We stop in Brindisi, Corfu, Patras. I book a deck passage without cabin, which is half price, but a friendly crew manages to get me a cabin both nights.

The most beautiful moment of the trip is docking at Piraeus in the night. The harbor is filled with a silence, broken only by occasional shouts and hammer blows. Some boats are garishly lighted, like the gigantic Greek Liner, "Patris" which is to sail today. Others sit silently moored, their hulls seeming more ephemeral and ghostlike than real. A large ship is being unloaded next to ours. It is the "Israel," bound for Haifa that same night. I leave the "Orebic" and walk to the "Israel" and ask for passage. I am told I must buy a ticket from the agent. For hours I watch the passengers board the ship. They are mostly American Jews and Israeli Jews... and I feel for the first time that I have a people—that these are my people... I am the only onlooker. The dock is empty, and everyone on the boat stares at me. I just watch without moving. Watching. Watching. I do not know why. I do not believe. I break every Jewish law invented and will continue to do so... but I am a Jew. And I feel that these are my people... And so I watch. I watch the drunk, dyed-blonde, middle-aged American woman from San Francisco making a loud-mouthed fool of herself. And yet I feel I belong with her, with this ship.

But I cannot sail with it and must wait in Piraeus until the next ship sails for Israel. Piraeus is a nightmare. I cannot take a step on the street without being accosted by a homosexual. It seems that almost everybody is homosexual. They pester me; they gape. But I am lonely, too. It has been more than three weeks since I slept with that girl in Vienna and I need a woman, so one night I venture out to the nightclub area of Piraeus. I find a sexy blonde bar girl with large firm breasts, a beautiful ass and gorgeous legs, and I ask her to come with me. But she says I must first buy her a drink and she will come with me later. Naturally, she orders champagne, which depletes my very low money supply. But I lust for her and I wait for her, and at closing time when I ask her to come, two gangsters stand between us and shove me away. I protest, and one of them pushes me very hard. I grab him while the other goes to the phone, and in seconds four policemen arrive, take me outside and start beating me up. I am on the ground and they are kicking me. I let myself go limp and, surprisingly, am not hurt. The girl is hustled to a car by the gangsters and they drive away. When the police have had their fill, they lift me up and ask me the usual police questions. When I tell them what happened they're sympathetic, and one of them says, "If you had told us before, we wouldn't have beaten you."

I return to my hotel room and wait for the boat to Israel.

Israel is sun, confusion, continual movement, girls in short khaki army skirts looking very sexy. I had planned to go to a kibbutz but I cannot find the office, and, by coincidence, end up on the street of an Israeli friend whom I knew in Paris. He is an actor and is shooting a film in the Negev. He arranges for me to get a job as an extra. The next morning I line up for the director, wearing my green army coat, and am chosen to play a British soldier. It is a war film, *The Best of Enemies* starring David Niven and Alberto Sordi.

Almost everyone in Beersheva is of French origin. I find a bed in the house of a French lesbian painter, two Israeli boys, and Danny and Milly, two Americans from Brooklyn who are living together. There are more Arabs than Jews in the area and the Bedouins come to town every Monday and Thursday with their camels, goats *et al*, and have a big market. Danny and I go to the market and I almost buy a goat.

We catch a bus at 6 o'clock each morning for a 40-mile ride to the set, which resembles a Second World War British army camp with tents and tanks. I get a haircut, but I don't get it cut short enough, so I spend most of the time hiding with Danny from the assistant director behind a tank... The desert is fascinating—Arabs dressed in long black and white gowns with veils roam the hillocks with their animals and camels. The animals nibble on the sparse growth that sprouts from the sand hills. The sand is dark, stony and hard. We are always thirsty, and we down quarts and quarts of carbonated soda water.

Danny and Milly have had a fight, and when the shooting ends, Milly comes with me to a new Kibbutz where I work in the vineyards—covered from head to toe to ward off the millions of attacking insects. We had been on the bus to Tel Aviv when a couple of Kibbutzniks boarded it and asked us and others to help with their harvest. Milly and I agree. We are living together, making love, but without real passion. She leaves after a few days and returns to Beersheva.

I go to Tel Aviv and visit the home of a distant cousin... She is an elderly cheerful woman and we communicate in broken German. I feel good sitting in her kitchen. I am in love with this country but I am not a part of it. The spirit of the people is wonderful. The Israelis are the most beautiful, proud, haughty and intelligent people I have ever met... but I am outside. I am always outside. I wonder if it will be that way my whole life. In Tel Aviv, two letters are waiting for me—from Tatyana and Carlos.

On Dizengoff Street I meet two army girls. They are entertainers who travel around to army bases performing for the troops. They are leaving that night for the Negev. Ilana is dark-haired, sultry, and beautiful. Liora is less pretty but has very muscular sexy legs and seems to like me. Ilana is engaged, so I turn my attention to Liora. She promises to meet me when she comes back and show me the country.

Mon cher Davidus

I write this on the pavement of the Monaco in a very depressed frame of mind. I spent the afternoon with Åsa reminiscing about past times. She is trying her best to cheer me up but I seem to be in my most impossible mood. I leave in three or four days' time for London. The thought that I may never possibly see you again weighs heavier and heavier in my mind. I also saw Jean-Pierre today and he said he saw you in Vienna. I am becoming some sort of hungry animal, hungry for the best news about your whereabouts and your doings. Even at this late date I am still hoping that you shall turn up in Paris before I leave. But this would be a miracle and, as you know, I have long ceased to believe in miracles. I am asking Åsa to hand this note to you.

Write to me as soon as you receive this letter. On second thought, I have decided to send this to Tel Aviv.

Love
Carlos

Liora falls in love with me, but I cannot fall in love with her. She is warm and assuages my sexual hunger, but her face is worse than plain. Yet she helps me feel at ease in the city and more a part of it. Yes, I have my Israeli girlfriend.

Together we explore this exciting country. The green Galilee, Jerusalem with its barbed wire down the center with Jordanian soldiers eyeing us... Tel Aviv's beaches, Moshavim, Kibbutzim with their farm lands and farmers in their round soft kibbutz caps.

When I return to Paris there are tanks in the street, anticipating an attack from the OAS that never materializes. Everyone has gone to Sweden, Germany, England, and the U.S. Jean Pierre, however, is in Paris and he has found an American girl —a Jewish girl... very nice but unattractive. I sit with them and we talk about Vienna, the future, life, meaning, art, France vs. the U.S., philosophy, sex. It is café conversation moved to the kitchen table.

A letter is waiting for me from Marlene. She wants me to come to Stuttgart to, finally, give herself to me.

> I will give my whole to you. Not as a martyr. You shall not believe it is a sacrifice. I want to love you so that one might compensate many lonesome, unhappy, destructed hours of your life. But how? Couldn't you come to Stuttgart? (If we would have time, a month or more, what a perfect lover I could become.)

I think of the fiasco in Munich, the mutual frustration... the agony... but how can I say no... The image of her voluptuous body is stronger than my common sense... I write to her and suggest she come to Paris. She agrees, but she has no money. I agree to pay for her ticket.

I am staying in a new hotel on the Rue de l'Hirondelle. She arrives at the hotel room in a short tight skirt, with her huge firm breasts thrusting forward beneath a white sweater. She tells me that all the men in the airport were standing around gaping at her and she felt uncomfortable. She is sexy but so aggravating... I want her but cannot like her... We sit on the bed and I rub my hand over her breasts. There is fear on her face... But there is no feeling... only lust and fear... no love. I undress her and look at her body dominated by the two huge breasts. This time she receives me and I enter her with difficulty and I come... She screams with pain and there is blood, so much blood... At last I've had her and yet it has meant nothing... I have all kinds of conflicting emotions churning in my mind... dislike, mixed with relief, sated lust mixed with a feeling of pity and hatred. She is bleeding terribly... She sits up, looking in disgust at her blood and starts crying. She caresses me, and wants to make love again, to enjoy it. I don't know why, but I cannot. I just want her to go. I don't know what's the matter with me. Is it me? Or is it Marlene? This was not the coming together of two human beings, but only of two bodies. Our souls did not touch... I can feel no affection for her. I only want her to leave.

She sits in the bed, naked, her back against the doorpost, tears rolling down her face. Her first time! What a disappointment it must be. I do not mean to be cruel, but I cannot like her. I cannot feel affection... Sated, I feel only disgust... an emptiness, a need to be alone. Poor Marlene, Poor David.

She leaves me a poem by Brecht to take back to the States.

The Flying Tiger plane loses a propeller after we have taken off from Le Bourget and we are forced to return and spend the day in the airport. I meet three new people: Gérard, a young, charming, handsome Frenchman about my age, off to New York for the first time. He works in the French schools as a monitor and tells me about some of the girls he has had. He seems to be without complexes, always cheerful, and I feel a certain envy. Then there is a French priest who talks to me about God and the church and the ultimate meaning of life, while I tell him I do not believe, that there is no objective morality, that everything is subjective, emanating from the human being. He says that I will change, but I do not believe him. He asks me if I am happy, and I tell him, "No, but I have to find my own path…"

And then there is Anne, who like Gérard is on her way to America for the first time. She has a sexy body and while I talk to the priest my eyes glance at her… and when we arrive in New York she comes with me to my parents' house. They are away, and Anne and I make love on every bed in the house. What a wonderful way to return to New York, a city that has so often beaten and defeated me.

I am supposed to leave for Berkeley soon to study history, even though I do not feel like being an academician.

America still seems to be a sterile, insensitive, hypocritical society. Money and conformity are king. Girlie magazines titillate and excite, but there is little fulfillment allowed. I go down to the Village and talk with friends. Gérard has found a cute, sexy American girl and seems very happy with New York. Anne is wandering somewhere in America, and after some days, despair, need and restlessness catch up with me again. The priest had told me that a period of despair is often the beginning of the spiritual quest. But all too often it is the end. It can lead to violence, self-destruction, suicide. I run into Michael who tells me that Nelly is out of town for the rest of the summer. We go to The Kettle for a drink, but there are no women there. Michael wants to do some painting. I am standing alone on Bleecker Street outside The Figaro, not knowing whether to turn to the right or the left, when a bum approaches me and asks for a handout. He says he is from Texas and has nothing to eat. I give him a quarter and watch him walk down the street. He, too, wanders through this city of darkness.

Priest and Hasid Manqué

RICHARD 1963

I'm painting her from memory and thinking about her ass, caressing it, full, round and incredible. It doesn't look exactly like her, yet the feeling of extraordinary voluptuousness is there. Thinking about her and looking at the painting gets me excited and I feel I have to hit the streets. I'm getting restless and jumpy and feeling closed in like when they used to make me sit in detention in Catholic School. Sometimes there are vague fears which come from nowhere. In the school, the priests and nuns would tell us about eternal punishment, and one had to cut it out of one's mind or one would go crazy. Think about something else... about a girl or baseball or food or anything to escape that fear. But there was confession and forgiveness and the striving for a pure soul, which was something that I wanted... a pure soul... a shining soul. And I knew I wanted to be a priest. Though sometimes seeing the thighs of Catherine MacDonald with the dress rolled up as she sat in the chair next to me... strong, full thighs—her image would pierce my nights and I knew I could not be pure enough to become a priest as the wet sticky stuff would soil the sheets and soil my soul. But sometimes I still get those fears, and then I just have to get out... try not to think.

I cross Canal Street heading towards the Village... moving at a fast pace. The streets are nearly empty: a few cars, lots of warehouses, not too many people. As I reach Houston Street at the edge of the Village there is always that pick-up of excitement. There will be crowds in the cafes—and girls, and maybe I'll find one. I need one tonight. I need to get away from these thoughts.

But then I see him... stocky, slightly drunk, sneering. He looks like my father and the whole flood of memory engulfs me... the beatings, the fights with my mother... and the night he called her a dirty Jew and he left her crying in the kitchen. And when I asked her why he called her a dirty Jew, she told me that she was Jewish—a killer of Jesus as we'd been taught—my whole world was shattered. I couldn't go to that school anymore... I started to cry and we cried together. And then she told me that according to the Jewish religion I was considered a Jew...

The next day after my father smacked me around for not going to school, I ran away, and not knowing where to go, I looked up the address of a synagogue and went there and spoke to the rabbi and cried. He called the Juvenile authorities, but eventually I went to the Yeshiva and learned Hebrew, and Torah and Talmud. But I felt uncomfortable there... The world was too narrow, too bourgeois for me. I was too wild. I liked to write poetry and paint and read novels and be near the girls. The sexual pull of the girls was strong. In the streets we were taught to avert our eyes, but I couldn't do it. I stared and desired. I read the Torah... I believed it was the truth. My head believed, but my eyes and my heart were pulling me away. While my fellow students would be crouching over their Talmud, I would sketch them. The language, the long debates between rabbis, the circuitous reasoning made my mind wander and one day I just hitchhiked to New York...

But sometimes the fears are there... The Catholic hell being replaced by Jewish punishment which awaits me in the world to come for not obeying God's commandments... But I am an artist; I want to create beauty... I need to get my insides on canvas... All the shit and agony... It really helps to paint it... The faces, the hands, the bodies... Images of *shabbos*, images of rabbis with deep haunted eyes... Women with their bodies; It all goes round and round and comes out... I had two paintings in a group show and both of them sold.

On Sullivan Street now, I pass Googie's Bar and look in to see if there are any chicks there. But there are only a couple of guys at the bar and a few scattered couples, so I decide to head to the park and sketch.

There are two games of chess in progress, a black guy and an unshaven white guy at one table have the biggest crowd. There's one chick looking on, long straight hair, a worn face that's seen too many beds, but I try to get closer to her. I feel the tension in my stomach. She looks at me and looks away. She doesn't seem very interested, and there's something about her that's not too inviting.

I wander into the park and this spade, high on something or other, is lurching back and forth but with a smile on his face, and he's followed by Winnie, the big black Negress, always a bit drunk. A lot of spades hang around the park to find drugs or white chicks. I see a white guy, drunk, three-day stubble, draped over a bench, soaking in the sunshine... Up from the bowery. Nothing much happening around the circle. The cops closed down the folk music. Won't allow anybody to have any fun... Neighbors complained, they said, but my guess is that they are envious of the bohemians... Thinking everybody's having a ball. Everybody pretends to have a ball, but there is a big emptiness, and terrible undefined needs.

I sit down on the bench and decide to sketch the bum. Who knows? Maybe some chick will come by to watch. It's usually the best way to pick up chicks and I need one now... but I seem to need one all the time.

Douglas wants me to live with him and his "commune" in that filthy loft on Greene Street. He says everybody shares everybody else and they have great orgies. Half of me wants to dive into a world of unlimited sex, but the other half is disgusted by it. Maybe later I'll wander over...

The bum is moving and is now watching me with a half grin/grimace on his face. He tries to get up but falls back on the bench. I start sketching... I want to see his eyes, but I don't feel like looking at him like an object. I'm sure the eyes are too clouded over... I feel someone staring at me and I look up. It's a guy, and I wonder if he's a homo. He has long hair but doesn't look like a homo.

An interesting face, one I'd like to sketch. He's watching me as if he wants to speak to me. I smile at him and he walks over.

His name is David. He's making a movie. He likes my face and wants to know if I want to act in a scene. Why not? He says it will be sort of a love scene with a girl, but no nudity, no sex, mostly faces, hands... Apparently another guy was supposed to do the scene but he never showed up, and the actress and a friend of his who is going to hold the lights are waiting in Rienzi's.

The walls in Rienzi's are covered with paintings for sale. Maybe I should talk to them about putting up my work. Probably not a bad place to show one's work, but I doubt you get many sales here, and I need to sell... They have two cute little waitresses, looking bored but arty, just like a coffee house waitress should. David leads me to a table and introduces me to Tom, a young guy with blonde hair, a nice open face, though perhaps a bit too ordinary to be interesting. Also sitting at the table is the most fascinating girl I've ever seen. I feel my heart start to pound... All I hear is the name "Kelly." She's not tall, but she has these huge tits and a smile that could melt anything... Apparently Kelly is the actress with whom I'm supposed to have the love scene. David and Kelly seem very familiar, so I imagine they're lovers... Just my luck, but who knows? I'll just have to wait and see. I can see David's eyes looking over the waitress, staring hard, so maybe this isn't a couple. One of the waitresses is at our table and I'm trying to decide whether to have an espresso for 35 cents or splurge 50 cents on a cappuccino. I'm also kind of hungry so I order the onion soup, "Onion soup les Halles—a meal in itself." It better be, because I can hardly afford the 95 cents. So instead of the coffee I ask for a glass of water to go with the soup. The waitress smiles... Maybe there's something there... but I hear Kelly's voice and am startled at the soft southern accent.

"I hear we're going to act together..."

I nod at David... "Yeah, that's what he says..."

She smiles and says nothing else. A southerner—like from another planet... I feel like reaching out and holding her. I can feel my excitement growing, and then I say stupidly, "Have you done anything with him before?"

"Yes... a couple of times."

She looks at David, smiles and reaches out and touches him. He imitates a smile... indifferent... I'm beginning to get the picture. She's crazy about him, but he's looking elsewhere. The usual story...

David says little. His eyes are everywhere, looking at everyone in the cafe. He has a young face, like a teenager, though I can tell he's older... He reaches down into a bag and pulls out a movie camera and fidgets with it. The eyes are piercing, but very sad. I think I'm going to like him. He has a nice smile and I wonder why he doesn't photograph himself, but I guess that's difficult. You'd need another cameraman whom you can trust. I don't know much about making movies, but this seems a long way from Hollywood... though it's better than being in my studio with my thoughts.

I ask David what the film is about and he shrugs. "Just scenes of things that are haunting me... It's hard to explain..." He taps his head several times... "I have it here. We'll work, we'll experiment..."

He walks over to speak to the manager who nods and David comes back smiling. "OK, he'll let us shoot here."

He starts explaining the scene to me. Kelly is sitting alone in Rienzi's when I walk in. I'm supposed to look over the cafe, see Kelly, hesitate, then walk up to her table and ask if I can sit. She'll nod OK... He'll then tell us what to do. There's no sound, so the picture has to tell the story... Then we'll go to an apartment in the East Village, which is supposed to be my place, and we'll shoot more. I won't have to do much acting to pick up Kelly.

David tells Tom where to stand with the light. He has two lights. One he sets up on a tripod and aims it at the ceiling so it reflects. There is something so gentle about Kelly's voice, and together with her voluptuous body I feel like crawling into her and being held and never letting go... I am shaking and later, when we have to lie in bed together, semi-naked for the scene, I get so excited I know she can feel it.

With Kelly I feel I have found what I need. Her face is incredible. There is a lot of suffering visible in her eyes, yet her mouth is the most kissable mouth I've ever seen. She is soft and voluptuous.

Kelly has the kind of tits and ass that we used to secretly look at in the magazines in Parochial School. Perhaps she is not as tall and lithe as some of those girls, but she reawakens images. She smiles and I feel strength coming from her.

Kelly, my mind is filled with images of you. I stand by your door every night for a week, but when you won't invite me upstairs I am crushed. Kelly, I must have you. You are a fever that is destroying my brain. I try to paint you, but just drawing the first line makes me so excited that I am forced to masturbate. I know you are in love with David, but I can see that he is not in love with you. I don't know why. But that's the way it is.

But nothing is ever easy for me. When I was 15 I saw a painting by Chagall and I wanted to be a Hasid and this has never left me. It is the mysticism that appeals to me. I read about Nachman of Breslov and the Baal Shem Tov and the secrets of creation. The Kabbalah explains how God began to withdraw, to contract. At first there was nothing physical, and then through countless contractions, infinite light began to emanate and finally a world of multiplicity with measures, boundaries, time, space, limitation... the humans with the impulse towards good, towards God, and the animal self, of passion and evil impulse. The Hasidim explain how the attraction to women is a reflection of the distortion of the sphere of divine love. Lust is the opposite side of the same coin. One must take the energy of lust, the desire for women and transform it to a higher sphere of holiness; passions must not be denied, but transmuted to raise one to the divine.

But there were few Hasidim where I grew up and I never felt comfortable in the Yeshiva, and my passions are too strong. I do not have the strength to either deny them or transmute them. But I would like to channel them into someone like Kelly. I wonder if she would become Jewish... but I mustn't think about it. I must forget, if I can, who I am.

But Kelly will not have me, it seems, and she doesn't come to the shootings. Every once in a while, I go around with David and shoot a scene for his movie. It is something to do. David also has an ever-roaming eye for girls. He talks about this French girl, Sonja, whom he's crazy about. One day we go to the Metropolitan Museum of Art together. He wants to shoot a scene where I am supposed to wander around wanting to pick up a girl, but I am unable to because of introversion, shyness, depression. And, of course, one girl wants me to pick her up but I am not interested. We find three girls to play the roles, one of whom, a German, is especially attractive with her beautiful dancer's legs. With the natural light coming from the overhead skylights, the beautiful legs and the extraordinary paintings, I have a momentary flash of eternity, a feeling of peace. I was looking at the German girl with lust, but suddenly the light and the pictures or whatever transformed this lust into a feeling of happiness, of peace.

Maybe this is the transmutation the Hasidim talk about. But it only lasts a few seconds and then I am back in the room watching the sexy German girl gliding on her dancer's legs as David films us. I do not have to act to look depressed.

There is one painting in the museum by a Russian named Repin, which fascinates me. It's a portrait of a writer staring with deep, sad eyes. The writer committed suicide at 38 and one can see it in the eyes. These are eyes that are seeking, searching for something. He writes political stories, but politics can never satisfy a soul such as his. Only God. And so he suffers and he doesn't know why. I stare at the painting and see myself in it. David, too, is taken with the painting. I think he also sees his reflection.

In many ways we are alike, though he has never had any religious beliefs. But perhaps it will come. We both think we can find something through women, through *the* woman... We never find her but we keep looking. I know Kelly would make me happy. I wonder if David is interested in the German girl, if she is a "kindling eye", as he calls the girls he likes who are attracted to him. I'm sure he wants her. I'll let him go after her if he'll invite Kelly to another filming. The German girl, however, has a boyfriend.

We are walking down Fifth Avenue near 30th Street. A girl with a great ass is walking ahead and we both notice her. David walks up to her, but she turns her head and gives him an icy stare. He shrugs, smiles and joins me and we continue walking quickly. The rhythm is good; we are in step, and we never have to stop for a light. I ask him if he wants to come to my loft to see my paintings and turn on. He agrees.

The loft is dark when we come in and, as usual, I have a hard time finding the light switch. David has never been here before, and though I pretend to be casual, I want him to like my paintings. We always need approval. The nude with the big ass is on the easel in the center of the room, sort of counter-pointed by a pile of dirty dishes in the sink. I watch David looking around. He looks at the nude and then at another big canvas hanging on the wall with its predominantly blacks and browns—a family lighting the Shabbat candles.

"I like your work," says David. "It has a lot of feeling."

"Thanks," I say.

David wanders around the loft looking at the paintings, the paints, newspapers, books. He picks up a book on Kabala and begins to leaf through it and then closes it. I go into the kitchen, glance at the mess, and then take a foil with hashish from the shelf. "Do you want to turn on? I have some great hash, strong but mellow."

David hesitates, then nods "OK." I wonder about his hesitation. I walk over to a table with the dead flowers, take two pipes, put the hash in them and hand one to David.

I don't know how to describe the high, but it is the only way I feel close to something transcendental. Perhaps it releases my soul and allows it to search for God. Maybe it just cuts off my rational mind and allows another part to take over. When I was in the Yeshiva we were visited by a wonder rabbi from Israel, a Sephardic, originally from Morocco, who could read your past and your future. He had dark piercing eyes and a long black and gray beard. A wild look. He inspired more fright than affection, though he loved to laugh and to drink arak. There was a power in his words, a sometimes-frightening power. He did not mince words. People would come to him for advice and to be cured from diseases. They said his blessings could reverse illness and help one find a marriage partner or bring financial success.

One morning he told me of a dream he had the night before. He had visited a house where a man was dying of cancer. The rabbi described the house, the room and the man, and he told me he had started the process of curing the man.

"Yaakov," he said, "before the end of the day, a relative of this man will come to me to ask for help."

By suppertime nobody had arrived, but around 9 pm a middle-aged man came to the Yeshiva and asked to see the rabbi. His brother had cancer, he told him, and the doctors had given up hope. They had heard that the rabbi could cure the ill. Would he visit the sick man?

The rabbi smiled and asked me to come with him. The house was exactly as he had described it, so was the room and the man. He recited a blessing and said to the brother, "He will get better."

The man did get better and the rabbi left the Yeshiva. I was on a spiritual high, compounded of knowledge, mysticism and fear, but after a few weeks of routine, Talmud, *Halacha*, prayers, and more Talmud, I began to get bored. I don't have the head for the Talmud and all its detail. I need the scope of philosophy and mysticism. I got restless. There wasn't anybody in the Yeshiva with whom I could relate. My spiritual high, my commitment to devote myself to God, my fear of breaking God's commandments —also elevated during the rabbi's visit—started to fade—I concentrated less and less and thought about things other than Torah.

But when I smoke, I sometimes get the feeling I had when the wonder rabbi was with me. I am witnessing a higher world, a glimpse of the world to come.

David is smiling. I smile at him. Time seems to stand still. I feel beyond time. It is no longer Sunday, 8 pm. We are moving timeless through space. I feel love; love for David, love for everyone.

However, David is restless. I can see it in his motions, his eyes. "Shall we go out?" he says.

I feel a knot in my stomach. "To go out" means to leave the security of the loft and its timelessness, and go into the streets and experience desire.

Bleecker Street is filled with passing bodies, and David has approached two of them who are looking in a store window near the Figaro. One is tall, blonde, the other short and dark. The tall one,

Melanie, is a high school girl with an extraordinary ass and a nice smile. Suddenly, I want her very badly.

David introduces me. "Melanie, Richard, Carol."

David knows Melanie (he seems to know everyone) and starts telling her that I'm a painter and maybe the girls want to see my loft and the paintings. They glance at each other, half excited, half fearful, but agree to come along.

The loft is the way we left it, hash pipes on the floor, dirty dishes, paintings, etc. The girls look at the paintings. I watch Melanie's ass. It is incredible, so round, so full, so firm. I offer the girls some hash, but Melanie asks if I have anything to drink. There is only some wine, but she wants a glass. Carol is withdrawing, feeling uncomfortable, obviously frightened. Melanie's eyes sparkle with excitement and fear. She is sitting on a mattress, leaning against the wall. Her father is French, her mother a Romanian. She is beautiful... When I was in the kitchen, David came in and whispered, "She's yours, if you want. I'll try to get Carol out of here..."

This will not be easy. They represent each other's security. My heart is beating fast. Asses like that turn me on. I walk over to the mattress and sit next to her and then I am caressing her face and her breasts and thinking about the ass. My head is still floating, and when I look around, David and Carol are gone. We are alone.

She is stiff. Could she be a virgin? But nothing matters except possessing her. I push her down on the couch. She lets herself go, but there is no passion. I start to kiss her and this time there is some response, but no abandon. It is almost like this is something she has to get over with. Something she had to do. My penis is so hard, it is about to come through my pants, so I start taking off her clothes. Her breasts are small. Little girl's breasts. I slip her skirt off. She is wearing white underwear and her thighs are lovely, the legs marred by thick shapeless calves. But the swell of her ass is what I want, and I turn her around to look at it, to feel it and I can hardly contain myself. I pull off her panties and tell her to get on all fours so the magnificence will be in the air... but she doesn't want to. She lies on her back and pulls me down on top of her... I cup my hands under her ass and enter her and she cries with pain... and I go in and in and she cries and there is blood and, yes, she is a virgin, and I come and she cries and I come and come and she cries and bleeds ... And as the coming is finished, the thought entered my mind that I hope she is not Jewish. My soul is being condemned to punishment and it would be worse if she were Jewish. And I rid myself of the thought, which robs the moment of all joy, because once the knowledge is there it never leaves you. But I must go on ... I pump a few more times... She moans... Pain or pleasure? I don't know. And then we lie there, each in our own thoughts. She, now deflowered, and me, another step away from the Yeshiva on a deliberate road to I don't know where. And then the thought of Kelly comes into my mind. I am in love with Kelly. There is no question about that...

I want Kelly more than I've ever wanted anything. It is the Southern accent that holds me, that speaks of mysteries I do not understand. Also, of course, the big tits and ass, but most of all the face. She has that look, that covering veil. There is a depth, a female mystery that can never be unraveled. I can enter her down below, but I will never grasp her essence.

She is living in the East Village with a roommate, a man who is always stoned, a half Irishman, half-Mexican named Jed. She assures me that their relationship is platonic. I am afraid to ask her out because a rejection from her would destroy me. I have no one now, no mother, no father, no wife, no God.

I decide I should just go over to her place, casually knock on the door and say "Hello." The sight of the street is a turnoff. Garbage cans, Puerto Ricans, some lost druggies, but this is her street. I walk up and down past her apartment building, but she doesn't come out and I don't dare go in. I don't want to be rejected. I recall the scene we did together. We were both nude except for our underwear and I was so excited I had to think of almost anything to stop from coming. She seemed indifferent, almost teasingly aware of my heat. I was embarrassed.

I remembered when I was in the Yeshiva and I wanted to marry for the *Mitzvah*, because one should marry and have children. I wanted to be a Hasid, but I was unable to keep all the commandments and to control my passions. I couldn't make it. I needed sex; I needed art; I needed something... but some of the Hasid is always with me, though I must reject it. Sometimes I think I screw women just to forget, because to remember has terrible implications. Maybe if I find a life with a wife and a child, it will be a compromise. I didn't make it as a Hasid, as a Jew, but I am an artist and I created a child. I picture Kelly pregnant, her breasts swelling even larger, but I don't dare speak to her. Instead I walk toward St. Mark's place and enter a jazz bar. Charlie Mingus is going to be playing. Surprise! David is there, sitting at the bar, tearing pieces of paper. He seems glad to see me and tells me he wants to shoot another scene with me tomorrow, if it's OK. I agree. He seems depressed and restless. We both order a beer. David is silent. The music doesn't start for another hour. David tells me that he likes Mingus's bass playing and his originality. I agree. We look around the club. No single women.

I ask David if he believes in God.

"I don't know," he says. "To believe in the God of the Bible means that there is an objective morality, a right and a wrong. It seems to me that the bourgeois, empty society with its restrictions is wrong. But what the Bible says is wrong... like about sex... I feel sex is right."

"You mean incest?"

"Oh, no," says David shocked.

"So maybe you do believe in something."

"Maybe... but right now I'd like to find a chick. Shall we go somewhere else?"

We leave the club. Dusk is falling. We are in stride together. David is talking. "My problem is that I'm too self-aware to ever enjoy anything. I can't appreciate the pleasure of the moment. Some thought is always telling me who I am or what I'm doing. Or what I need, or what I lack. It's a beautiful evening tonight, but I can't feel it. I do feel it, but it's like there has to be a result, like finding a sexy chick and getting laid. I can't enjoy the moment in itself. I read the books on Zen and for a day I study the leaves on trees and absorb the veins... you know what I mean... but it's not me..."

It is a clear night. There might even be stars but the city lights outshine them so they cannot be seen. We head west towards the Village to get a drink, to try and find a woman, and to forget.

Film and Philosophy

DAVID 1963

The knot in my stomach is there as I walk along MacDougal Street, alive with more promise than fulfillment. The colleges are on their Christmas vacation and it is always an exciting time of year. There are more girls in town and more life and magic in the air. And more need. Bob and I have found a place together on University Place near 12th Street, a few blocks from the Living Theatre. Bob has met a pretty German girl, found a job and seems happy. My life is the usual confusion.

I had been in Berkeley where I was supposed to go to graduate school but did not register. Instead I box in the gym against all comers. I am lonely, without a woman, too bitter and, thus, too withdrawn to talk to anyone, so when a notice arrives from my draft board in New York for a physical I am almost relieved .Berkeley is chaos. It is time to leave.

We are hitchhiking. California to New York. Two days before leaving New York I met this thin, sexless, sour girl who wants to hitchhike to New York.. It is easier if there are two, I provide protection for her while she helps me get lifts.

I remember Wyoming in the morning, the sun just rising over a corral with real cattle and real cowboys. The image remains etched in my mind. I also remember sleeping in jail on metal springs without a mattress because we had no money for a hotel. I remember the Salvation Army finding a hotel room for us. I remember sitting in a cafe in Iowa, when a man, who had been staring at me, approached me and asked if he could sit down. He told us that he'd been in Iowa for two years and hadn't met anyone he could talk to. The emptiness of Middle America.

Back in New York my loneliness is so overwhelming that I am paralyzed with inaction. There seems to be little purpose in going on. When I go for my Army exam, they take one look at my long hair and send me to the psychiatrist. I have my 4F.

In the Village I see a help wanted sign for a new cafe, The Bizarre, and I get a job as a waiter. It is difficult. My frustrations, anger and bitterness are churning inside me and it is hard to relate to the customers. On my third day, a short, stocky, well-built, arrogant guy comes in with a tall, sexy girl. When I ask for their order, he says nastily, "Bum off ... get outta here..." This is too much for me; "Fuck you," I respond. He leaps up from his seat and starts throwing punches, showing off to his girlfriend. He is strong and muscular, but I am taller and quicker and

I just keep jabbing him in the face. The fight goes on for ten minutes before the police arrive. No one is hurt, but I have lost my job.

>   My dear waiter,
>
>   I can see you with a white shirt—starched well— and black tie. I'm eating now ice-cream and reading your letter and cannot find any difference. They are very cold and very, very sweet.

>   Dear David,
>
>   I'm sorry but I tried to think of a way to get money for you and I couldn't—-it's impossible, but just a moment! —-I have a great idea—-to do every- thing in order to get permission to leave the USA... go by ship... because in Paris I have a little money for beginning... for you also—-and we shall find a way to live. I promise...with me you will never be hungry, anyway—-not with me. Try David, and make it. It will be wonderful.
>
> Love,
> Liora

But I cannot go to Liora or live with Liora because she is not really pretty enough and I will look at others.

I dream of getting away from New York and its oppressive atmo- sphere. I see only two New Yorks, the New York of the bums lying on the streets having long ago given up———-the New York of crime, dirt— -and the middle-class New York, crew-cut, sitting in offices shuffling paper from one basket to another, never having an original thought. I do not like either world. The Village is a third world, but it, too, is unsatisfactory. Eyes that do not meet, restlessness, wasting time, real hunger, sexual hunger and aimlessness.

To get away I go to a hiring hall for seamen in Brooklyn and sign up for a ship. I have dreams of getting on a freighter, going to Japan and the Far East, wandering around strange and exciting cities, sleeping with geishas and whores... It is an exciting vision. I am told I must take the first job offered, which turns out not to be a freighter, but a tanker going to Venezuela ... I am the Cabin Boy on the Norwegian tanker M/S Sir James Lithgow, departing New Year's Day for Venezuela.

The ship is berthed in Philadelphia, and while I wait to be driven there I listen to Edith Piaf records. They make me think of Tatyana who is writing to me often from Germany. We keep making plans to join each other. I have been reading poems by Rimbaud and biographies of various people like Sergei Eisenstein. I have also been going to films: *La Dolce Vita, Breathless, Ashes and Diamonds, Judgment at Nuremberg, Les Tricheurs*. I dream of getting back to Europe and acting in films, getting away from American women and their complexes. I write to Tatyana and tell her I will co-star with her in a tragedy.

People from Paris keep showing up in New York. Tom Morrissey, the red-bearded American who lived in the 'Beat Hotel' at 9 Git-le-Coeur, and Vibeke, the gorgeous Blue Bell girl, are here. She married a Negro homosexual whom she met while dancing in Vegas. I listen to the Piaf records thinking of Nelly, crying.

A week of 12-hour seasick days in the kitchen washing dishes and serving the almost always drunk Norwegian seamen, dreaming of Nelly, singing "Wildwood Flower" over and over again with tears in my eyes. My depression overwhelms me. I think of suicide. As a cabin boy I am the lowest of the low, so every member of the crew can boss me around, and because of their own frustrations they take pleasure in doing just that. There is one seaman, Karl, who enjoys reading, and we sit and chat in my spare time. Half of the crew have come down with gonorrhea or syphilis after a visit to Brazil, but this seems to be accepted as part of the seaman's life. I only wish for the trip to be over. Eight days later we are in Venezuela in an oil field. I am allowed to leave the ship for four hours and I visit a French ship berthed next to us. Talking to the French sailors makes me nostalgic for France. I miss it. Seventeen days after sailing from Philadelphia, we are back in New York and I sign off.

The only good thing to come from the trip is that it rekindled my desire to read and I devour novels by Maurois, Mauriac and Mann. They are all such great stylists, so disciplined ... something I can never achieve. There is a letter from Tatyana waiting for me. Her mood parallels my own.

Neither of us fits in anywhere. We skim the earth, but are caught up in its passions and sufferings. I wonder if we will ever find a way out.

One day my father sees an ad for a film school at City College and suggests I attend. I go to the school for a month and do not learn very much, but my father gives me his old Kodak 8mm camera and I begin shooting little scenes.

The Cedar Tavern on University Place and the Figaro Café on Bleecker Street become my two main hangouts. The Cedar Tavern is the home of the Abstract Expressionists, getting famous in the New York art scene. One day Gregory Corso drops in and invites me to go with him to Italy. I decline. A few days later, walking with Gregory on 8th Street, I am introduced to Allen Ginsberg and his lover, Peter Orlovsky, heading towards their pad in the East Village. A weak handshake and we continue in opposite directions.

Tom, the 'Amphetamine Christ,' is talking to me in the Figaro. "Amphetamine is another high. I turn on ... people give me things... 'A', reefers. It's a way to pass the time. I function the same way with or without. 'A' keeps me up all night. I take it because it's there. I wouldn't mind taking 'A' all my life if someone gave it to me. They all need something to live for; they don't have that something. They're just going on because tomorrow they got the same thing to do. Yeah, I'm here for people. For them. For their benefit and my benefit ... I'm tired of giving. I want something back.

"My mother wants to put me into the nut-house. They thought Christ was crazy, too. He was a funny guy. Walking around saying he was the son of God. Still, these kids on the scene, they're all taking 'A', flipping out, going to hospitals, getting sicker and sicker, more bitter ... It affects their brain cells. My brain cells don't function in the same pattern as a human being. Om Rani Krishna. I'm going out to California just to do something new.

"You gotta love. I don't mean you gotta love one person, you gotta love a lot of people. Chicks can't understand that. I sent George $200. He flew to Acapulco to see us because he needs us. Joyce wanted to get out of there, but George was bound up in Ouspensky and Gurdjieff. He flipped out and someone took him to the hospital. Sasha told me he was using a lot of psychedelics and other stuff."

Sasha walks in, tall, nice-looking, working as a short-order cook in a cafe. He's with Joyce now. We nod, say a few words, but never get into each other's mind or soul. So many people passing in and out of cafes. We know them and yet we do not.

I see a girl with long curly hair, a notebook in front of her, sort of slouched in a chair. She is staring straight ahead and crying. Sobbing would be a better word, softly and steadily sobbing. Her eyes devour everyone, inviting, appealing, anguished.

I look at her, take a deep breath and slowly walk over to her. I stand by the side of her chair and say "Do you mind if I join you?"

She turns her head, and her face is streaked where the tears have run. Though not exactly beautiful, there is something appealing about her face... a face that is both knowledgeable and soft. She looks at me and smiles: "If you can stand the sight of me, then I guess I can stand the sight of you."

She has an unmistakable Southern accent so I ask her where she is from. "Alabama, home of red-blooded American men," she says sarcastically. "It doesn't sound like you like it there," I say.

"Why, honey child, I just adore it there. Where else can a girl have the honor of getting gang banged, just because she spent a year or two in New York's sinful Greenwich Village."

And piece-by-piece her story comes out. Her name is Kelly. She is 24, married, divorced, certifiably insane (in Alabama). Married at 18 to a local workman, who left her on her marriage night, went out drinking, returned home and beat her. Repeated this "delightful custom" regularly. Mother of two children. After her mother had her declared insane because "I wrote poetry," her mother took her children away. "I'm not allowed near them." Left the mental hospital, fled to New York, wrote for a Village newspaper, waitressed. "Had hands laid on me by every junkie, con artist and fat tourist." She spent meaningless nights with unbathed folk singers who told her she had "real soul," while they pawed her body and threw her out in the morning. Needing affection, she drifted from one to the other, smoked pot, took pills, sat on the floors of cockroach "pads." She ate less ("a diet of orange juice and chocolate") developed a cough, never saw the sun, scurried along garbage strewn East Village streets like a rat, sold her tourists 3-dollar cups of "blood coffee." Sometimes she would meet a man who attracted her and seemed decent, but he was looking for "it" with some nice-assed, well dressed, perfumed high heeled chick... This she certainly wasn't, anymore at least.

One day she'd had enough and she decided to go down to Alabama and maybe, just maybe, see her kids, and put her hands in the earth where things grow and don't decay. Her mother took one look at her, sent the kids out of the house, told her she could stay for one night.

She went out, met the local crowd, who figured that anybody who had lived in Greenwich Village was a bit of a whore. There were five of them who took her down to the Mill by the river, smacked her face, held her down and "in the great gallant tradition of Alabama, the gentlemen took their pleasure in little ole me before retiring for cigars in the drawing room."

She didn't dare go to the police or local hospital, but got a bus to New York. Turned uptown instead of downtown when she came out of the Port Authority. Went to a hotel, cried herself to sleep, bought a paper the next day, looked at the want ads, and got herself a poorly paid job as a secretary in a publishing firm.

Though "my poetry is better than my typing," she managed the job for six weeks, getting up, going to work, going to bed. She bought some new clothes, washed her hair, ate meat and vegetables. Then one night the hunger returned, the restless feeling. She spent the night with another out-of-towner at his hotel, overslept, and called in sick. She repeated this several times, said "screw the job," spent her nights in bars looking for "it" and needing to be held.

Her money dwindling, she went to the Welfare office, but couldn't stand the waiting or the atmosphere and fled. In the middle of the street her stomach nerves got so intense that she had to lean against a building. She began moaning and when a middle-aged man asked if he could help her she screamed "no" and ran.

She started the round of bars and cafes trying to drive the desperation from her gut and that's where I found her.

Behind the bright smile, there is a desperate lonely look. She shows me her poetry, which she carries around in her bag. It is beautiful, moving, powerful, tragic.

Her eyes are dark, many shadows betraying sleepless nights. A fascinating face, and a personality which switches in a fraction of a second from bright ironic humor to deep unfathomable despair.

In the streets, I put my arm around her and softly sing. She snuggles up to me.

The stairway is dark and we have to grope up one flight to our apartment. A mattress on the floor, a bookcase, some pillows. Bob has cleaned the dirty dishes in the sink. We take off our coats. There is nowhere to sit except on the bed. I take her hand and gently pull her to a sitting position on the bed. My hand rests on top of her full breast and I caress her. My mouth kisses her neck. Kelly starts panting and grabs me. We make love.

In the morning I wake up to the sound of coughing. Kelly is sitting up in bed, her body racked by coughs. She's been coughing like that for a long time, and when she tells me that her diet consists of chocolate and orange juice, I talk to her about going on a macrobiotic diet. I tried macrobiotics for a few days but soon became fed up with brown rice. I get up and make some brown rice for Kelly and give it to her with a few protein pills... I can sense that Kelly does not want to leave, but I don't really want to have her hanging around all day. I like her; she attracts me, but not that much. Sonja gets me far more excited.

I had met Sonja in the Cedar Bar almost a year ago. She was visiting the States from France and I fell in love with her beauty and her perfect body. For a week we made love in a room I rented near 125th street. When she returned to France I hitchhiked an airplane ride to Paris on a charter, but when I knocked on her door her father wouldn't let me see her. She ran away to Paris, but he hired detectives to drag her back home. Completely broke, I slept in Gerard's rat-infested apartment and we would spend the day playing *baby-foot* in the downstairs café until I got a job writing a column on art for the *International Herald Tribune* and a job dubbing German war films into English.

Bob Miller, an American whom I had met at the Figaro with Gerard, is in Paris and living in the Hotel des Balkans in the 6e. Leaving his room to go to a café we run into a girl with brownish/blondish hair, about 5'7" with an intriguing face. She gives us a warm smile and I say, "Hello, are you coming to have a drink with us?" The three of us go to the Monaco.

Her name is Anne-Sophie from Switzerland. She is in Paris to paint. We go back to her room and she shows me her paintings, mostly of birds. An interesting style. We make love. She is warm and giving. I like her and the fact she's 10 years older than me intrigues me. Perhaps she would be good for me.

Bob and I have decided to go to Lisbon and then return to the States and room together. Bob has picked up an American girl, Kathy, who is high on LSD, and he is trying to help her get control of herself. I am with Anne-Sophie. She leans her face into mine and says softly, "You know what I like about you ... You're observant... You look at people to find out what's inside of them, to feel their vibrations, to know what's behind their faces…"

Sometimes I can sit in a café and barely get enough courage to order a drink from a waiter. I just stare and stare, all wrapped up in myself. Anne-Sophie understands how introverted and shy I am most of the time because she is the same way. Yet she is more organized, more purposeful. Maybe because she's Swiss or because she's older. She tells me that her mother is ill and she has to return to Switzerland. Bob and I will leave for Lisbon. I doubt we will see each other again. She promises to paint me from memory…

Portugal is a joy unsurpassed. In Lisbon we watched the women endlessly carrying baskets of fish on their heads from the port like a scene from Goya's "Witches' Sabbath", played soccer on the beach in the Algarve, haunted cafés and tapas bars, listened to sad Fado music, slept and played rummy with friendly whores before returning to New York on the slow-moving Italian ship, SS Vulcania. The Statue of Liberty, the tall buildings, the concrete, the need to start all over again to find a place to stay, a job and a woman.

In New York letters keep arriving from Sonja declaring her love for me and promises to return to New York.

Thoughts of Sonja's body simply weaken me. With Kelly it is easy; I feel at ease; there is no bullshit… but I do not have the passion I feel when I am with someone like Sonja.

Kelly tells me where she is working, and I tell her I'll drop by and see her. She clings to me as she leaves. I feel she is falling in love. Those incredible eyes hold me as she backs out the door.

The mailman delivers a letter from Sonja. She writes about her family. Everyone is asking her if she is in love "I said, 'Yes I am. I think it's true.'" Her problems in getting a visa to come to the U.S. would fill a novel. I think about her and get so horny that I have to run around in circles to stop from masturbating. She drives me crazy. But she's far away.

I've been offered a job as a bartender in a new bar that is about to open up. It is run by the owner of Googie's on Sullivan Street and he's asked me to come by to discuss details.

Ray must be 40, dark eyed—always seems calm, a mystery. He spent most of the fifties in Paris, an expatriate, doing vague and mysterious things. We never really get to know about each other. A lot of people who come into Googie's lived in Paris, but our conversations are like warm showers... soothing, but non-sticking. Ray is opening a new bar near Sheridan Square and he wants me to be one of his bartenders "to attract the girls." This is kind of ironic, because I'm not attracting too many girls for myself. He's going to have pictures of the bartenders on the wall ... a kind of cult of personality. I accept. It's always been a romantic dream of mine to be a bartender in the Village. I mean, that's to be really in.

After leaving Ray, I take the subway to 42nd Street and walk over to Ninth Avenue. There's a small photo shop selling out-of-date reversal 16mm film for 50 cents a hundred feet, and I buy a stock of it. I put a roll in the used Bolex camera I'd bought and begin walking up 42nd Street, looking at the faces of the defeated and the insane. When I see an interesting person, I film him. At the corner of 7th Avenue, a heavyset preacher and his companion, a slender, wild-eyed, fiery woman called Rosie are screaming their message to a crowd of about 30 people. I look for the best angle and begin shooting. I move in closer, in order to capture the insane passion that drives her. They are preaching salvation to the denizens of a Bruegel 42nd Street Hell, and I know that I am only one step removed from being with them. It is easier for me to relate to the woman sitting with her piles of clothes and junk against a wall between two sexploitation movie theatres than the well-dressed and carefully-coiffed secretary entering the glass building on Sixth Avenue, one block away. There is a mad music to Rosie and her friend. Why are they there? Is it to bring the listeners to God, or is it for themselves, a way of fending off their own madness? I don't know, but I film them... Dusk is approaching and the flashing lights of 42nd Street begin to shine clearer. A bum with long, fatty hair has his face illuminated by a neon sign. His eyes are wild, seeing some inner vision which I can never probe. The only instrument I have is the camera... I back a few feet away and aim the camera at his face. I press the button. The film turns. He stares at me, but doesn't see me... No, he doesn't see me. He sees only his inner madness. And then he grins, a grin so mad that there are universes and infinite spaces of deranged floating souls and disembodied spirits captured in this grin.

He turns away from me waving his arm drunkenly and ambles towards Rosie and the Preacher. I watch him as he pushes his way through the crowd and walks right up to Rosie, stops before her and begins laughing, a frighteningly crazy laugh. I, too, am frightened, because I know that there is such a thin line between sanity and insanity, and I can easily be on either side of this line.

When I get home, Kelly is in my bed waiting for me. She has brought a friend, a light-skinned Negress—Mona. Mona is putting on makeup, sitting at the edge of the bed, looking at herself in the mirror. She has a round face, but an interesting one. Her hair is short. She glances up, looks at me and then continues putting on makeup. Kelly sits up and smiles.

"How did you get in?" I ask.

"Your door was open," she says.

"Bob's not here?"

Kelly shakes her head and then leans over Mona and caresses her on the shoulder. She takes the eyeliner pencil from Mona's hand and begins penciling Mona's eyebrows... I watch fascinated. I put a clip-on light on top of a tri-pod, bounce the light off the ceiling and take the Bolex and shoot the girls. Kelly's delicate hand carefully applying makeup to Mona's sculptured face. The door opens and Anka walks in. She is Bob's fiancée living with Bob in the other room. I decide to film a scene with the three of them. Anka will be Kelly's girlfriend who is jealous of Mona.

We film the scene, and when I see it a few days later I know that I am on to something good. Kelly's face is incredible, those sad deep eyes grip and hold and pierce the viewer. I have got to shoot more scenes with her, to capture the despair and aimlessness of her life and my life and all our lives.

The result of our film work is more successful than our relationship. I sleep with Kelly, but I think of Sonja, and I become craven, weak, nothing. Her letters become a lifeline. I know Kelly is better for me; we are more alike. She would be the rational choice. But my gut desire is Sonja. It is like a pressure, a longing, an urge that grips me. My desire for her is so strong that it consumes me. Her body so perfect, so firm, so round, so slender, so long, so slim, so voluptuous, so sexy. Kelly lies next to me, but my mind is with Sonja.

The letters keep arriving from Sonja...

> My dearest love David,
>
> Received your letter. Thinking of you all day... Oh yes, don't think I'm lying. Oh no. Are you really seriously probing Japanese Zen philosophy and diet?
>
> I passed one week skiing in Briançon and now I'm in Lyon. I just received a letter from the embassy asking for more information. They write:
>
> At such time as your turn is reached—on the waiting list for final consideration of your case, you will be notified of the date when you may present your documents at this office, and execute your formal application.'
>
> So, I'm just waiting, it's terrible. Find a solution, what can I do? Find a solution for my coming to USA as soon as you can.

All my love, Sonja

I try Zen meditation instead of Sonja, but it doesn't work. Every time I get into either a lotus position or any other 'relaxed position' my mind tells me that I'm meditating so it becomes impossible to meditate... Like another voice saying 'look at David meditate.' I've never been fortunate enough to have control over my thought process.

One night Kelly, Anka and I go to Googie's to shoot a scene and inside we find Alan who has just returned from Paris. He must weigh close to 300 pounds. Alan agrees to play a John who gets picked up by Kelly for $25... Anka again is to play Kelly's jealous girlfriend. I shoot the interplay among the three and also film some of the customers in the bar. The scene seems to work.

Kelly and I roam the city with a camera... Wall Street, Times Square, the Village... I try to capture her aimlessness, her despair ... She is in love with me, but I am not attracted enough to her... My eyes restlessly seek out others... And one night in a cafe, I see this extraordinary blonde dancer and I ask Kelly to pick her up for me. I am not being mean or cold. It is simply the sexual/sensual nature is stronger than the virtuous side. It is also a way of signaling her that our romance is over.

There is a guy named John whom we know from the various cafes. He's a folk singer and very handsome, and since I would like to start shooting scenes with a man, I ask him if he would like to act. He agrees, though without much enthusiasm. We plan to meet the following day at Rienzi's, and I will shoot a scene with him and Kelly... a scene where he picks her up, takes her back to his pad but does not desire her... a scene ending in the heavy silence of despair. A scene from my life. The next day Kelly and I are in Rienzi's, but no John. He doesn't show.

"I'll go look in the park, sometimes he sings at the circle," I say. Kelly smiles. I leave and walk over to the park, but there is no sign of John... Passing the benches on the way back, I see this guy with the most extraordinary face. He has long, dark, straight hair and is wearing a black cape. I watch him sketch for a minute and then approach him.

"You have a great face. I'm looking for someone to be in a movie."

He looks at me, smiles, waits. His name is Richard. We walk together towards Rienzi's and towards Kelly.

A few days later I am speaking to Ron Rice, the filmmaker. He says films should be comic because people want to laugh. To act, he says, one needs to make oneself ridiculous and people will laugh at you. This is the essence of comedy—make oneself an utter ridiculous fool. Films should portray a world that is unreal. They should bring the audience into another world... I have the exact opposite view. My scenes with Kelly and Richard are real, taken from my life, their lives and the lives of the people I know. With the movement of the camera, the movement of a hand on the close-up, one can emphasize a certain aspect, a specific sensation. I can extract from reality what I want to show, but make it true nevertheless.

Ron laughs at the world. I see its tragic side.

"All good films should have some fucking in them," he says. "However, mine don't because I deal with perverted and impotent people who do everything else but fuck."

I am standing in a loft near my apartment watching Ron film with Taylor Mead and Winnie, the heavy-set funny personable Negress. There is something so free in his approach, so honest. Yet I do not want to do comedy. I want to reflect the search, the suffering, the irony, the aimlessness, the frustrations of our lives.

A long letter arrives from Melvin, who is studying in Providence. It is filled with references to 'aesthetic truth,' and 'reconciling concepts of art with my work in philosophy of history.' He writes about Leo Gershoy, Carl Becker, Cassirer, Whitehead, Joyce, Camus, Dewey. "I must follow my intellectual tangents where they take me, relying only on existential subjective artistic sense of value, which if rigorous and self-critical enough, will constitute the authentic inquiry. One must be a great person to be a great writer. One must consider the search for love and beauty a part of the whole—to be followed when one needs to. Time must be ignored, along with economics if possible. Camus' all or nothing... and the search must be primarily considered a moral one... But not in the sense of Western writing—where morality is only conventional, and art and morality appear contradictory. Quite to the contrary—Pascal's morality is thought, with the implication that it is good enough thought. Freud's analytic attitude is the fundamental ethical imperative and Camus also, but with the 20th Century afterthought that we have murdered by philosophy, that the delusion of certainty that Science presented must be ever exposed by tenaciously evaluating all philosophy, value and ethics by whether..." etc.

The bottom line: he broke up with an English girl to whom he was engaged (a "kindling eye") and seems to feel that he must devote his life to his intellectual search. He has nice things to say about the letters he's received from me.

"They are magnificent. You have a great gift. You can write; you could write something that would last. But you must not cross the line into madness—you must promise yourself that you will never—you can stop if you know that you are right... but you *are* completely and wholly and totally right. Everything you do and did is completely right. I have thought all of it over. You must only do what you feel you must. This is not true for all men. It is true for you. Edmund Wilson now—"the conflict of the essentially Romantic conception of one's duty to one's own personality with the conception of one's duty to society." Gérard de Nerval suffered from spells of insanity. He believed... and no doubt Whitehead would approve his metaphysics—that the world which we see about is involved in some more intimate fashion than is ordinarily supposed with the things that go on in our minds, that even our dreams and hallucinations are somehow bound up with reality."

He asks me if I've seen Nelly. I haven't in a long time, but then one of those coincidences occurs. With his letter still in my pocket I go into the San Remo and Nelly is sitting at a table drinking. She embraces me, slurring her words. She is drunk... but she looks great and sexy and I desire her. She is so tall, well built and accessible. Since I stopped sleeping with Kelly, I haven't had a woman and the need is taking over. I take a beer, and Nelly starts complaining about some guy she knows and about the restraints imposed on her life by her parents.

We go to my apartment. Nelly lays on the bed, her legs spread, her eyes shut, between sleeping and waking. She doesn't wake up and my desire is so overwhelming. I deplore my weakness, my desires. Nelly sleeps and I hold her in her sleep.

The next morning, she tells me that she can't see me again because her life is out of control and she has to stop drinking and sleeping with men. I give her some breakfast before she leaves. When the door closes I start wanting her again. I know something is wrong with me but I don't know what to change...

The scenes I shoot with Richard and Kelly fascinate me, but I don't know if I should take it seriously. How does one know if one has talent or not? We are all lost children, groping, but unable to find a better path. Maya is in a mental hospital in Milwaukee. Nelly is on the verge of madness; Melvin writes (rationally, of course) about suicide. Kelly has slit her wrists twice and is kind of bravely holding on.

Richard lives in metaphysical despair. However, there are others who seem happy, seem to be with it. They have a girl, a job, an art... They seem to escape madness. I envy them.

Maya writes to me...

> Dearest David Dot,
>
> I miss you. I wish I knew how we'd get along if we were together. As you know the 'Barry thing' was a mess and helped me to get sick. Right now, I should be getting out of the hospital soon, but the sickening part is that I'll have to stay in Milwaukee for maybe six weeks. Why didn't you like me modeling? Actually, it's kind of fun. Either that or movies seem like my kind of stuff. Still with the guitar? I hope so. Heard Josh White the other night.
>
> Avec amour
>
> Maya

I take a job with a TV producer in the City Center building in midtown. Mostly perfunctory work, but the job is enhanced because the New York City Ballet rehearses and performs in the building. Sometimes I sneak away and watch rehearsals. I spend some time with the lovely ballerinas in a coffee shop across the street, and though I would like to have one for a girlfriend nothing works out. However, one day a ballet troupe from Washington D.C. arrives to perform and I meet the lead ballerina in the coffee shop and she invites me to her hotel room after the performance. We make love. She has beautiful legs, but when I ask to see her again she is not interested. The next afternoon I go to an office supply store to buy something for the producer and I am told that President Kennedy has been shot. It is like a frightening stillness, a dark cloud, chaos, the earth loosening under my feet. My immediate reaction is that Hoover or LBJ finally got him. I think of one of the earliest memories of my life, the day FDR died. I am walking with my father, hand in hand, around the block near our apartment. He is somber, stunned, mournful. I remember little else from those early years, but the powerful mood of my father when he learned of FDR's death remains with me.

I read a lot of books — Somerset Maugham, Evelyn Waugh, Henry Miller, Jack Kerouac, Alan Watts. Maugham and Waugh are such great stylists. Their use of the English language is incredible. I envy that ability... Kerouac and Miller have such a joie de vivre though Kerouac has his dark, depressive side. Miller is totally amoral... anything goes for him, while Kerouac is more the observer... but they are living, while I seem to be stagnating. Dean Moriarty drives fast cars and fucks high school girls. I play the guitar, read poems by Rilke and—considering Nelly—fuck high school girls. But he seems too extroverted, manic, happy. Whereas I am more introverted, despairing, depressive. Why?

Mel calls me from Providence. He wants to commit suicide with me once again. He is very serious; he has thought it all out rationally. A 'rational' decision in the prime of life, so to speak. He says that since the pain out-weighs the pleasure, and since pleasure is just momentary and extracts too high a price, it is not worth living.

Mel refuses to accept the limitation of life. Life can know no real love, no real giving, no real accomplishment. It is a kind of absurd joke lived by scurrying animals, most of whom are fortunate enough not to examine what it all means, or why they go through the daily motions. When one faces truth, the inevitable result is suicide, he writes.

Mel says that the only possible pleasure for him in the future is the occasional intellectual pleasure of a philosophy paper. This is not enough to live for, when one considers all the pain. I understand him. Every day brings fear; fear of loneliness, of frustration, of responsibility. There is little else but fear.

He claims he does not want a woman. I am skeptical. If he had a good fuck he wouldn't be talking like he is. He wants me to come to Providence with a gun. Why involve me? I ask him. This would lend more spontaneity to the act ... to die in friendship.

But I cannot accept this rational suicide. The power of reason is limited. Logic is only a part of man's makeup. He is governed as much by the non-verbal, non-logical elements. Committing suicide as a logical conclusion is nonsense. It has to be an emotional thing, a despair too great.

I decide to go to Providence without a gun. Another friend of mine, Jimmy Levesque—a painter and would-be filmmaker—is living there and he says I can stay with him.

Providence is lonely. After New York, the streets seem empty. Mel has met a Pembroke girl and is now more cheerful. No more talk about suicide. "It may still be rational," he says, "but I guess I'll wait." I am hired by the *Providence Journal* as a cub reporter, and I work nights, traveling to town meetings, sewer commission meetings, etc., all over the state. I buy a small used Studebaker, a 'tub on wheels' and travel the lonely roads, striving to make deadlines. Sometimes I am assigned to local offices in small towns in Rhode Island, checking in with the police, reading police reports. With my long hair, I am not really accepted as one of the boys, but I do my best, though sometimes I have to copy the news out of the local paper. I write a couple of feature stories that are well received. The letters keep arriving from Sonja almost every other day. Her love for me is greater than ever; she is coming to the States in the fall; we will live and be happy together, etc.

Sonja is having difficulty getting her visa, and she keeps me informed of the details. Her father is resigned to her departure.

> But the important thing is that I am in the USA so that we can be together. I have such a terrible need for you — in the shower, in bed or just speaking. I need you.
>
> If you could only see how I am jealous knowing that the other girls have you for themselves... even if it's only for one night. But all that will finish soon, and I will have you to myself. I'm celebrating in advance...
>
> You are right to sacrifice everything to make a film. But don't sacrifice me. I love you, I adore you and hope soon to be with you.
>
> Yours always,
> love, Sonja

In Providence I am celibate, working, reading, talking to Mel and Jimmy about life, nihilism, literature, sex... No cafe here, but we have cafe conversation in the apartments. Sonja's letters sustain me... It seems she is really coming. The most beautiful, sexy woman in the world will soon be mine on a steady basis.

I am tired most of the time in Providence... Feeling weak. I crawl into bed at one o'clock each morning after delivering my copy and sleep for 10-12 hours, eat, and then report to work. I have little desire for anything. My throat starts to hurt and I go to a doctor who tells me my tonsils will have to come out.

I have been in the hospital for a week and my throat is still painful… I am feeling weak and listless. I drag myself out of bed, get in the car and drive to Truro on the Cape where Jimmy has a little shack. I run into the soothing salt water and after a half hour swim I am cured. I leave the water, drops falling on the sand, the sun shining, my body tired from the swim but restored to health, and for a little while, at least, I know peace.

In Provincetown the highlight of the summer is "THE TRIAL." Five people on trial for marijuana charges, and one, a Negro musician, on trial for giving drugs to a minor (a white girl). Since four of the five defendants either live or go to school in Rhode Island, the *Journal* agrees to let me cover the trial. One of the defendants is my friend Jimmy Levesque, who fills me in on some of the pre-trial details.

I lose interest in the outcome of the trial when I get the incredible news that Sonja will be arriving at last. She has gotten her visa, now all she needs is money for the ticket. All summer I have been trying to decide what to do with myself. I have started painting. The German expressionists fascinate me… but I do not have the talent to capture their style… And my own style? Well, I like it. At one point I decide to do a photo book about the Village, like "Love on the Left Bank," and then go to the UCLA department of Theatre Arts to study acting and film-making. But first Sonja has to arrive. I write to my parents and tell them that Sonja will "prove to be the stabilizing influence I need to concentrate 100 percent on work and stick to it," etc. I have saved some money from the *Journal* job, but not enough. I ask my parents if they will help and they agree.

It is now a month later. I am sitting on the bed in a New York room rented by the week, crying. Sonja has been here and is now gone.

I sent her the money. I drove to New York from Provincetown. We met and hugged, but I never felt at ease. We went to this room and made love, but there was something not quite passionate about her. The day after her arrival she got a job as a waitress in a key club similar to the Playboy Club. She arrived on a Sunday. On Thursday, when I came back to the room, all her things were gone. Just a note that I should call her friend Lucien who would explain.

I called Lucien who told me that she felt it wasn't right between us, and that she had met a rich man at the club and left with him for Las Vegas. Finish the Sonja saga. I stare at the walls. There are no more tears. I get up, put on my jacket, walk down the stairs, turn left, walk to Seventh Avenue and get on the IRT uptown. I will go home to my parents. They are always there with love. We are close. When I travel I always write to them. They don't understand me, but I don't understand me either.

Blood Coffee

KELLY 1963

Weak we were
with knowing eyes
And weakened by our knowledge,
We sipped blood-coffee
by candle light—
For we were bled much.
Recovering from our
Thought's inflicted
Surgery,
We neither laughed
nor cried,

Lest the wounds
Tear.
And watched we
carefully
for those who watched our
Pain to
Laugh
or take away our self-
rolled medicines.
Some cut too deep
with Searching's knife,
Dying grateful
in the lights,
But we who
survived—
Weak we were
with knowing eyes.

I am in love with David. "Love," I don't know anymore what that means, but we have to use words as they are understood, even if they're not completely accurate. Anyway, I want him; I want to touch him, to caress him, to lean against him. I write letters to him, which I will never send and he will never read. The thought of him sustains me, but if he leaves me for another I might cut again. A razor cuts much bloodier than love.

David... Two days ago when I left you I was sick. It was snowing and I ate the snow, the pure white snow. Not like me. The snow melted in my fingers because my fingers were warm. It melted in my mouth, cold and fragile and disappeared. There was nothing left under my tongue, nothing between my fingers and I thought of you, because I can do nothing else but think of you. I pressed my cheek against the white surface and I saw the trace of my profile. And I thought about those who succeed in suicide. Me, I belong to those who try. I am not strong enough to die. Suicide would be a victory over life. I scratched my fingernails along the side of a wall, but I didn't cry. I wanted to die; sometimes I want to die... Just like that. Why can't one die just like one walks or breathes? My heart was beating in my stomach and I saw your eyes. I wanted you. I didn't want to go home, to be with myself once again. I needed someone to hold me and protect me, but I had nothing. You left me without a gesture, and me, I need someone to show me his approval. You, you don't need to show me anything. You live only for yourself because you have enough of your flesh without having to worry about others. But my flesh needs yours so as to not feel naked. I wanted to cry but everything was blocked up in side of me, as you had destroyed everything I had inside me for you. Why? You look for love but you have lost it...

> Come sit with me in
> dark times rising and
> count the weeping in
> these stones, For I
> have taken hands for
> loving, and found them
> cold as immortals' bones.

I am walking with David down the street... I love walking with him. I feel flattered because he is so beautiful. And I feel that we have things to do together, that we belong together... that we have a lot in common... a lot to say to each other. People look at us as we walk. Inside we are alike, and outside, he, tall and dark, me petite and up to his shoulder. To walk in the streets with David makes me feel good.

David is cutting a scene from the film he is making and I am watching him with an almost uncontrollable desire. I sit on his lap. He tries to ignore me and continues working, but I can feel that he is starting to get excited and soon we are on the floor together. I love making love in forbidden places. This excites me.

When we leave the cutting room it is night and we head to the Village streets to hear some folk music. David wants to go to Charlie Washburn's cafe and I'll go wherever he wants to go. The cafe is filled mostly with tourists... clean-cut, uptown/New Jersey/Long Island types... having a thrill watching the beatniks in the Village. But my heart does a little plop when I see that tonight's featured singer is none other than Lenny.

Lenny's on the stage emoting folk songs and looking soulful. David is looking at everyone in the cafe, especially the women. I see him tense when he sees a leggy blonde sitting by herself near the stage. I know he wants her and I am already hurting but we have to be cool, oh so cool and pretend that we're not anything more than "Just Friends." David is fidgeting with the paper napkin, tearing it into pieces and staring at people in the cafe. He has this way of looking at someone as if to unveil the inside and the outside of the person, to know all of his secrets. He's an observer, but I know the only thing he wants to observe is that leggy Scandinavian blonde... and to observe her at close range.

David—

Yesterday I wanted to be with you. You knew it, but you didn't need my affection. Sometimes I think that you love me but I know that it really means nothing. So I left, dragging my heart because it didn't want to follow me. I wanted so much to stay there next to you. I wanted you to rest your head against me. I wanted to caress you.

The other day you were sick... the flu. You were complaining. I took care of you and I prepared your food. I always liked to take care of my men. Perhaps it's because they became the son or the little brother that I was finally able to protect. And by doing it I could have power over them. They were in a state of weakness and they finally needed me. All of that because I'm not sure of myself. Unconsciously I think that—by myself—I'm not able to keep a man. When you are sick you need me; when you are well you tell me that you want other girls. You are very sensitive in your awareness of the world, but you must know how much you hurt me.

I need you; you know it, I'm sure. When I saw you, I felt my heart enlarge inside of me like a huge sun—immense—immense. I was troubled because I was happy. The intellectuals call it the masochism of happiness. It's still snowing. You know how I like the city when it is covered by white snow, before it gets dirty and slushy... like love before it fades. I would like to write the word "hope" on my forehead.

I try to understand your attitude towards me by comparing it to Paul. He loves me, he follows me, he wants me, but I don't want him. Perhaps you feel towards me as I feel towards him. Now the snow has become soiled. I don't want to bore you; I want to love you. I try to act, to play the game, but I play it poorly when it's a question of heart. I don't want to look like a stupid lovesick girl, but this is the way I feel. I act badly and you feel it; you run from me, and you escape, and I stay there, without saying anything, wounded, disoriented, incapable of concentrating on anything else. Thus, I have the strange impression of only living through you, for you, when I want to live *with* you. Why isn't it possible? Bit by bit you withdraw all hope, all of my will to live, to act.

Where are the beautiful promises that you made? Do you remember you spoke of the marvelous relationship we could have intellectually and psychologically? But it's far from that. Is it my fault? Is it yours? I don't know anymore—I'm lost, and the more I try to find myself, the more lost I become.

At any rate, tonight I don't feel too depressed thanks to some pills I took, which puts me in a different world. I'm not happy, but I'm not sad. My mind is filled with thoughts. Thoughts. Thoughts. I've met a lot of interesting people in New York and I'm glad that a lot of people know me and like me. This comforts me, envelops me. Otherwise, I would slowly die. My body, this traitor, needs you.

When I saw you take off your shirt this afternoon and saw your torso, I began to shiver. I had an overwhelming desire to throw myself against you so that you would warm me. Don't you desire me? I love the world because it is like me, alone and in despair. And you? You are alone; I know it. It is written on your face, a loud cry of loneliness. I recognized this the first time I met you. I understood your smile; I understood your eyes. Why don't you want me? I would do anything for you. I will try to bandage my wounds, but I would also like to cure yours. Think of me from time to time.

David doesn't love me but he is fascinated by my face and my expression and he uses me in the film he is shooting. When I see myself on the screen in his apartment, it is strange. I recognize myself, but I do not. Sad eyes, aimlessness. Is that me? I am sitting in Rienzi's sipping an espresso, waiting for David who is roaming the streets looking for an actor to play a scene with me. John didn't show up, so he's got to find someone else. I took a pill before, so I'm feeling reasonably placid, trying not to think of anything. Anyway, David comes in with this strange looking guy, like he dragged him out of the night—thin, wearing a cape, a tortured, troubled face. I notice he's got no socks in his shoes. He introduces him as Richard, and from the way he looks at me I can tell he likes me. Always the wrong ones. I've got to do a love scene with him. An interesting face, but not the kind to turn me on. He seems to be in the clouds. He sits, smiles, says nothing. I feel I have to break the silence, and say inanely: "I hear we're going to act together."

Shyly he says, "That's what I hear."

David seems happy about our scene together. When Richard was in bed with me for the lovemaking part I could feel he was really excited, which made me feel uncomfortable. It's David I want in bed with me.

Oh, David
Oh, we must walk down
Streets, not meadows, and
We will speak words of Now.
Not dreams, and there will
be no castles, only us
but
I will hold your hand.
When you are tired.

When I come home the next night, Richard is waiting for me. I make excuses that I'm tired so as not to invite him up. He looks hurt, but he leaves. With his long cape, walking down the dim street, he looks a bit like Dracula. He makes me a little bit afraid. The next night he is also in front of my door. This time I speak to him and I can tell he is in love with me—at least it seems that way... Perhaps it's just sex, but anyway he's attracted to me... but I can't get interested in him.

David wants to shoot more scenes with Richard, and he asks me to come because he may do another scene with the two of us. Anyway, when I arrive at the apartment in the East Village, Richard is in on the bed kissing this pretty girl and at that moment something happens to me. Because we're all so complicated, filled with contradictions, because we're always searching for what we can't have. Suddenly I want him to love me; I need him to love me. Seeing him with the other girl makes me jealous and I can't take the idea that Richard doesn't love me. It's crazy, but that's the way it is.

Richard can tell that something has changed in my manner, and he looks at me with other eyes. Suddenly he jumps up from the bed, fully clothed, and goes into the shower and turns on the water. As the water flows, I can hear sobs. The other girl goes to the shower and comforts him; she puts her arms around him. She comes back to me and tells me that he is crying because of me. I feel flattered. I like having someone suffer because of me. The other night, Richard had left a bouquet of violets and a poem in front of my door. I find this romantic and now he is crying, fully clothed, in the shower. With the rejections and the cruelty I've had all my life from my parents, the romantic appeals to me, grips me. It is beautiful. Someone crying because of me. Someone leaving me flowers and poems. I smile at Richard. He looks at me with sad eyes and smiles back. And suddenly I am under the shower with him and we are kissing.

During the next two weeks we pour out our blocked passions. We stay in his loft, leaving only to buy bread and some food. I think we were thrown together because our pasts are similar. I think we found in each the reflection of the other, a kind of brother or sister, but linked emotionally. That's not completely true because we each have so many problems, our own problems. Thus, we retreat to our own isolated chambers.

Both of us were rejected by our parents and, thus, we desperately needed someone to unite with. We think we can find it through physical love, but that's not possible. The union of physical love is a mirage, a trap. Something tells me I am walking into a trap... but I cannot stop.

False Stones and Chips of Glass

DAVID 1965

I try being everything, and therefore am nothing. Maeterlinck expressed it well: "In some strange way we devalue things as soon as we give utterance to them. We believe we have dived to the uttermost depths of the abyss, and yet when we return to the surface the drops of water on our own pallid fingertips no longer resembles the sea from which it came. We think we have discovered a hoard of wonderful treasure-trove, and yet when we emerge again into the light of day we see that all we have brought back with us is false stones and chips of glass. But for all this, the treasure goes on glimmering in the darkness, unchanged."

It is the dark mysterious world with the glimmering treasure that is never reached, that becomes banal and fades as soon as one approaches it, that I try to discover. It is a world apart from my parents, which has its foundation in honesty, family, work, and the everyday material things. My generation seeks unconsciously to discover this other world, a world that can never be defined, a world which is at once sensual and bohemian, and where everyday morality ceases to exist.

We look for the answer in sex, art, drugs, mysticism... the promise, the glitter... but we never seem to find it. One night in Paris this German guy, Erhardt, was homeless and came into my hotel room to sleep. I went out to an all-night café. There was a young girl there with some friends. When I left the café, she ran after me and said, "My friends say I'm drunk, but I'm not," and asked to come with me. She had been on a camping trip with her friends and didn't want to go home to her mother. So we went to my hotel. When she saw Erhardt, she asked, "Is that your mother?" She lay down on the floor and asked me to hold her hand so she could fall asleep. I did.

I didn't know what she was, a young girl, a woman or what. As time passed, we started to get more affectionate, and I began falling in love with her face, which was beautifully angelic. I stroked it; we kissed. Finally, she said, pointing at Erhardt, "If he wasn't here, I would like to sleep all nude in your arms."

I told Erhardt to get out, which he did. The girl got undressed and fell naked on the bed. I knew a disaster was going to occur. I didn't desire her body. It didn't arouse me. We made love, but I forced it. She sensed it and when we finished, she said, "You bastard."

She was 18 and had made love to one man, her fiancé who was with the army in Algeria. The most important thing in the world for her was to become a woman. She felt inadequate. She didn't know whether to join her fiancé or sleep with every man she could find in the streets. Now she had slept with me and I had rejected her. At one point, she tried to commit suicide by jumping out the window. She attacked me with a knife. This went on for days because I had rejected her physically. I suffered as well, because I wanted a woman, and I didn't want her body; the right curves were not in the right places. I needed so much to desire her, and yet I couldn't. Physical desires are not dictated by the will.

She returned to the streets and slept under the bridges by the Seine, keeping herself alive by stealing. I met her again, two days before I left Paris. I was living in another place, but she found the address. We spent two days together and parted indifferently, solely because of the lack of physical passion on my part.

It is night. I am wandering through the warehouse area of SOHO. There is a visual fascination about this area. There is a total aloneness. Houses without people. All of a sudden the world is left behind and you are alone with yourself and your echoing footsteps.

Soon SOHO becomes the bright lights of The Village. I turn left and walk to the Figaro. The cafe is three-quarters full: spades, beats, junkies, artists and restless searchers of both sexes looking to pick up and get picked up. The atmosphere is charged, restless. A slender girl with blonde hair almost down to her waist is sitting alone. She must be about 18 and has a tense, charged look on her face. I would love to sit next to her, but I feel too depressed and too shy to do so. I notice Jimmy sitting alone a few tables away from a girl. He signals me and I join him. He has returned from Providence and is now living in the East Village. Jimmy has been thinking about drugs and Vietnam.

Several young men enter the cafe, their eyes scanning for women or a connection, grasping for life in a seemingly never-ending circle.

I recognize a couple of them, but don't remember their names. I nod "Hello." One of them goes up to a girl in tight sexy clothes and sits down with her. I feel a twinge of envy. Another—I think his name is John—joins three spades and a white chick at a nearby table. Must be his connection. The other girl has also been picked up now. I'm feeling too depressed to try to pick up anyone, so I just watch the people. Most are dressed in the latest Bohemian fads, their coolness contrasting with my shyness and tension.

I would love to have the ability to *be* in the moment, to savor the present, with the mind alive and happy. Instead I dwell on images of the past and fears of the future, loneliness, sickness and futility. I want to be optimistic, but life seems more of a burden... a terrible chasm into which one can plunge at any moment.

Maybe music, art, film, poetry can save me, because it gives the sadness a beauty. But I experience no salvation. My mind is too active; it cannot let go and just *be*.

Jimmy breaks the silence. "Where are you living now?"

"With my parents most of the time. But my friend, Bill—I don't know if you met him—has gone to Mexico and has given me the key to his pad in the warehouse district below Canal Street. The trouble is, no one's allowed to live there... I can only use it between 9 p.m. and 9 a.m. so the bar owner downstairs doesn't know I'm there... I'd invite you to come over, but I can't take the chance."

The furnishings in Bill's semi-condemned apartment are a mattress on the floor, an old bookcase, a record player, strewn clothes, a fridge and an old bathtub and toilet. I lie down on the mattress and turn to the sports section of the paper, but the images of the girls I have seen in the Figaro fill my mind. I wander into the bathroom and turn on the hot water. The phone rings. It's my father. He tells me that my uncle, my mother's brother, has died of a heart attack. The funeral is tomorrow... My sleep is restless. My dreams are of death and sex.

Seeing my relatives at the funeral home increases my feelings of alienation. We are a family but I live in a different world. At the cemetery my mother is crying and I put my arms around her. She is lovely and sweet and is always nice to me. I love her... but I am uncomfortable. I am considerate—always—of others, but my own suffering does not allow me to feel anyone else's pain.

My father is talking to me. He finds it more difficult to display affection, but beneath it he is a warm man. He wants to know why I didn't call last night, why I don't get a haircut, and why I don't get a job. I mumble that I plan to look for a job that afternoon. I kiss my parents goodbye.

I am on the 45th floor of the TIME LIFE building, the glass and steel monster of Sixth Avenue, symbol of the dominant bourgeois culture. Sitting behind his desk is an employment manager; he is looking at my resume. He glances at me, his face showing his distaste. I am wearing a suit, but my hair is too long. He looks again at my resume and then looks up.

"After college you went to the Sorbonne?"

"Yes."

"And then after that, odd jobs, bumming around, a little film-school, a little journalism."

"Yes, but now I want to start a career."

"That's not how a TIME man would have spent his time."

I am on Sixth Avenue looking up at the building, picturing with pleasure blowing it up.

The next day is spent on 42nd Street going to one movie after another for $1. Walking under the marquees after seeing my third film, I imagine assassinating the president of the United States. The vision becomes real. I then imagine taking the gun and shooting everybody in the streets, killing several people on 42nd Street and then fleeing in the subway. My bitterness has now become so intense that I have become a murderer in my mind. I take the train downtown, leaving the corpses lying under movie marquees, the flashing neon lights adding a garish aspect to the massacre.

In the Figaro a young girl enters, rather attractive, long hair, and sits down at a nearby table. I look at her, but am too much embroiled in my bitterness to speak to her. I am paralyzed by depression. Near the entrance of the cafe, a waitress is arguing with a bum. He sees me and walks over, his drunken eyes only half focusing.

"She won't serve me," he said. "I'm a citizen." The attractive girl is looking at us. She smiles at the bum. He grins. I smile at her. She smiles back. The bum has provided enough of a spark to enable me to conquer my depression, stand up and join the girl at her table. She is a freshman at Barnard College, 17 years old. I invite her to my place and she agrees. Her name is Doreen.

We wander through the empty warehouse district. I put my arm around her and hum a song. Up a flight of stairs to the apartment. We enter.

"Well, this is it. Excuse the mess, but, uh... This isn't mine... It belongs to a friend who's down in Mexico. Let me take your coat and I'll find some place to put it."

She gives me her coat. I throw it on a chair and then sit down next to her. We really have nothing to say to each other, a 17-year-old college girl and me, both here for the experience, for sex, a temporary end to loneliness.

"Isn't it great the way the light comes in here," I say feigning enthusiasm. "Look at our shadows..."

I get up... stand awkwardly. "Let me put some music on. What kind do you like?"

"Oh, anything... Something. Whatever you like."

I put on a folk music record, Joan Baez singing "Plaisir D'Amour," walk to the refrigerator and open it. It is nearly empty.

"There's not much here," I tell her. "Only an orange. Would you like that or some pot?"

"I'll take pot," she says casually.

I take out a small bag of marijuana, pull some paper from the shelf and start to roll a joint.

"Is there a bathroom back there?"

"Yes."

"Excuse me for a moment." She takes her purse and goes into the bathroom. With nervous anticipation I continue to roll the cigarette. When I finish rolling the joint, I lick it and light it. The smoke burns my lungs. After a few puffs, the girl emerges from the bathroom. I offer her the joint.

"This is strong stuff. You probably won't need much."

She takes the joint, shuts her eyes, takes a deep puff and starts coughing. We walk to the bed and sit down on it. I start caressing her face and her arms.

I push her on the bed. We are both high from the pot, and we pull off our clothes as fast as we can. She has a fair body with full breasts, and the pot has made me excited. I want her desperately. I am inside of her and we both come together sharing our pot high. As I am coming, I cry... there is pleasure but there is something missing; I pull away from her and smile. She smiles back. I look at the roaches on the floor. Here I am in a rundown pad, clothes strewn all over, joints on the floor, an under-age chick in the bed. The epitome of Beatnik heaven.

I don't know if I'll ever see Doreen again, but sleeping with her postponed the nightmare... For a few hours I fooled myself into believing I held a treasure... instead of stones and chips of glass.

Bellevue Interlude

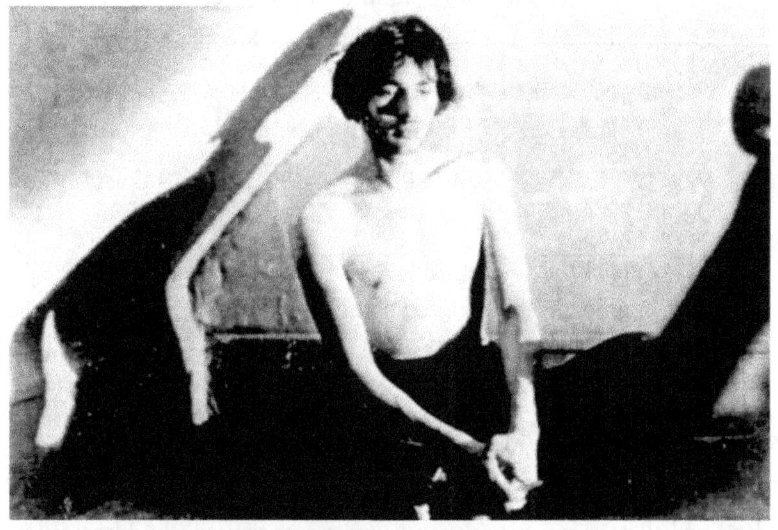

DAVID 1965

Leaving Charlie Washburn's Creative Workshop with a young folk singer in tow, Hal and I walk in the drizzle on Third Street. A young girl walks by looking lost, perhaps drugged. I reach out my hand and put it on her shoulder and turn her around. Without breaking stride she comes with me and hands me a clown-like doll that she is carrying. We are on our way to the Improvisation, and Hal figures it's a chick I knew who is stoned. In her hand is an envelope containing, amongst other things, an airplane ticket from California, a brochure from Alcoholics Anonymous, and a check for $12.64 from the Juvenile Court of San Francisco.

She tells me she arrived from San Francisco that night, was met at the airport by her mother who was drunk, and by her mother's boyfriend. They took her to a few bars; the boyfriend gave her the little doll and left, leaving her to wander around the street. Her name is Pamela.

Into the subway, Pamela smiling, saying nothing, questioning nothing, obeying everything. Her hair disheveled, her face covered with pimples. A suede jacket covers a white cotton blouse. Leaving the subway at 42nd Street, we walk to the Improv which is crowded. Hal asks the owner to let the folksinger play, while Pamela and I wander to the front looking for a table. We find a place to sit in the area that serves as a stage. The cafe begins to quiet down and I put my finger to my mouth, "SHHHH." Silence. Pamela sits on the stage, alone, completely oblivious to everything.

She sits with the doll, smiling. The girls at the next table want to see the doll. She gives it to them… red and white clown eye, a red nose, dancing ballet, *relevé, pas de chat*. Pamela, eyes slanted, shudder, smiles, no words. The Improv quiet. Hal kneeling down next to the table talking about some television gig.

Pamela growing more tired…

Leaving the Improv, Pamela says, "I like it here, but let's go somewhere else." Outside it is raining. Pamela skipping. I've told her that I'll let her sleep in my place. I tell Hal, "She has no money. All her clothes are in San Francisco or at her mother's place in Pennsylvania."

Hal nods.

Pamela walks quickly; her mother is an alcoholic. I ask her if she is one too; she says she doesn't know.

Home, small room, one bed. I go into the bathroom and when I come back Pamela is completely nude under the blanket. I don't want to sleep with her overly much, and I told Hal I would go back to the Improv.

Four a.m., Hal and Bernie off with two chicks, a third one playing up to me. She's a bit too ugly and, anyway, my room is a bit crowded now. I buy an apple to bring back to Pamela if she's awake.

Pamela is waiting.

"How are you?"

No answer.

"Do you want an apple?"

"Yes."

She has a scar on her neck.

"Where did you get it?"

"When I tried to free a little boy's soul."

"OK, but how did you get it?"

"With a razor blade."

And then the story about the nine months of heroin, amphetamine, and finally an LSD trip ending with a cut throat in the hospital in San Francisco. Bit by bit, parts of her life come together. She attended Performing Arts High School in New York, started roaming the Village at the age of 12, creating fantasy worlds filled with fairy princesses and witches. Her world would be destroyed by some contact with reality, and then she would move on. Married in Texas under an assumed name, she says she is 17.

She seems lucid and says she doesn't want to become an alcoholic. She looks at me. "Why are men so superior to women?" She asks. And our bodies touched with great hesitation on my part, but touch they do. She didn't want me to use a rubber. I tried anyway but the thing fell off and I said the hell with it. Afterwards, her hands went over my body with a pinching movement.

"What are bodies for except to make others?"

"We'll have you dancing," I said.

Pamela off on an LSD trip after three months of heroin, cutting her throat, and I am touching the scar and pimples on her forehead.

"Pamela, you've got to talk in complete sentences."

"Poison, poison… look at the molecules on my body."

"All right, baby, that's where we start. No more drinking, just you and I."

And the next day, Pamela still naked, David dressed…clothes neatly folded on the bed.

"Put your clothes on Pamela."

"Oh?"

Breakfast at Radley's… for Pamela, a chicken salad sandwich, milk and tea. She calls her mother at the hotel. Her mother wants to meet her in a bar but Pamela doesn't want to.

Walking in the rain, I am singing French songs, Pamela smiling.

"I think I'll become your father, Pamela."

"OK."

"Courez, courez, vite si vous le pouvez. Jamais, jamais…"

We arrive at Hal's pad on 3rd Street. He puts her to work cleaning dishes, which she does willingly enough. "You can stay here," he says, "in the little room there, as long as you keep out of the way when I have a chick," and to me- "Can I ball her?"

"Sure."

Hal goes to his closet and takes out an Oriental two-piece suit. He throws it to Pamela and tells her to try it on. She strips completely nude, feeling her long thin body with her hands and puts on the outfit. Two long slits up the side of the skirt leave very little covered. Off comes the top and Pamela dances. She is a beautiful dancer, much to my surprise; her long Botticelli hair has been pinned up in a bun. I join the dance, while Hal photographs the pas de deux. Pamela still lost, Pamela nude, dancing, dancing.

Dishes cleaned, spaghetti with marijuana sauce served. I eat quickly as I have to run, leaving my 'daughter' with her new 'husband'.

I returned the next night. Hal is not there. Pamela is crouching nude on all fours on the mattress. She says nothing, but looks around strangely, her hands moving in the air. For minutes she stares at her hands. I ask her questions, "Where's Hal… did you go out?" No answer.

She is obviously wandering; her eyes do not focus. I ask again, "Did you go out?"

"Yes."

"Where?"

"To Tangier."

"Oh? Where else?"

She begins to cry: "I've been poisoned, I'm going to die… ah… hmmm.. Yes.. what will you do with me when I die or crack up … hmmmm … Am I sick?"

"You're a bit disconnected," I say. "But you're not going to die or crack up."

The hands are in the air.

"Pamela, have you eaten? Are you hungry?"

No answer. She gets dressed and I take her to Katz's. When I let go of her hand she begins wandering around. Her slip is showing beneath her dress and her hands are drawing pictures in the air. She doesn't speak, just answers "yes" to every question.

Roast beef sandwiches. Pamela not eating. In the rain, back to 3rd Street. Pamela undressing, while I am watching. Pamela crying, "Take me away. I don't want to be alone with that big black dog." Hal's dog,

Diogenes, licks her face. "Take me away with you, take me home," she cries.

"Don't you like it here?"

No answer.

And then — "Why are men superior to women? Do little boys become men?" Pointing to her genitals, "What happened to this? If I lie down and go to sleep or hang myself… au revoir Francois… What would have happened at the Improvisation if I hadn't asked you to live with me?"

She is wandering. She sees her shadow on the curtain, and begins to growl, arms twitching in the air. "Through a glass darkly," she yells… "Ah, *N'est-ce-pas?*… hmmmm… ah…"

Her expression is marvelous, imp-like, excitable. Her French accent is good. She sits on the toilet, eyes closed, muttering French phrases. "Where is my…? Where is my … soul? Is he on the john? Did I sell it?"

"No, Pamela, souls are funny things. You can't force them. The harder you look, the more elusive they are."

She is crying again. I had been planning to leave, but I must stay. I undress and fall down next to her on the mattress.

"Pamela, are you high on anything?"

She smiles and doesn't answer.

"We'll go to sleep, Pamela. Let's go to sleep."

I fall asleep. She cries out. I sleep again.

Hal returns from balling some chick, apparently a de-virgination.

"We've got a schizophrenic here…"

"You really picked a beauty, my boy."

"Did you sleep with her?" I ask him.

"All day and night."

He recounts some of her adventures of the night before; her whipping out a knife at this painter's house and doing a wild knife dance, scaring everybody. Pamela, oh beautiful Pamela, what will we do with you?

"Hello Pamela," says Hal.

"My name is Judy tonight."

"My name is Punch." She laughs. Hal and Pam dance; she's still nude. The radio is playing some rock and roll. She looks at me and laughs while trying to pull Hal's shirt off.

Hal: "Will a little schizoid from a mining town in Pennsylvania make it here in the big city with two potheads?"

Pamela: "Bugs by the wayside." She hits her hips several times while a cockroach crawls on her leg. She picks it up and plays with it and then places it on her shoulder. "Mush… grrr…er… music, music… music… music, music. You cung piss." She is on her feet stalking her shadow. "Bubble gum makes me sick. Health, health, *santé.*"

Pamela continues: "What is it? It's all there by itself. It has something to do with Alice. Did you see a horse without any skin with icicles dripping off it…"

One of her favorite themes is "Hot and cold fire and ice." She repeats this over and over: "bones, bones, bones… halibut by the wayside."

The dance continues, her lithe nude body extending, her wild hair waving. "What about pirates and swashbuckling things. They're for little boys. Could I be a dragon… no ice…no fire… in the bathroom. Shit."

And then louder — "True love — someone should tell me about it."

She pauses, smiles, "Hmmm, oh… hmmmmm. Blessing and curse, and overfilled purse."

She begins reciting as if in a drama class, "I can raise you hosts of ghosts. Hey boys, what are we doing here? Hey, let's go swimming. What are we going to do without our songs."

Hal explains that it is too cold to go swimming.

"Oh," says Pamela.

"Hey, Jean Pierre. Hey, voltage. What do you do with all that voltage? It's used for dams and bridges."

"Oh, oh," I say.

"Oh, *c'est possible*," says Pam.

She is on the bed still nude. Hal speaks to her in Spanish.

"Deirdre, Deirdre, Deirdre," cries Pam. "I've been poisoned; I'm paranoiac."

She jumps up. "Don't you dare, don't you dare," she yells and then smiles. "Oh you are? That's nice… huh."

I prepare to leave. I am beat and want to head home and sack out. I kiss Pamela goodbye and tell her I'll see her tomorrow.

"I wonder," she says, "what it would feel like to have a machete go through and cut me in half… Fractions… Geometry."

The next time I heard Pamela's voice was the following afternoon on the telephone. Hal was calling me, screaming into the phone, trying to drown out the screams and tortured laughter coming from Pamela in the background.

"She's reached the cosmic breakthrough," he yells. "She's flipped. I'm going to take her to Bellevue. Meet me in a half hour."

There it was. I had sort of expected it and had a vision of Pamela wandering down 3rd Street nude. My visions were nearly realized.

Hal is still yelling on the phone. "She burned up all my money and then tried to climb out of the window with no clothes on. We're going to walk up. See you in a half hour."

Taxi to Bellevue. Hal and Pam walking along. Her limbs are wandering, her body trailing along. She's singing and muttering in Italian and Spanish with remarkable fluency. At the information desk in somber Bellevue, Pamela takes leave of my hand and writhes on the floor screaming.

"What do you want?" The girl at the information desk asks.

"That should explain it," says Hal, pointing to the body twisting on the floor. I reach down to pick her up. There is no escape in her insanity. It is all suffering, a despair with limitless bounds. I start to sing to her, *"Ma petite est comme de l'eau, elle est comme de l'eau vive."*

We lead her down a corridor into myriad offices until I get the attention of a doctor. Pam is rattling in Italian and Spanish to the line of patients in the waiting room.

"I'm Eliza Doolittle," says Pamela in cockney. "Margot Fonteyn. Why can't the English teach their..." And then into Spanish. She begins cursing in Spanish at some Negro who starts to answer. It looks like we're going to have a fight, but the doctor stops it. We are now in the hands of the doctor. Bellevue bureaucracy begins.

If a place gloomier than Bellevue exists, I have yet to see it. Age and poverty appear to be its outstanding characteristics. The doctors, dressed in new white coats, seem to be out of place. Pamela is uncontrolled, but her language fluency is startling. It is a genius we have on our hands.

A nurse addresses her. *"En Anglais,"* says Pam.

"Does she speak English?" asks the nurse.

"Yes, I speeeeaaaaak Eeeeeenglish," Pam jibes in a Spanish accent and then continues muttering in Italian.

We wait and wait and wait. I sing to her. A nurse enters.

"Are you sick?"

"Yes."

"Do you have a rash?"

Pamela eyes her contemptuously.

"What's wrong?" asks the nurse.

"I have a headache."

"How long have you had the headache?"

"Ten thousand years."

"She's the only sane one here," says Hal.

We wait. Our angel is to leave us. Our positions, our feelings, our attachments still unknown. An attendant brings in a wheelchair. We tell him that she can walk. We wait. A guard is needed. Pamela is becoming more agitated.

"Give her 25cc's of Thorazine," says the nurse.

"We have no Thorazine."

"Then give her Benadryl."

We explain all we know about her to three different nurses — LSD and heroin in San Francisco, alcoholic mother, etc.

Pamela screams, "Switzerland, F. Scott Fitzgerald… Tender is the Night…"

"Why Tender is the Night?" I ask.

"James Joyce. En Anglais… Beetlebub, Beezlebub.." and she is off again. The guard arrives and the underground journey from 27th Street to 30th Street begins.

We have discovered that Pamela is afraid of Negro men. Apparently she was married to or had lived with a Negro who had harmed her. Now, whenever she sees a Negro, she becomes upset. And Bellevue is staffed by Negroes, which contributed greatly to what was to follow.

First a corridor… Blank wall at the end. Pamela limping, very reluctant to walk. Hal and I holding her by the arms. Policemen passing. Negroes passing. The long corridor… The screams begin, unearthly, terrifying screams. There is no stopping her. Her eyes squint in fright, in horror. Everyone turns to stare.

An elevator ride down one floor and we are in the basement, a long, murky, gloomy basement. Three figures walking along step by step. The feeling of imprisonment is overpowering. At the end of the corridor we pass the bars. Yes, we are now committed. It is too much for Pam… Her screams come without pause.

She had been smiling, but now she is not smiling. She is screaming, hating, revolting against the inhuman corridor in the basement of Bellevue.

Another waiting room, another nurse, the same questions, the same unreceptive minds who do not understand any of the information they are being given. Pamela yelling and yelling, her throat getting hoarse. She stops a minute; "Let's take a walk, Babe," she says bitterly and sarcastically and lucidly to Hal. I go to a telephone and call a chick and tell her I have to break our date. The screams reach a crescendo.

When I return, Pamela is gone. Hal tells me that two huge Negro attendants took her away, causing the final throat-splitting yells. We hand over Pam's used airplane ticket, her check for $12.64, a photo of her from a magazine where she posed as a model, and one dime.

A big, semi-illiterate Irish nurse slowly takes down the information. We are told that visiting hours are from 2-3, and that we can speak to the doctor at that time. There is no more.

Outside. Hal explaining that he had read some of Lorca's poems to Pamela and that she learned Spanish from them. Her retention is extraordinary. Hal tells me that just before she was taken away a doctor came in and had the following conversation:

"What are you here for?" he asked.

"To be killed," said Pamela.

"How?"

"With medicine."

Hal and I walk the cold streets. I am thinking of Pamela with her light suede jacket, no money, no home. Pamela, who has become a lump of screaming clay, with no resistance, no will to live or function. Beautiful, brilliant Pamela, lost in her own world, communicating with me by feeling my body and face, nudging her nose into mine and smiling.

Pamela, locked away in impersonal, uncaring Bellevue, a cipher, a psychotic. She will be classified, examined, given a toothbrush, yelled at by nurses who have seen too much and no longer care. She will be examined by doctors who have too many patients and don't have the time to care. Food will be put in her; food will come out. And then I realize how deep our commitment is. We cannot let her drown.

Our immediate thoughts are of syphilis and gonorrhea. What have we caught from her? A body, which had been led every night somewhere by someone. A body which has fucked and fucked since the age of 12, Negro and white, tall and small. In this way, she is like a wood nymph running nude, and indiscriminately laying with all. She told me that at first she feared men and found little pleasure.

I feel itching on my body, as does Hal. We turn on with a marijuana/opium mixture. Syph, the clap, leprosy, bubonic plague, unknown diseases, the crabs, the Grand Slam. We are in hysterics… laughter… laughter. Every disease in the books is ours. Oh, Pamela, what have you given us in your innocence? Lovemaking pacifies, but whom have we made love to, and what did she have? We cannot stop laughing. Morbid jokes about making medical history render us helpless with mirth. It is the ecstasy of fear, of doom. We are doomed. Did she sleep with Diogenes, the dog? Who knows? Diogenes is silent, and Pamela has spoken of "White penises… an aesthetically anemic, ugly, spider-leg albino penis between nose and mouth over eye." What penis? What men have you known, our little, sweet, pure, beautiful angel who has seen too much and is too intelligent for this world. (Two days later a Bellevue secretary asks Hal over the phone if Pamela is "weak minded.") "What are bodies for except to make others?" I still cannot answer you, Pamela.

The next day we are at Bellevue at two. A line waits to get in. We get our passes and wait in front of the elevator to take up to the disturbed ward where they have placed her. Minutes go by, no elevator. Hal fondles his copies of "No Exit" and "Fanny Hill." I have a small camera in my pocket for Hal to use to take pictures with. It will be tricky to get the shots but we will try. The elevator arrives. Up to the seventh floor where the door to the ward is securely locked.

Pamela is lying on a bed in oversized blue pajamas. She says nothing. The older patients and nurses are sitting on benches. Everything is old, surrounded by bare and cell-like walls. The atmosphere is oppressive. Pamela is lying down, drugged, listless and helpless.

"Ah, David," she says with a French accent and leans against my hip.

"Jensen!" the nurse yells at Pamela, "You can lie better than that." Pam receives the venom stoically and assumes another position.

"They've given you some shots?" I ask.

No answer.

"We'll see if we can get some amphetamine and horse for you," Hal says jokingly. Pamela smiles.

We give her a water coloring set, but she takes the brushes and puts them in her mouth. The nurse takes it away. Pamela moans and jabbers completely disconnected. She is suddenly lucid, "I want to get out." She then, returns to her own world, uttering meaningless phrases.

"Pam, you must talk in complete sentences if you want to get out of here," I tell her. "You've got to use complete phrases. Do you understand? Even if you hate the doctors, play their games. You've got to show them you're controlled and connected. Do you want anything to eat?"

"A little beedele doodle…"

"Pam, complete phrases."

"OK, complete phrases. I'll talk in complete sentences."

The resident physician is a young Korean. I speak to him.

"She very sick girl," he says.

"OK, I know, but what's wrong with her?"

"We send her to state hospital."

"OK, but what's wrong with her? And then I notice he's reading the wrong form. He's talking about another patient.

"I'm here for Jensen," I say.

He picks up Pamela's form. "She very sick girl."

"Well can't you tell me a bit of what's wrong with her?"

"Are you a relative?"

"No, a friend."

He smirks. "Ah, a boyfriend? She very pretty girl."

I notice a column that says "final diagnosis." There are some letters there. "What do those letters mean?" I ask.

"I explain that to her mother."

"But you don't understand; her mother is an alcoholic who is who-knows-where. We're the only friends she has."

"I explain to her mother. We will contact her mother. You not relative. I can't tell you anything."

"All I want to do is help the girl."

He smirks again. "She very pretty girl. Very sick. She go to state hospital in two days."

"And who's going to be informed of this?"

"We tell her mother."

"But her mother doesn't exist." I am getting furious. It is like talking to a wooden Buddha who sits and smiles. I try again. "Take down our address. You have my friend's name. I will give you his address."

"We want her mother's address."

"Nobody knows her mother's address."

I take the form he is holding and write my address under Hal's name. "There, we can be contacted there." The Buddha smiles.

"Had she been physically examined?" I ask.

"All patients are physically examined."

"And?"

"All patients examined," he repeats.

"Perhaps there is something physically wrong with her that is affecting her mind," I say. But he is no longer interested and smiles me out of his office.

Back to Pamela who is humming my French song, *"Courez, courez, vite si vous le pouvez…"* We are now sitting inside on benches. Pamela leans backwards, making faces, and I have to hold her. "Control, Pam, control… It's the only way to get out of here." Hal is snapping his camera like a madman, shooting from the hip so that the nurses and attendants don't see it. A woman complains because they would not let her keep some flowers.

Jane, an overweight and ugly girl who had run away from a hospital in Massachusetts, comes by. She is in a straightjacket having been a fire engine today and gotten a bit violent. "Sane" people wouldn't understand what it means to be a fire engine, but I understand. Hal continues to take pictures as "Momma" wanders by for a cigarette. She is a Negress, either with a very fat belly or very pregnant. Hair standing on end, blackheads all over her face, she shuffles along in her hospital slippers.

Pamela says that she needs another husband.

"Who?" I ask.

"You," she says.

What can I say? Here I have taken on a half commitment, and am trying to tread a very thin line between no commitment and full commitment. I can't marry or adopt her or support her or anything, and yet, I can't let her drown. All that lies ahead of her is a future of captivity in a hospital or an equally black future of aimless wandering, violent emotional seizures and a constant misery. Pamela will never be normal, but neither will I. We have that in common.

Pamela is off again on her deceiving kick, "Everyone's face is deceiving," she says. "I trust faces, that's why I'm always hurt."

She has put purple paint on her face and gold on her lips. Her hair no longer flows. It's knotted in a little braid. Golden hair, golden eyes, golden lips and purple skin. "How can you love a girl with purple skin?" she asks me. Someone has given her *The Brothers Karamazov.* I read to her from the "The Grand Inquisitor." She is not interested.

"How old are you, baby?" Hal asks her.

She smiles. This is her favorite game. Today she was Joyce and 21. Now she is 19. (17 turns out to be her real age.) "Teach me Russian," she says to me.

"I'll bring a book," I promise.

"Switzerland," she says suddenly.

"What's in Switzerland?" I ask.

"F. Scott Fitzgerald and better hospitals."

The visiting hour is up. We prepare to leave.

"I hate you," Pamela cries out, and then she turns towards me, kisses goodbye and says, "I love you."

They move Pamela to Creedmoor in Queens and I plan to visit her there to make sure she is ok, while Hal and I continue to meet, smoke pot, hunt chicks. I have been spending a lot of time with a tall Jewish redhead named Janice. She's crazy about me and I can do anything with her that I like. I make a date with her for tonight and then set off to Washington Square Park to meet Hal, so we can hunt chicks together. As I'm walking to the park I start thinking about this cycle of continual hunting and fucking and restlessness and never being satisfied. I pass someone I know and see the look in his eyes. He is also hunting. Maybe he fucked last night and maybe he didn't, but it would hardly make any difference… only add a little desperation to hunt.

On the corner outside the Figaro, Bob Browning is talking to some chick. He says he's working in the Columbia Library and that the girls there are beautiful. "I've had enough of this scene," he tells me. "I'm going to move uptown. I move every two months. Two months in the Village, two months uptown."

I continue along MacDougal Street and then enter the park. The crowd around the folk singers is thinner than usual. Sandy is walking with her sister. She wants me to take some model photos of her. Scott Foster comes along and shows me some pictures of his paintings. They're really extraordinary. A couple of weeks ago, I bought a sketch of his for a dollar when he was starving.

I spot Hal and join him. A couple of square-looking cats are playing some folk music. They're very good. Hal starts coming on to a cute little blonde girl standing next to him. He's pretty aggressive in his approach, although he says he lacks confidence now. I wander off, spot two girls, look at their legs and decide not to pursue. Jean-Michel, a handsome

Frenchman, hails me to ask a question about a missing car. He is tailing, more or less, two girls, but he has his eye on two beautiful blondes standing next to us who are talking to some guys. "Beautiful, beautiful, beautiful," he keeps muttering. One of the blondes leaves and says she's going to the Figaro. We'll find her later, I say to Jean-Michel.

Hal comes over while I'm talking to two girls. I can't decide whether or not to stay with them. The one I am talking to is pretty ugly, but has fairly sexy legs. She might make a good fuck. We invite the girls for coffee and walk off ahead of them. They linger behind, hesitant, and we leave them. Jean-Michel curses. Passing the Judson Church, we see a seated row of girls inside listening to a piano recital, their expressions ranging from boredom to frustration. Hal has his camera with him, and we take turns snapping pictures. Passing another window, we see two girls by themselves. Jean-Michel knocks at the door and starts speaking in French. He's another professional Frenchman, but he's very extroverted and for me he's good to be with. The girls are both very cold and defensive. Everybody is defensive in this city, I tell Jean-Michel.

We arrive at the Figaro and Jean-Michel joins some friends, while Hal and I sit down at an empty table. Julie is working as a waitress. We're good friends, having spent a weekend together at the Cape. We've remained close platonic friends since, our paths crossing in New York, Cambridge and elsewhere. I put my arm around her and ask her about a beautiful waitress whom I saw working last night. She tells me her name is Jill and she'll be in at eight. Klaus, a painter for whom I did some photos, sits down at another table.

I speak to him and then go back to Hal.

A girl comes in, all excited because she's gotten John Barrymore's signature on 42nd Street. We invite her to sit down and she joins us. She is waiting for a friend to go to a play. Hal and I begin competing for her, but we both lose interest in her after a while. Sergio comes in. He's stoned, and sits silently with a far-away smile. Finally, the waitress I've been waiting for comes in. I follow her down to the discotheque and stop her. "Your name Jill?" She nods, "yes" and starts walking away. "I'm Julie's brother," I tell her. "Do you have a few minutes?" She comes with me and we talk. She's from Massachusetts and wants to go back. We make a date for Tuesday, the first day she has time off. I can't seem to get through; she seems very distant, though pretty hip. She's 18. We'll see.

Upstairs, Hal is sitting with three people and arguing with a chick about politics. I'm standing behind Hal and looking over the customers. A chick smiles at me, a young impressionable type. A bit square.

Hal and I leave the cafe. He asks me if I saw the girl's legs. He's made a date with her but couldn't see her legs. I tell him that I saw them and they were fair. We circle the block, head over to Sixth Avenue and have a pizza. Janice is due at my place between eight and nine. I start walking downtown and pass two chicks—one of them carrying a flower. They're not very attractive, sort of slutty, Brooklyn, and stupid looking. I walk up to them anyway and take the flower. We begin talking. She's receptive. She's from the Lower East Side and works in advertising and wants to watch me develop film. I take her phone number. She dresses sexy, so maybe I'll give her a ring. I leave her, and as I'm walking home a real beauty passes, wearing sexy black stockings on beautiful legs. We look at each other's eyes, but I continue.

Arriving home, I do some shooting from the screen. Janice enters and I show her some of the photos I've done. She likes them. Janice isn't feeling well. She asks me to be gentle when we fuck, and I am gentle, ever so gentle. Abated passion for the moment, for the moment only.

FRANCINE

DAVID 1965

I am sitting in the Figaro reading Lawrence Durrell's *Justine*. I don't really like Durrell; his style is too obscure, almost passionless. I like only the idea of Durrell, his interwoven lives... novels without plots, like Miller, like Kerouac. In Paris I had met the real Justine and we spent an evening together, but we didn't make love.

Durrell calls his novels a "word continuum," and he is right. Life doesn't fit into any neat plots and sub-plots.

Lately I have been reading works by Krishnamurti and Ramakrishna after learning about them in Miller's book, *The Books in My Life*. Perhaps there is an objective morality in the universe... good and evil, right and wrong, ordained by a Supreme Being, God. I had always thought that life was a continuum, if not as words, as Durrell wrote, but of dots... lines, no meaning... morality being totally subjective. But Ramakrishna has frightened me. If there is a soul and the soul is striving for God, for perfection, and if there is an afterlife and reincarnation, and when we sin, we suffer and are punished, then the universe becomes at the same time more meaningful but far more frightening. We will be called to account for our actions. And so a new element of fear is added to my life.

I glance up from the book and I see her — tall, red-haired, voluptuous, perhaps a bit heavy, but wild-looking and friendly. She is standing between some tables looking around, searching for someone... A date? A friend? I walk up to her. "Hi, would you like to join me?" She comes to my table. We have an immediate *rapport*; there are no barriers. She is attracted to me. She is mine.

Her name is Francine, from Paris, working as an au pair in New Jersey... wild... untamed. Her father is Danish and her mother French. They are divorced. She has been living with her mother in Paris, visits her father in Denmark, and speaks both languages fluently.

An hour later we are on the subway going to my apartment. Francine has huge breasts and must weigh about 30 pounds more than me. But she is well proportioned.

Francine is insatiable. We make love twice in the night and once the next morning. I am exhausted all day; my strength is drained.

Going downtown to drop off some film I can hardly walk. I have been conquered, quartered and eaten.

I am glad she has to go back to Jersey, but she will return the day after, she says.

I feel like a skinny sacrifice given to the ancient idols by this tall red-haired Amazon.

She is in love with me; I am the adventure she has been looking for since coming to New York from her bourgeois background in France. She is experiencing Bohemia.

We roam the city together... Chinatown, Midtown, the Village. Men stare at her; cars crash.

I read Ramakrishna and think of asceticism, but Francine demands my body. One day she shows up at my door with a suitcase and moves in. She has quit her job in Jersey. She will find work in New York.

We talk about going to France together.

My fatigue doesn't disappear. I wonder if I'm allergic to her. It seems there is always something, either in the body, mind or soul, to destroy happiness, peace, tranquility.

We move uptown to Washington Heights... I edit my film ...

Sometimes I stay up all night on amphetamines, thinking I've done a wonderful editing job, but the results are usually mediocre. One night, high on amphetamine, I crawl along 42nd Street, talking to the bums and the junkies, black and white, the denizens of the 42nd Street lower depths.

With my camera I film them in extreme slow motion and their faces appear on the screen, haunted and desperate. This is New York as I see it—a city of loneliness, apartness, despair, hopelessness. I long to leave and return to France.

A college friend, Fred Sontag, calls from Boston and asks if I want to journey to Mississippi with him and a friend to fight for Negro civil rights. I am not interested. I tell him that the Negroes won't appreciate the help and will turn on the whites when they have a chance, but that they're welcome to stay overnight on their way south. Fred and his friend, Tom, arrive with duffel bags, and Francine and I find two mattresses for them. The next morning they are gone. My apartment has become a way station for the civil rights workers, but I do not feel it is my battle. Someone once wrote, "When you raise your right hand in protest, be prepared to have it cut off." I admire Fred's passion, but I am not prepared to lose my right hand.

The film with Richard and Kelly is finished and I summon up enough nerve to show it at a midnight screening in the Village. A week later an article in the newspaper declares it a masterpiece. It is hard to believe, because I was always only potential, afraid to put anything into form... because this was compromise. I touched the anguish I was feeling, as well as the anguish of my friends, and shaped it with images, camera movement and faces into something that could communicate, at least in part, to another person. I have become real. I exist.

THE TRIP

DAVID 1966

It's tingling, almost like a Dexedrine high. The first thing I'm aware of is that it's very hard to talk. I hear every word but it doesn't sound clear. My legs are starting to twitch. My whole body feels like it's being touched by sparks.

I've taken LSD for the first time, after being talked into it by my friend, Arthur, and after reading the persuasive articles by Alpert and Leary. We're sitting on the floor of the living room, Francine, Arthur and myself.

"I see you all coming and going. It looks like a Charlie Chaplin movie. It's like my eyes aren't so good..."

I'm a bit frightened... perhaps this was a mistake, but so far the effect hasn't been too strong.

I feel my blood circulating in my body; it's like everything is more alive. It's different from anything I've tried before. Every cell has awakened.

"All my cells want to do something," I say to Francine and Arthur who are watching me, "I don't know what. It's not a physical feeling... It's a weird feeling."

I begin to understand the fear of being different, of being separated from others, of living on a different plane. I can't communicate with the rest of the world. This feeling of alienation is getting stronger. My whole body is starting to feel crazy, tired, nervous, twitching, like I've been running and I'm out of breath.

"It's like a snake but it's not a snake, like neon lights, Coney Island. Do I sound funny?"

The words start to pour out of my mouth. "My arm's beginning to stretch now. I don't know if I like this. I can't imagine living like this... functioning would be impossible. The nerves couldn't take it; the body would go... I'm a very nervous person... there's a blue haze in the distance. WHOOOOOH. It's moving! The door's moving in and out and faces are moving closer. I can still control it. It's funny, everything is moving now, but I know it's not. Your hair looks red like fire. Everything's moving; my fingers are moving..."

I begin to shake my hand strangely and get up and walk to the door. "The walls are moving, in and out, in and out. I'm not scared of it. Is my sight distorted or is it real? Everything is curved. You're moving and getting smaller, more distant... You're like Alice in Wonderland, after she got tall."

I turn to Arthur. "You're a serious devil," I say to him.

My body is now feeling ticklish. Strange sensations all over. "This is too much. I don't know what to do with all these sensations. I can see why people become LSD dropouts. I feel insane now."

"No, you're not going insane," says Arthur.

Then I see something moving, a figure, a person, something. I'm frightened. "I... I see something."

"Stay calm, David," says Francine.

"Lie down," says Arthur.

"Let's eat something," I say. "Let's eat."

We went to the table and had some sandwiches and fruit, and after eating, the nightmare began. The drug became too strong, and I went insane and didn't recover for five days. Everything was moving. I was totally out of control, removed from people and objects. I was no longer in touch with the world as I knew it. The new world was a nightmare world. I wanted to leave it but I couldn't. I knew only fear.

The worst part of the trip was between midnight and 6 a.m. Then I fell asleep for three hours and the sensations had lessened somewhat. But the fear and the feeling of detachment didn't leave for five days. I was dizzy during that entire period. I would touch something, be aware that I was touching it, yet it didn't register directly in my brain. The world looked like it was being seen through a shimmering wide-angle lens. At no time was there any escape from the madness. If I closed my eyes I felt it in my stomach. Constant images coming at me and over me. I had absolutely no sex drive. The horror was so encompassing that relating to anyone else was impossible. Fortunately, Geraldine, who lived above us, came downstairs. She and Francine talked and I held on to my sanity because they kept me calm and told me it was only a drug that would wear off.

Geraldine tried to get Thorazine for me but was unable to. I was feeling out of breath all the time and on the verge of screaming and doing something desperate. My mind no longer had a focus, only this interior screaming and loss of control. The fear was so great I wanted to end everything. At times it was unbearable; at times the agony would lessen. The only lesson to be learned from an LSD trip is to know what it feels like to be totally insane, of having no control. One small part of me stayed sane and so I was able to talk. The rest of me was on a nightmarish voyage, with faces moving and changing, things leaping at me, claws grabbing me.

The second day I cried for hours. It was only then that Francine realized how bad it was.

Reflections on a Mexican Vision

DAVID 1966

Taxco is built on the side of a rock-green mountain. Thus, the town is on many levels connected by steep rock-strewn streets. Large houses (casas ricas) mingle with old dirty huts.

The main road from the bus stop leads down a slope and David comes upon a group of Mexicans selling various merchandise: chickens, fruits, orange crush sodas, lemonade, breads. Other merchants are leaving the marketplace and attempting to force their way into the buses with their unsold goods. Taxco is one big market, the streets lined with squatting men and women selling everything conceivable. Narrow rows of booths and open-air stores stretch far into the distance, up and down the hills. It is a market which never closes.

David buys a pair of *guaraches* for 15 pesos and replaces his too-slippery shoes with these rubber-soled sandals.

The Hotel Colonial is a short distance from the bus stop. The rooms connect to balconies surrounding a large courtyard. For 12 pesos (one dollar) David gets a room with a bath. There are no towels and no hot water.

Outside, David is struck by the contrast between the luxurious buildings, mostly hotels, and the animals living with their owners in dirty shacks. People go to the bathroom everywhere. David sees little girls squatting in front of their houses. Skinny dogs roam the streets looking for food. *Platerias* (stores that sell silver) are ubiquitous, since silver jewelry is what Taxco is known for. Most of the *Platerias* are located in one section of town. Another section is predominantly burros and their manure overlooking a magnificent park with a beautiful church.

Evening—David goes to the park, which is filled with people promenading and buying sodas and magazines from vendors. A drunken policeman accosts David and takes out his gun. He points it at his head and says, "si o no?" and then shows David his belly which is swollen fat from drinking too much beer. David smiles, nods, turns, and walks up the hill to his room.

Nine p.m. and the rain starts like it does every night. It pours for an hour, leaving the other 23 hours of the day dry. David watches the rain from his small room. This is his second time in Taxco. He breathes in the clean air, the quiet, the peaceful night.

In a few days, David is supposed to meet Anka and her friend, Eva, in Acapulco and shoot a film with them.

However, he has written nothing and he is hoping that a few days in Taxco will result in some ideas and images for the film.

Anka and Bob have broken up, and now Anka is engaged to a musician named Philip who may also come to Acapulco. David is hoping that Francine will join them, but for the present she doesn't have enough money for the trip.

The rain stops, leaving that cool, fresh after-rain smell in the air. David puts on his rubber-tire sandals and goes out into the dimly lit quiet streets.

The whorehouse is exactly the same as it was seven years ago—a large room with ceiling rafters and bare wooden walls with huge rats running along the exposed wooden beams. The room is filled with women sitting on cot-like beds, half of them with large pregnant bellies. There are a dozen children playing in the room. None of the women are the least attractive and David wonders how anyone can have sex with them. But some of the curtains surrounding the beds are drawn, so he imagines that there must be a few customers.

One corner of the room is taken up by a small bar where several men are drinking. David orders a Carta Blanca, takes a few sips and pulls the Bolex from the bag he is carrying. The bartender seems friendly and David asks him if he can film the scene. "I'll pay for it, of course," says David. The bartender shrugs, smiles, and David hands him a few dollars, glad that he is paying to use his camera and not some other part of him.

The camera pans the room, and the film captures the poverty, the sadness, the degradation of this quiet inferno-like scene... The women, the bellies, the children, the rats, the beer-drinking men, the dim lights, the bare wood, the hopelessness.

Midnight, and I am back in my room preparing to get undressed, read a Ross Macdonald book and fall asleep. There is a banging on the door and I experience a momentary sensation of fright, but I go to the door and open it. Several Mexican men are outside telling me to come with them. They have something interesting to show me.

We walk down the mountain—down... down... down. And at the bottom is a scene out of the Middle Ages. People wearing large masks, death heads, some carrying crosses and torches, giving the whole scene an eerie illumination. It is a ceremony for the dead, Christian and pagan at the same time, and I'm sure I'm one of the few foreigners to ever have witnessed it. I ask one of the men to explain it to me, but his words are too fast and my Spanish has gotten rusty.

When I was here seven years ago, having completed an intensive Spanish course in summer school, I was much more fluent. I had come with guitar to visit Mexico and practice my Spanish.

I remember walking along a country road near a stream when I saw a beautiful young girl washing her clothes in the water. I walked up to her, smiled, and spoke to her. She was shy, sweet and obviously interested. I asked her if I could meet her later that evening and she agreed, giving me her address. Her name was Esmeralda.

That night Esmerelda and I walked together, accompanied several paces behind by her brother, sister, cousin and two aunts. I am young, horny, sensitive, longing, wanting to go to bed with her. Esmeralda, charming, virginal, wanting to get married to the gringo and live in America.

I glance behind; the procession is still following. I ask her if she'll come to my room.

"No puedo," she says.

"Mi corazon esta roto porque tu no me amas," I reply.

"No es eso," she says sadly. "Yo solamente no puedo."

Sitting in a restaurant a few days later the owner approaches me and asks if I would like to marry his daughter. "Only $100 and you can take her back to America. She's very beautiful, very hard working, good wife."

I went south and swam in the warm bath-like waters in a small town near Acapulco. Then it was time to return and begin another semester at school.

I hitchhiked a ride with two callous, half-drunk Americans in a red convertible. They tear along the winding Mexican road without a thought about oncoming traffic. I am scared. There's no way we'll make it back to New York alive. Finally, we stop at a roadside restaurant where I order a meal.

An hour later the terrible stomach pains begin. I ask the driver to stop the car so I can throw up on the side of the road. I am very sick—pain, nausea, high fever... standing on the side of an empty road in the middle of Mexico. I can't go on, and the two insensitive guys in the car are not going to help me. I ask them to drive me back to a gas station we had passed a few miles back and they agree to do that and leave me there.

At the gas station I am almost delirious. "Doctor, doctor, I need a doctor," I tell the attendant. I collapse against the wall of the building, too weak to stand. Just then a huge American car drives up and a young man gets out.

"He's a bullfighter," the attendant tells me. "He'll take you to a doctor."

The bullfighter notices my guitar. "Play me a song," he says.

I can't believe it. I am burning with fever, semiconscious, semi-delirious, and he wants me to play a song. Somehow I manage to sing "Deep Blue Sea."

"Bueno," he says, "Come with me."

But I am too weak to walk and he has to help me into the car. He drives me to a clinic in a small town. The clinic is clean, neat, modern. My temperature is 105 degrees and the doctor gives me an antibiotic shot and puts me to bed.

The next day the fever and the pain are gone.

I take a bus to Mexico City and use my last money to buy an airplane ticket to New York.

Acapulco is heat, hotter than New York on its hottest day. I'm sipping coffee in a small out-of-the way café. Arrived yesterday but unable to sleep. Have a large room with four walls, bugs and heat. At night one sweats.

My sister is waiting for me with a friend and with two English boys they picked up hitchhiking. She takes me to a room in the center of town. We live with a family that runs a laundry and rents out three rooms. Anka, Eva and I have the three rooms... There is a shower head in my room but no water, no sink either. I have to get water from Anka's room and cook it on the primitive stove.

Mexico is color as well as heat. Open restaurants along the beach, but I prefer to buy food in the old market place, which will soon be torn down as a health hazard. I miss Francine. For me she is everything good. I trust no one in this world and don't believe in love... except for Francine. Is she being faithful to me while I'm gone? I worry that she is fickle.

I study Anka and Eva. I learn something, and yet learn nothing. Fragments, images, visions.

When one speaks of visions they are not always mystical events but often everyday occurrences which become visions only in retrospect. They are occurrences that return to the mind over and over again, always posing the same questions, always seeking an elusive answer. Such is my Mexican vision.

I see Eva on these mornings talking and laughing with Anka. For Eva, Mexico is abandon, and sensuality. But the loneliness is always there... inescapable.

They spend much time together. Eva grasping at everything Mexican. Anka, pretty and aloof.

Anka is waiting for her fiancé, Philip, to arrive from New York, torn between promiscuity and fidelity.

Philip arrives with Francine. They have taken the bus all the way from New York. We stand in front of a juice kiosk on the main street, Francine and I hugging, Philip and Anka holding each other. I am so glad to see Francine, though instinct tells me she's slept with Philip.

Images of Philip and Anka together. Philip is dependent on her. He is afraid of the future alone.

The day on the beach when they meet the beach boy, Sergio. Philip's instinctive reaction is jealousy, a jealousy he tried to hide but cannot. Anka, torn in half, wants to do something new and exciting, something flirtatious and cool, while also wanting and believing in love, kindness and dependability.

I remember how shocked Philip was when Anka, in whom he believed, walked off and left him because he spoke too long with people she did not like.

They fought and broke up. It was all over. Days pass. They are together again. It is as if the fight did not happen. It made me realize that life is not made up of climaxes or sudden decisions, as in books and films, but rather slow change and many repetitions.

Philip has gone again on a trip and Anka begins getting restless and withdrawn. She sees omens in objects and starts wondering if all things are symbolically related and meaningful, or is life merely a chaotic happening, minute succeeding minute.

The fortuneteller says that the man she is thinking of will not be her great love. Anka, worried, sees evil symbols in everything. The nightmare begins. The same world and the same people she saw in one light yesterday are totally different today. What was beautiful yesterday is ugly today.

Anka tries to conquer her fears and her nightmare but her mind will not let her alone.

The jealousy and the loneliness are in control. She has lost Philip; she is afraid; she wants to die.

Philip has returned... her fears unfounded. Time has again changed the problem. Yesterday Anka discovered the ultimate truth: life is a nightmare. It will be different tomorrow again. A person's life is a cycle... it is ever changing. He will rarely want the same thing two days in succession. He is made of many parts, disappearing and reappearing, and as the parts change, the truths change and the answers change.

This is the end of my vision... Anka swimming, Philip walking, Eva painting, Francine undressing. This is motion, doing, action. It is the closest I can come to an answer.

The Room

DAVID 1966

ONE

It would be difficult to describe how small the room is. Try and imagine an enclosure where the only place you can stand is right by the door. And that is if you are under six feet. I am just about six feet tall, and when I stand straight my head grazes the top. From the door, the ceiling slants down at almost a 45-degree angle until it reaches the opposite wall about two feet above the floor. On the ceiling is a window, which opens toward the sky, and from which, if you care to look, other

Paris rooftops can be seen. There are no lights in the room, there is no water; only two mattresses with blankets, a shelf with some books, a suitcase full of clothes, papers, photos, a few candles and some food scattered here and there.

I have been in the room two weeks without leaving it, and I doubt I will ever leave. Francine, who lives with me, does the shopping every day, bringing back enough bread, cheese, apple cider and yogurt to survive on. I love apple cider and yogurt—and bread and cheese go well with them, which explains my diet. Francine is a girl with whom I have lived for ten months now since I met her in New York. When we came to Paris we stayed in a hotel room, but after we ran out of money we found this room through a friend. It is hard to find anything cheaper than 60 francs a month.

To be honest, Francine doesn't attract me that much anymore, which is one reason I choose to stay in the room. If I were to journey into the streets I would see more beautiful women, desire them, and not feel happy with Francine. Remaining in my room removes the visual stimulus and leaves me quite satisfied with her.

There is another reason I stay in the room: I want to know the answer. THE answer. I want to find God.

Francine came home around lunchtime joyfully reporting that she had been offered a job as an art model and had accepted. It struck me that as an art model she would be posing nude and would not do so if she had a poorly shaped body. I wondered if it were possible that other people looked on her as an attractive and desirable female, while only I often thought her undesirable, simply because I had her. This increased my sexual excitement and I actually enjoyed making love to Francine this time. When the lovemaking was over, Francine descended those seven long flights of stairs, which I doubt I will ever descend.

I get nervous attacks. This has been true only in the last six weeks. The first one came three weeks after moving into the hotel room. I had decided to go to a movie halfway across Paris. Quickening my step, I reached the Metro entrance where I became one with the descending crowd. I felt a part of the crowd. Each person ahead of me presented a brown or green ticket to a girl with a hole puncher. I did the same. This automatic action gave me a sense of being linked to humanity, a part of the great mass of men. Even while waiting on the station platform this elated feeling of belonging did not disappear. I felt love for all the Metro riders, identification with their suffering; I was their brother and guide. We were not separate, but one—all emanating from the same source. The roar of the approaching train brought us back into action. Those who were sitting, arose; those standing at the edge of the platform took a step backwards. The train halted, the doors flew open, and as one person we entered the car, waiting to be carried off. There were no seats available, but I was happy to lean against a pole and watch the faces of my fellow passengers.

It was then that it began. I was staring at a fat oldish woman who was complaining to her friend about people's impoliteness. The change occurred in what must have been less than a tenth of a second. When that tenth of a second was finished I was totally alone. Not only was I alone, but I was shaking uncontrollably. I had lost control of my body. I felt like screaming and smashing things. It was not I who wanted to, but my cells and my nerves were acting independently from my conscious mind. Every cell was screaming for release. I was struggling to hold my body in check. My lungs wanted to shout, my arms wanted to flail. My head was light. I was no longer in any sort of contact with the people on the train. They were no longer in my world. Within a tenth of a second, I had entered another world, a strange, frightening, nightmarish world where I was all alone. The most horrifying aspect was that no one else could enter my world no matter how much I wanted him to. Because there were no longer any people; there were no longer any objects; there was nothing but a continuing horror in which each cell of my body had declared its independence from the conscious controlling force. I was terrified; I did not want to become insane. For five Metro stops I was struggling for my sanity and no one was aware of it.

When I reached my stop, the open door released me from one prison, but the prison in my mind followed me as I walked down the station platform, up the stairs, and into the streets. There was no street, no people—only the crashing cells and the desire to scream. My legs moved automatically, as one small part of me remained in control, and it wanted desperately to get home to Francine. She was my only hope.

I flew up the hotel stairs, opened the door to the room and fell on the bed crying: "Hold me, hold me, hold me... I'm scared, I'm scared..." Francine enveloped me, pressing me tightly against her, moaning, "poor baby, poor baby..."

Several hours and several tranquilizers later the crisis subsided. Since that day, however, I have never been without fear.

TWO

I believe in reincarnation. The soul or entity is reborn and reborn, living through many lives, re-seeking the original spirit state from which it came. It lives according to the law; 'As ye sow so shall ye reap.' This is Karma.

Each act or thought of man is buried in his unconscious life after life. The soul, by being reborn according to the degree of its spiritual growth, is punished and rewarded as a consequence of actions and thoughts in past lives. Thus, the soul learns the lessons it is supposed to learn.

This is an extremely moral doctrine; in fact it is the only valid morality I have ever come across. Be cruel or deceitful in this life, pass through the dreaming and relearning of "death," reappear in a new body, years or centuries later, and in a similar situation find yourself on the receiving end. The cycle continues until goodness is attained. But when I look too deep I see only blackness and the void. The light has so far been denied me. But I shall stay in this room until I find the light or until I go insane. For I do not feel like being reborn to this earth of little rooms and empty souls, this state of unknowing, of fear, of frustration, of sickness, cut off from knowing who we really are, frightened entities drifting alone, unconsciously searching for God in an endless void.

It is not like I haven't been warned; my soul is on notice. I cannot claim ignorance. Just yesterday, during my reading I came across the following:

> *Be not deceived; do not misunderstand; God is not mocked. For what man sows, man reaps. Man constantly meets himself.*
>
> *The unpardonable sin is knowingly and willfully to reject spiritual truth. In a certain sense all sins are unpar-*

donable because they all cause effects which have to be exhausted before they can cease. But if a person knowingly and willfully rejects the truth it proves that he has a determinate preference for evil, and that he is therefore amalgamated with evil. Only the good will survive, and he who chooses evil will perish in evil. It is therefore dangerous for men to acquire occult knowledge before they have become sufficiently wise to select only that which is good.

You must renounce all feelings of possession. It is possible that Karma will take away the things you hold to the most, perhaps the people you love best. Even then you must be prepared to separate yourself with joy from anything and from anyone.

These words do not give me joy, but only fear of the punishment that awaits my soul because I cannot rid myself of ego, sin, desires, and accept that everything comes from God and is good.

I am not able to perform an act or have a thought these days without asking "Why?" and relating it to the universal law of right and wrong. But the answers are denied me. I do not think that I am any more of a saint now than I was two weeks ago. I am just more nervous. But I go on, because I must go on. My soul refuses to accept it; it questions and questions. In this respect I am without will.

Let me give an example of this ceaseless questioning. Francine has just returned from work. She has bought some new makeup and wants my opinion while chattering about this and that. All her talk is about earthly matters, especially love. I know what she is leading up to—bed. It seems that the more meditative and distant I become, the sexually hotter she gets, an emotional seesaw. All I feel is annoyance, but I know she will not shut up until I comply with her wishes. My meditations have been interrupted, probably for the rest of the afternoon.

In spite of my behavior, Francine loves me; in fact I am her life. As long as I make love to her three or four times a week she does not mind if I sit unshaven on the floor in lotus position. She also frequently wants to talk about the future and does not take me at all seriously when I explain that I am never going away from this room. Even my nervous attacks leave her unfazed. "They will go away," she explains.

I find these interruptions most annoying and I have arrived at the point where I feel little or no passion for Francine. In short, I wish she would leave me alone. But if I were to tell her that, or even hint at it, I would hurt her cruelly. And I cannot do this. I do not have the right to wound Francine, for she is good and truly loving. So I must not only suffer her presence, but I shall learn to accept that two souls must struggle selflessly together towards self-perfection. Because if I do not make a success of my "marriage" in this life, by learning love and selflessness, I will return to work it out again in the next. It is difficult to live with this knowledge.

Francine's hand is touching my face. I smile and kiss her. Somewhere, perhaps, there is love.

THREE

The walls of the church are everywhere, transparent and opaque at the same time. Sometimes they are moving, sometimes still. The stones that make up the facade are trying to tell me something. I can see their faces. They are screaming, the scream of the eternally insane. White, black, blue, and gray molecules are moving at fantastic speed to compose the stone. I have seen this church for centuries; I am a part of it but I will not enter it. It will not have me this time, for I am not ready. I try not to scream in reply. I want to tell them that I have seen them, but the people who are in the streets would not understand. The stones are pleading with me to help.

High up on the left is a small window. Often when I pass, the light is on, though sometimes it is not. I have never been in that room during this lifetime, but I know every inch of it. The gray stone walls, the small wooden bed, the cross carved in the stone above the door. I have lived in that room and I am both fascinated and afraid of it.

From where the church stands I turn left and walk along a narrow street until I cross the Boulevard. On the other side of the Boulevard the streets are all dark and silent. Shadow forms are moving back and forth or standing in small clusters on the corners. The shoulders are hunched, the eyes furtive. Occasionally a form approaches one of the women and they move off together up a flight of stairs. The shadows are everywhere, dimly illuminated by hallway lights where the women are waiting. I move quickly through the shifting silhouettes with embarrassed glances at the waiting flesh, the dream-like forms in tight sweaters and short skirts. Ashamed, I glide past them until they are no more. Now there are crowds and bright lights, but the lure of the dark streets is too great and I turn back. The one I approach is tall, large breasted, shapely-legged. For twenty francs she is to be mine. She leads the way up a small flight of stairs, the incredible sway of her ass hypnotizing me into complete submission. I am afraid as I follow, but of what I am afraid of I do not know. Perhaps fear of inadequacy, perhaps fear of disease, perhaps fear of God. The screaming stones are far behind but they have been replaced by a new fear.

At the top of the stairs we turn right and enter one of several identical doors. The room is small, brightly lit, containing a bed, a chair, a washbasin and a bidet. I do not belong here. My world is elsewhere. But the woman is there and she controls me. I have come to her; I am but one of the voiceless phantoms moving along the dark street.

The woman moves slowly past the washbasin and then sits on the bidet. I do not know what she is doing. It is part of the ritual, the ceremonial magic. The water is flowing, but she is not washing herself. I realize that she is merely pissing. The room has been invaded by the smell of her imperfection.

She goes to the bed, lies down, her head on the pillow, her feet flat, her knees in the air. Then she spreads her legs. She is wearing no pants, just a round circle in the middle of her garter belt filled with black pubic hair. Every hair is visible in the bright light. I shift my gaze to her breasts, then to her calves but I can get no erection. My excitement has vanished, leaving only the fear. The voice is saying, "What are you waiting for? Undress yourself."

Slowly I obey. My sweater, my shirt, my shoes, my pants, my underwear, and I am naked and small, pitifully exposed in the merciless glare of the bright room. I approach the bed slowly, knowing that the warm shower is but a gas chamber and that it is too late. She has not moved; the legs are still spread at the same angle. The smell of the gas is strong as I reach her and place my frail body on top of her rounded flesh. I rub against her, shutting my eyes, seeking out images of other full and firm bodies. But nothing helps. There is only the glare of the light and the voice saying, "Hurry up, I haven't got all night."

And then she is no longer there and I am no longer there. We have ceased to exist. We have passed beyond life. And I am in the dim streets again, slipping by the moving shadows until I come to a street where there are no forms and no flesh, a street where there is only stillness. Here are no human shadows, only spirit forms, invisible to the eyes. But I sense their presence. Like the stones, they are trying to shout a warning to me. It is not things human of which I am afraid but of the spirits' eternal suffering. I have been given the vision to see them and so I know the horror of these agonized spirits. I did not ask to be given this vision. It has led me to the border of another world but is denying me the pleasures of this one.

No, I did not ask for it. And I do not know if they are real spirits or phantoms of the mind. But I wish they were not there.

The form that is coming toward me is large. Everywhere it is black except for the face and the hands, which are white, a pale sickly white. The hands are holding a knife. I am too paralyzed to scream or to flee. I watch without motion. The voice is asking for my money. I am unable to move. The presences are in the air around me. I stare at the knife and watch it while it plunges into my chest. I am screaming, the blood is flowing from me into the room, a white light is pouring through the window. The room has become large; the walls are moving. I see them moving. Hands are coming from the walls reaching for me. The hands are there even when I shut my eyes. The light is full of terrified faces also screaming.

FOUR

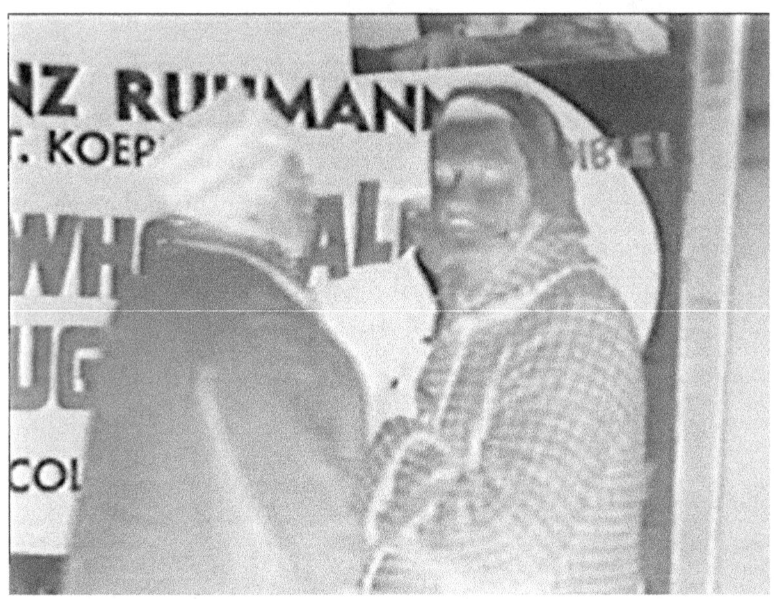

That was yesterday. Francine said she found me crying in a corner and that I did not stop crying for three hours. Yesterday's feelings are still with me today, though not as strong. I am nervous, and when I shut my eyes, vague little dancing nightmare figures are everywhere. I am also depressed; it appears I will go insane before I discover the answers. And there is no illness or human malady worse than insanity. Francine wants me to leave the room and walk in the streets with her. For me there is no turning back, however. I am committed.

Holding Francine's hand, I timidly follow her to the toilet in the hall. I ask her to wait outside the door while I squat over the hole. I look at the little window, the pull handle, the lined metal plaques where one places one's feet, but they do not seem the same as they did two days ago. They have not changed; something in my mind has. I pull the string, watching the water flooding into the little hole taking the brown lumps with it. Francine is waiting outside the WC and she takes me to the wash basin. The cold water startles me for a moment. I turn the tap off and hold on to Francine as we approach our little room. For a moment the hallway reminds me of another place I had lived.

It was in New York. I had bought a gun, a .38 Webley, from a guy I knew who made a living selling dirty photos of his wife. Why anyone would want to buy these photos was beyond me, but he apparently sold enough to live in stylized poverty. Stylized poverty means a two-room cockroach flat in a Spanish quarter complete with tuxedo and color TV. I had bought the gun for one reason: To kill myself. Having entered a new kind of despair, it is difficult to describe the old. At the time I had no purpose in life, was terribly shy and had nothing to do that seemed important, outside of the immediate. And the immediate was a continuity of senseless wandering, loneliness and frustration. Some weeks would be more bearable than other weeks. The day that I bought the gun was a low point, and since depression breeds more depression it is a difficult state to break out of.

I took the gun and placed it in an old blue canvas bag. Next to the gun I put a half-filled box of bullets. Closing the bag I said "goodbye" and walked down the foul smelling stairs into the street. The building was situated on 22nd Street between Eighth and Ninth Avenues. I walked to Eighth Avenue and hesitated. I was living in a small apartment in the warehouse district below Canal Street, a fast 20-minute walk from the corner where I was standing. Should I go directly home and shoot myself or should I wait? The presence of the gun calmed me slightly. The fact that I could now effortlessly kill myself seemed to comfort me. Every step I took now was on borrowed time, so to speak. This thought, while it did not make me happy, did elevate me slightly above the real pain I was undergoing. It was similar to the relief one sometimes feels after a long cry.

I decided to wait until night to shoot myself. I was anxious to see how I reacted to life walking around with the gun in my bag. And, of course, there was always the faint hope that something good would happen to me. Perhaps a beautiful woman seeing the agony in my eyes would take me in her arms. I was too bitter and too negated to approach any woman myself.

I do not remember much of the 20-block walk along Eighth Avenue, though I must have passed cafeterias, bars, Penn Station, the Post Office and the Bus Terminal. On 42nd Street I veered right and examined the marquees of the movie houses on both sides of the street. I entered what seemed to be the most interesting film, a psychological study by a new French filmmaker. The huge theatre was only one-quarter filled, as most of the afternoon homosexual trade was sitting in the balcony of the horror film across the street. About 30 minutes remained of the first film, an Italian bedroom farce showing plenty of bosom and little talent. Although I was more interested in bosom than in talent that day, I was beyond the stage where I could get any vicarious satisfaction. The French film proved to be much more interesting and, as I can see now, rather prophetic. It was about a man who slowly gave up his worldly posses-sions, including his wife, to lock himself in an empty room, sit on the floor in lotus position and meditate. At the end he is carted away to a mental institution where he happily sits on the floor in his new room. In an Eastern culture he would have probably been considered a saint. I was rather moved by the film, and I wish I had been in a more appreciative mood that day. Now that I, too, am permanently enclosed in my room, it will be impossible to see this film again should it reappear. This is one of the few regrets I have concerning my present course of action.

When I left the cinema, it was dark in the streets and I immediately become conscious of the task that awaited me. I thought of the gun in the canvas bag and began imagining what it would be like to take it out and begin shooting at the passing people, felling them one by one. I played the scene in my mind: I am shooting at random—people are screaming and falling everywhere. A police car siren. I am running into the subway. The train pulls in and I am safe.

I replayed the scene with a different escape but the same ending. Perhaps if I had actually done this I would no longer have felt like suicide. The killing may have served as a temporary release. But I did not shoot; instead I turned East on 42nd Street, walking until I reached Fifth Avenue where I headed downtown. It was the hour when the office buildings are disgorging their 9-5 automatons. The streets were filled with people—and beautiful women were everywhere. I walked, a ghost among the living, or was I the living amongst the ghosts? I was slowly walking towards my death, but all I would need to avert it would be one friendly smile or touch. Click, clack, click, clack, click, clack. Eyes looking straight ahead—automatic bodies.

By the time I had reached the Village the crowds were gone and night had arrived. I walked along the endless deserted warehouse streets with the strange night lighting from dim street lamps and arrived at my street, even more silent and more deserted than the others. Opening the door I climbed a flight of stairs, turned right and opened a second door. My apartment consisted of two rooms separated from each other by a semi-partition. Removing my jacket, I sat on the bed, took the gun and the bullets out of the canvas bag, and set them beside me. I released the catch and let the gun fall open. It was a big gun with a six-bullet revolving chamber. Closing the gun, I held it before me and sat staring at an image of myself in the mirror, which lay against the wall facing my bed. After a while I opened the gun again, took three bullets from the box, and placed them in the chamber. Why three bullets and not six? I wanted to die and, yet, I was afraid to kill myself. Putting three bullets in the chamber would give me three chances out of six of living. I would leave myself in the hands of fate, having made the odds even. I took the gun and placed it against my temple. Time passed; I did nothing. I had reached the nadir of despair and yet my mind was setting up roadblocks. I was incapable of action. What I needed was an emotional situation, which would make me react automatically. Like Hamlet, I was incapable of killing without it. I knew exactly which person would provide the necessary catalyst.

Several nights previously I had been with her. I had wanted her desperately and she had refused me, saying that although she liked me, she had a boyfriend and she was not able to split herself in two. If I saw her tonight she would probably refuse me again, and at the peak of frustration I would have the emotional impetus necessary to shoot myself. If she did not refuse me, small chance that there was, it would no longer be necessary to kill myself. I would have a temporary respite until the next crisis.

I phoned her, asking if I could come over, saying it was important. She agreed. I put the gun with the three bullets in the chamber back into the bag, zippered it, put on my coat and went out. She lived in the West Village, a 15-minute walk from my place. During the walk I was conscious of nothing except the impending scene which would end in either death or life.

I arrived at her building and rang her bell. The buzzer sounded, the door opened and she was there waiting for me by the entrance of her apartment. She looked more sensational than the last time. Her body in a tight fitting colorful silk dress, cut several inches above the knees, had me excited before I entered her apartment. She asked me if I were hungry. I said no. Would I like a beer? Yes, I would. She opened the refrigerator, the movement of her ass causing my excitement to near the breaking point. Carrying two glasses of beer she sat down across from me. We drank in silence.

"How are you?" she asked.

"So, so," I replied, "and you?"

"Fine," she smiled.

I got up from the couch and pretended to be studying the books propped against the wall. Her dress was half way up her extraordinary thighs. I turned, came to her, placed a hand on her thigh, drew her to me and kissed her. As the kiss lengthened I moved my hand up her thigh, but she grabbed my wrist and drew away from me.

"No, please—I can't," she said.

I had heard it before, but I said nothing and stared bitterly into the corner.

"Would you like another beer?" she said.

"No," I muttered. I sat down on the couch again.

"I would." She went to the refrigerator and as I watched her, it was all I could do stay in control. She came back with the beer, sitting down next to me on the couch. "Why are you so sad?" she asked.

"I don't know," I smiled. "Because you refuse me." I tried to make it sound like a joke.

She touched my cheek with her hand. "I like you very much. But you know why I can't."

I took her hand and pulled her toward me, kissing her on the mouth. We fell on the couch together both panting hard. My hand was at her sex and I was removing her dress. Underneath she was wearing a white slip.

I tried to remove this but she fought back. We struggled. I was not able to rape her. I was not capable of real violence.

She pulled herself upright and I did the same. Slowly I walked to the canvas bag, every nerve and muscle tensed. Unzipping the bag, I placed my hand inside of it and felt the gun. At last I was going to use it on myself. I turned my face to her and said softly: "Are you sure you won't change your mind?"

"I can't," she said.

I turned away and stared at the wall. Slowly I pulled the gun out of the bag. I moved to face the girl so she could watch me shoot myself, but she was no longer there. I saw her through the window. She was running in her white slip along the black street. For a moment it seemed comical. I laughed, put the gun back, and left.

FIVE

I am afraid of the moving walls and the phantoms in my mind. But Francine says she must go out for one hour. I tell her I am afraid of the footsteps. When they come to get me, I will hear them climbing the stairs, slowly, steadily. Who is coming to get you? she asks. I don't know, I tell her, but I am afraid of them. I put my head on Francine's lap and she strokes me. I am frightened again. I try to touch something; I know I am touching a material but it does not register in my brain. Something has been severed. Suppose the walls should start moving again when she is gone, and suppose I hear the footsteps climbing the stairs.

Francine is looking at her image in a pocket mirror. I watch the reflection. She looks pretty. I hope I have not sounded too negative about Francine. She is a wonderful girl and we have had much fun together. In the hotel we had a radio, and one day we found some good folk music and jazz. This led to a half hour of wild dancing. My mind was clear of problems and I was totally caught up in the rhythm and Francine. After the dancing we fell on the bed and made love very passionately.

Another time walking along the Boulevard Raspail... Francine very well dressed and looking sexy. I'm sucking a baby pacifier and taking funny steps like a Mongoloid idiot. We dash behind trees hiding from each other, running around and through the surprised people. Everybody staring, while we laugh.

Or the time we went with Francine's friend Isabelle to a strip tease place near Pigalle. The girls on stage were interesting, but before long the whole place was staring at us. Francine and Isabelle were making out, playing at being dikes, while I sat in the corner sucking my thumb. They kicked us out.

In the Metro we found an old clochard sitting on a bench underneath a huge ad for a soft drink. His pants were torn in many places. We sat down, talked to him and I gave him some money to buy another pair of pants.

Francine is applying her makeup, giving it her full concentration. I can concentrate on nothing earthy any more. Every thought immediately transforms itself into an awareness of God and the supernatural, a quest for something I know exists but cannot touch. It is as if I cannot help myself because the quest is certainly an uncomfortable and frightening one. Trying to contact the supernatural, even trying to pray, has led only to nervous attacks so far—but I am unable to stop. Though I am afraid of the truth, I must find it. For a modern man to try and find God in a world that worships material things, worships ambition, success, money, pretty women, requires more courage than I feel I possess. But I must try. If the truth lies in doing good, eschewing evil and ego, loving God and thy neighbor... What then? Through incarnation after incarnation the soul tries to find its way back to its spiritual source and fails. Each generation of men makes it more difficult. Values become more and more material; the soul drifts further and further away from its true vision. And though I am deathly frightened by yesterday's nervous attack—by the hallucinations—though I cling to Francine like a terrified child, I must stay in this room until I discover my vision, or until it destroys me.

Francine is cleaning the room and I am watching every movement. It all must be accomplished on hands and knees.

During the first week in the room we would often forget about the low ceilings and bang our heads. Now we are accustomed to it.

Francine has picked up a used yogurt container and is about to throw it out. I ask her not to. She tosses it to me. I squeeze and mold it into as round a shape as possible. I now have a ball. I get on my knees, take a stretch position and pitch at the door...I throw a direct strike, which makes me happy. I crawl after the ball and pick it up. I will wait until Francine leaves before continuing the game. I must remember—strike one on the first batter. It is too bad I can't stand up here.

For a moment it appears... one of yesterday's phantoms, one of the tortured faces... but it is soon gone. It has frightened me, however, and I crawl over to Francine and huddle against her. "It will be all right," she says. "Don't worry, baby, it will be all right." She is so understanding and does not seemed frightened. I crawl away and return to stretch position; a full windup would be impossible. I try a curve ball that misses by two feet to the left. BALL ONE. I let the ball lie where it fell and return to sitting position on the floor. I try praying silently but God seems distant as usual. My ears are clogging up and the nervousness continues. I lie on my back and do leg raising exercises. Through the window I can see only the sky, but that, too, seems to be moving and making faces. I quickly turn my head away.

Francine is putting on her coat. She says she will be back in less than an hour. She kisses me on the forehead and leaves, closing the door. As soon as she is gone I crawl over to the ball and resume my game. The first pitch is BALL TWO, but then I strike out the batter with two fast balls over the inside corner. The next batter is left-handed and so I try a screwball which misses low and outside. I watch the ball hit the wall and roll away at an angle. I do not feel like chasing it. I stare at the wall but turn away as one of the faces appears. How can I stop them from coming? I crawl into a corner and wait. There is nothing, only silence. My hands are shaking and I am afraid to keep my eyes open. I shut my eyes, but then I am afraid of the sounds. Suppose I hear the footsteps on the stairs. I do not want them to come for me when Francine is not here. Please come back Francine... quickly... please! I am crying now and gasping for breath. I roar like a lion, once, twice. This helps me regain my control.

And so I wait, huddled in the corner, afraid of what I see, afraid of what I hear. I feel like screaming, but I do not. I look up and see a black angel hovering above me. On the walls the faces are appearing and disappearing. I shut my eyes and try to sleep but I cannot. My ears are listening. And then I hear them—the footsteps. They are coming. I want to cry out but I do nothing. My voice is soundless. But my cells are screaming. The footsteps are louder and closer. They are coming. My body is writhing and shouting and seeking release. The door opens and it is Francine, out of breath, rushing into the room with a big smile on her face.

SIX

I have been outside. It was not easy. I walked the streets clinging to Francine, staring at things which were there but did not seem real. I even nodded to someone I knew.

That was yesterday. We stayed outside for 15 minutes; we will try for a half hour today. Most of the time I walked with my hand on her stomach, but of course there was nothing to feel yet. No, I have not discovered the answers I was seeking. But maybe my son or daughter will.

Birth, Death, and Rebirth

DAVID 1967-68

I

The contractions are coming more quickly as the taxi races towards Nørrebro and Sankt Joseph's Hospital. Francine is so huge, I'm surprised she can fit in the taxi. We had a false alarm before, but this seems like the real thing. I'm going to be a father!

She preferred giving birth in Copenhagen and not in Paris, and so we moved, finding a two-bedroom apartment in Ostebro. I was reluctant to leave Paris because I had joined a baseball team, the Paris Pirates, and we were vying for the French championship. I was walking with Francine in the Bois de Boulogne and I saw some people playing baseball. Thinking they were Americans I walked over to the field and was surprised to discover they were French. I learned that the French had a baseball league and that most of the players had been taught by the GIs who had been stationed in France. After a tryout I became the third baseman for the Paris Pirates. We played our games in St. Germain en Laye. We weren't terribly good, but neither was the rest of the league.

I remember when the Six Day War broke out—the headlines in *France Soir, Le Figaro, Le Monde.* I was standing on the Boulevard Rochechouart when I saw the headlines. A sensation of fear and doom overwhelmed me. Tiny Israel being attacked by those large Arab states. I again became a Jew, and even went to the synagogue asking how I could help. Of course, there was nothing to do and the war was soon over with a total Israeli victory.

Walking the streets with Francine, sometimes experiencing flashbacks from the LSD. We'd go into a café and play pinball machines, using the numbers and the ball's movement to try and ground me.

I'd given up trying to be a saint, though it lurked in the back of my mind. Francine's pregnancy, her morning sickness, where to have the baby, became our primary concerns.

My problems really started when I went to England to edit a film. That summer, the girls were wearing short mini-skirts and hot pants. It was too much for me—a pregnant wife at home, visits to spiritualists while still harboring ascetic religious ideas and lusting after the mini-skirted girls. Something cracked, and my lower spine began burning, which produced a strange sort of irritation and continual sexual desire.

However, sex didn't alleviate the sensation. Only alcohol dulled it. Again, I plunged into depression with the thought of suicide. I knew that suicide is a great sin, but I couldn't take any more suffering. Only Francine's pregnancy kept me alive. I went through the motions of living. There was nothing else except for the burning in the spine.

The head is emerging and an exhausted Francine is pushing. The doctor's hands are pulling and the body emerges. "En dreng," says the doctor. A boy. They wash him, weigh him and give him to Francine. I look at his face and I am in love. Dark hair, smooth, beautiful features. So perfect. I can't believe I'm a father.

I leave to make phone calls—Francine's mother, Francine's father, my parents.

Out in the street I speak to the first person I meet, a man selling fruit. "I just got a son, just born." He congratulates me. I'm too excited to go home so I walk and walk until I arrive at Søren's apartment near Nørreport Station. We drink beer after beer. He has a gun hanging on the wall. It falls and hits me on the head. I have a headache, but it's nothing serious...

Later, I go back to the hospital and see my son. I can't stop looking at him and kissing him. All these years I've been the center of my universe and now this little person is more important to me than I am. I kiss him, I kiss Francine ... and momentarily I am reborn.

II

Francine is pregnant again and ill. Morning sickness—morning, afternoon and night. She can't get out of bed and I have to take care of Serge. We've moved to France and I've gotten most of the money for a film. Francine is supposed to play in the film, but now it will be impossible. If she's pregnant and sick all the time like her last pregnancy, there will be no film. Nine months illness, a worn-down body, varicose veins... and no money. An impossible situation. I've been trying to put this film together for years. So much work, so much frustration. No film, no career, no money... only more chaos, more thoughts, more void. I must do this film. Aside from Serge, it's my life.

We decide to get an abortion. It seems like a choice between death and death.

We go to Holland where a woman squirts some water into Francine's womb. Lots of pain but no abortion.

We return to France and visit an abortionist in Villiers-le-Bel, a 15-minute train ride from Paris.

When we arrive at the doctor's office the nurse tells us he will not be in for three hours, so we walk through the gray suburban streets, and then sit in a café. Francine is unable to eat; she is simply too weak. When she tries to stand, she topples and I have to catch her. We return to the office and I ask the nurse if she can lie down. The woman points to a couch in the waiting room.

The doctor arrives and invites us into his office. He is a short, brusque man. It is clear that some sort of failure has forced him to perform illegal abortions. He is no idealist; all business, no compassion. He tells us to come back the next day, and he will open the uterus and pierce the egg. Then a surgeon, a friend of his, will finish the operation in a clinic near Paris. The price is $300, one hundred for the doctor, one hundred for the surgeon and one hundred for the clinic. We agree to come to his office at 8:30 the following morning.

I call a friend, Lucien, and ask him if he can drive us to the doctor the next morning. He agrees and says he'll bring along our mutual friend, Lazlo. I want to stop thinking, but the thoughts keep churning. There is no sleep.

Lucien and Lazlo arrive at 7:30. It takes us about 45 minutes to drive to Villiers-le-Bel. We hardly say a word in the car; we are too exhausted. The doctor is waiting for us. He heats his instruments, puts Francine on a stirrup table and begins stabbing at her with a metal implement. Francine screams with pain and turns completely white. The doctor tells her to keep quiet, but she cannot stand the pain. Finally, it is over. Francine looks barely alive. I've never seen anyone so pale.

The doctor says we should call his friend, the surgeon, at 1:30 in the afternoon and then go to his office in Neuilly. I help Francine out to the parking lot, but she starts throwing up before we reach the car. I leave her sitting in the lot and run to get Lucien and Lazlo who have been waiting for us in a café. We put Francine in the car and drive to Paris. She is groaning with pain and we practically have to carry her up the five flights of stairs to our apartment. I decide not to wait until 1:30 and call the surgeon immediately. He tells us to come to his office right away. He is a tall, kindly man and he arranges a bed in a clinic in Asnières. He will perform the *curettage* in the afternoon. "Don't worry, everything will be all right," he says. But we are worried. I'm afraid something has gone wrong. There shouldn't be so much pain. Lucien drives us to the clinic, but when we arrive they tell us that they do not have an available bed.

Francine is led upstairs into a private room and she falls asleep. I walk to a small neighborhood café to get something to eat. When I return, Francine is awake and scared. I hold her, saying nothing. At 3:30 they come for her. I leave and go to a café and watch 15 minutes of a rugby match. But the game cannot take away the morbid thoughts. I return to the clinic and by four o'clock she is finished and asleep in the room. I frantically look for the doctor, and when I find him, he says she is all right.

"Do you want to see the fetus?" he asks me.

"No," I say, surprised and annoyed at the question.

"It was a girl," he says, and walks away.

His words pierce me. The fetus has become real, a child, a sister for Serge, whom he will never see. What have we done?

When I look in the room, Francine is awake. I put my arms around her, but she says she wants to sleep more. I again go out for a walk. In the street I begin crying. I feel we've committed a great sin. We have caused death. But did we really have a choice? We were placed in a trap without exit, I tell myself.

When I return, Francine is awake and feeling better. I lay my head on the bed next to her and continue crying. I stay like that for an hour. Night has fallen. I must get back to Serge and relieve the babysitter.

Serge is sitting on the floor playing. He is so beautiful and I'm glad to see him. I love him so much.

I give him a toy I bought while I was walking around in Asnières. He is very happy for it. I hug Serge and find I cannot stop crying. It is only later, after I've fed him, bathed him and put him to bed that the irony hits me. The film I am supposed to do is about reincarnation—the rebirth of a soul.

III

Back and forth, back and forth... Denmark to France to Denmark to France. Never settling, nervous system deteriorating.

In Paris the student revolt breaks out in May. We are living in the suburbs and I am re-editing a film in Montparnasse. Every day I commute to Gare St. Lazare and have almost a feeling of normalcy. However, when the revolt begins, I must stop editing because the film is not "revolutionary" and I retreat to the suburbs and drink beer to dull the discomfort in my spine. One day I receive an invitation to show one of my films at a *faculté* at the Sorbonne, now occupied by the students.

The anarchy and chaos in the Paris streets are both frightening and fascinating as I walk towards the building. I have had two beers and am a bit tipsy. In the *carrefour* near the university hundreds of policemen are gathered, a force without power, direction or leadership, their hard-edged capes inactive in spite of the growing anarchy and societal dissolution. They mill about, talking, smoking, staring, waiting for orders to crack heads... more frustrated by the minute.

I pass the *flics* and walk down the small side street towards the *faculté*. Garbage and humans are lying about. There is an end-of-the world feeling. I pass a man with a gun, a small pistol, holding up another man. However, I am too tipsy to react and just walk by.

The French love films; for them it is high art. Even grade B Hollywood films are art. I received a letter recently from a provincial film club telling me that Jerry Lewis and I are their favorite directors. But today the students' attentions are elsewhere. There is so much movement and so much coming and going in the auditorium that I don't believe anyone can see the film.

Back in the suburbs I drink more beer, take walks along tree-lined avenues with baby Serge, watch television and grow more depressed. I listen to DeGaulle's two televised speeches, the first one a failure, the second a masterpiece, which results in a million Frenchmen massing on the Champs Elysées in support of the government. The revolt is broken.

My condition worsens and I consult a famous psychic doctor who recommends that I live in the calm of the countryside. Francine and I decide to rent a farmhouse in Denmark.

But Denmark doesn't cure the problem. Bike rides, badminton, baths and beer. One day I meet a girl with beautiful legs in a railroad station. We go to a hotel and make love. Several weeks later I stupidly tell Francine, who almost leaves me.

The marriage goes on but it is deteriorating. I am deteriorating. Only Serge's smile saves me. I pinch his cheeks, his hand, and kiss him gently on the lips.

Walked Together Miles

KELLY 1968

He has gone
and with him inside smiles
Walked together miles
and cotton candy streets.

He has gone
there'll be no joy in flashing lights
There'll be a sometime solace
crying in blue rooms,
I'll become a folk song
drifting through a dusty mike
and tears will not bring him back.

I'll sit softly
in empty echoing rooms
'You have sad eyes'
my friends will say to me.

I'll become a folk song
drifting through a dusty mike
and tears will not bring him back.

And it was a trap. Today I am alone with a baby daughter, Amantha, and I am desperately trying not to cut my wrists again. It's true, Richard and I were both seeking things, but we couldn't really get along, find harmony, a balance. I think that the way we met guaranteed that we would have a life together of ups and downs, with terrible anguish and conflict. We were simply too young, too immature, especially Richard. He never accepted a wife and child. Now he has become religious; he is growing up; perhaps it would be different now. Richard needed protection, a structure. Without a structure he would fall. I'm sure he would have committed suicide or become crazy. He had had a Jewish education, but he couldn't forget that before he had been raised a Catholic, and it always bothered him that he was born Catholic. Even from his childhood, Richard was a mystic and he wanted to become a priest before discovering that he was a Jew. Then he wanted to become a Rabbi, but the lure of women destroyed that ambition. With a friend, he started writing pornography about girls and boys, plunging into his own sensual hell. He even had sexual relations with boys. He had a need to run as far from himself as he could and shortly before I met him, when we were doing the film, he had been with an awful Colombian—a disgusting type. It was purely a sexual relationship and it was destroying Richard.

I think he saw his salvation in me, at least a step out of the mud which he had voluntarily entered, but couldn't find his way out. His painting helped, but everything about him was mystical or semi-pornographic. Like a yo-yo, he'd go from one extreme to the other. I was to be his rope, but when he had hold of it, he threw it away.

He thought that I was very strong and even if he left me I wouldn't be hurt. We all project masks to the outside, and I tried not to show people how much it hurt inside. Kelly smiles; Kelly jokes; Kelly's got big tits; Kelly's a coffee house waitress. She's cool. But inside is the knife, the need, the hurt. But he didn't see this when he placed violets at my door. He saw the other and something else... I don't know what it was, but it was something he needed. Inside I was as weak as he was. Two children in a forest.

Anyway, he started to love me, to idolize me, and as idols always get destroyed, he destroyed me. I let him destroy me. Soon he realized that I wasn't so strong, and eventually our relationship became almost sado-masochist. He was expecting a mother, a strong mother, but instead I was a victim and he lost respect for me.

Richard isn't talking; he's nervously pacing. There is this heavy silence, but I have to talk. I'm pregnant, but it's like we can't talk to each other anymore. I take a deep breath and plunge.

"Richard, the doctor says I'm pregnant."

He stops, stares at me and smiles. "Good, we'll have a baby."

And he comes to me and hugs me and I feel secure and I think everything is going to be OK.

He says we'll have the baby and we'll get married. He seems animated. I was raised to marry, to listen, to obey. That was my education. A southern lady's education.

We married, Amantha was born, but it was all a mirage. He escaped into the idea of family, the triangle. Mother, Father, child. He tried to play the role of the father and loving husband, but it was all role-playing. He made a lot of drawings of a child in a baby carriage, but I know that he was forcing himself to be good. In reality, there was the devil in him. There was something of the monster that always rose up, and he was not happy, not well.

Even with Amantha he was starting to go crazy. Men have the right to go crazy. Van Gogh was crazy and he was placed in an asylum. Artaud was crazy; Pound was crazy... They were placed in asylums and admired. A woman doesn't have the right to go crazy, to be abnormal. Yet my insanity is the same as his. I was not allowed to express myself, and I put all my energy into Richard and Amantha. I was really a good mother and wife. But Richard really didn't want a child's mother—he wanted a strong, sexy girl.

He started staying away with a friend, the pornographic publisher, and, of course, he plunged right back into the life he knew before. He was running away from Amantha and me. When he'd come home, we'd fuck. I can't call it love making... He made love very well, and I needed that. But when he would be with us he started to get nervous, nasty. He felt trapped. Once he smacked me in the eye and I went to my waitress job with a black eye. But I tolerated his violence. I don't know why I didn't say "No." I was scared to go back to being alone.

I know he was filled with guilt because he had run away from his Judaism. He was also filled with fear... fear of punishment. He started to bring Jewish things into the house. He asked me to keep a Kosher home. I agreed. We even lit the Sabbath candles. He would paint pictures of a family lighting the Sabbath candles and then run off to his friend and probably fuck other girls. One day he tells me he is going to Israel and he leaves.

I take Amantha and visit a friend in the country—in Vermont. Woods, hills, mountains, old houses, old bridges. Jeanne is patient; she listens to me. She's divorced from her husband, quit the city with her 5-year-old daughter and came to Vermont to live a "natural" life. She tells me to divorce him. I know I should. I know it cannot get any better. He treats me like a rag, but I still love him and need him and want his body and his face. I tell Jeanne that I'll start divorce proceedings, but when I get back to New York I can only feel disappointment because there is a single post card from him, nothing more. He's my husband; why doesn't he write?

I am still the victim. I can hardly function as a mother, but somehow I get Amantha fed and clothed and to the doctor. But I cannot make it through the day without pills. Instead of Cocaine, I'm now on Valium. My depression deepens. Why can't he have a family? I try to psychoanalyze him. His father was a shit, and maybe he's afraid of a family. Maybe he can get help. Maybe a psychiatrist... Maybe... maybe... maybe... After six weeks with only one post card, I go to a lawyer to start divorce proceedings. I write to him to tell him, and two weeks later he is home.

When he was away, I'd re-dyed my hair blonde and started wearing miniskirts. I'm looking very sexy when he arrives and I can see his eyes light up. He embraces me, rips off my clothes and we make love.

The aching feeling in the gut is gone. It doesn't matter how many times your head tells you that the marriage can't work, that I'm being mistreated. But the heart refuses to let go. At night, I'd sometimes think of him with other girls and my guts would knot up. I'd listen for the sound of the mail in front of the door... hoping for a letter from him.

We are a family again. He tells me he has to become a Jew and that I'll have to convert. I don't know what to say. He says I have to see a Rabbi. I agree, but put off the decision... I do not really want to become a Jew. It would not be a true conversion... I cannot forget the church and the fear; and I tell Jesus that if I do convert it is only the outside and I won't forget him. I take a piece of paper and write it down and hide it away...

But again, it is up and down. One day we are a family, a Jewish family to be, the next day, Richard is moody... his eyes scan the street for women... One day religious, the next day, who knows... One day Kosher, the next day not.

I see a rabbi in Brooklyn who asks me if I really want to become Jewish. I tell him I don't know, but I don't want to lose my husband. He tells me about all the obligations a Jew must fulfill, all the commandments, and that without a burning desire, they will only be a burden, a source of unhappiness and not a source of joy. He gives me a book to read and says I should contact him when I feel surer.

At home I bake bread the way his mother baked, and I keep the kitchen kosher... But it is clear that Richard is troubled, that it's not working... but neither of us is willing to face a permanent split. At least when he is there, there is no knot in the stomach, not the awful emptiness and loneliness, and so I go through the motions of buying kosher food and reading the book the Rabbi gave me.

Richard starts drawing again, but he is also smoking a lot of pot. Each day he is high. He visits his friend who has a studio in the East Village and I know there are girls there... always girls. I take more Valium... and also start smoking pot. It is the only way to drown out the fear, the loneliness, the inevitable.

Amantha is adorable. She looks more like him than like me... dark... I concentrate on her.

Richard wants to be religious; he talks about it. About the Torah, about God, about fulfilling the commandments, about the soul and the world to come. But he is too weak when he is with his friend—I can't even write his name—a Jewish friend, but a sensualist. He breaks down. He is influenced by the environment and he succumbs. All his religion vanishes... Richard has to surround himself with religious people or he will fall. And he falls. I know he is sleeping with other girls, and I dull my mind with pot.

One night he is away all night and when he comes back he smells. He starts crying and crying and crying... sobs and screams. He'd been with his friend and they'd gone to an orgy at some producer's house; he'd slept with two girls, and now he was sick and guilty and he holds on to me... But I'm starting to lose feeling... I am feeling disgusted and I know it is all ending. Yet I've invested so much in the family that I do not leave. I think of Amantha and put all my efforts into Amantha. Like a robot. I feed her, I smoke pot; I go to work. I come home and pick her up at the nursery. I shop.

We are married, but we no longer have a marriage. He is there sometimes and sometimes he is not. I try not to care. I take more pills. I play with Amantha. I touch objects and stare at them—a vase, a lamp, a typewriter—to keep me fastened to the earth. My guitar saves me. I cannot perform in public anymore because I am too depressed to even pretend to be happy, but at home I can play those beautiful melodies and cry. At least when I cry I am alive. I will not go crazy. Maybe Richard will, but not me.

One day he starts screaming at me again. "You let me treat you like a dog. Why do you let me?" And he grabs his head between his hands and starts crying, but when he looks at me there is hatred. I am too nice and, thus, I am hated. He has to take his suffering out on something, and it is me. Suddenly he leaps up from the floor and grabs me by the shoulders and starts shaking me until I become afraid, and he finally begs my forgiveness.

He is hugging me now, "Please hold me... I'll be better... Just convert. Please convert... We'll have a Jewish home... We'll live by Jewish law... We'll bring God into our marriage. You'll see, everything will be fine. You will? You will? Please, please I beg you... please."

I agree and go to the rabbi again. He tells me it will take about six months to convert. In my heart I know it is false. My background is too strong. I am afraid of Jesus, of being punished, of betrayal... But I cannot let go. I start to read the book and there is a logic to it... but in spite of the fact that I haven't thought about God in years and years I am afraid to let completely go. I just want my husband and a family.

Richard seems happy that I am going to the rabbi. He starts putting on *tefillin* in the morning and going to shul on the Sabbath. And then he stops putting on *tefillin* and he vanishes. I find out that he has gone with a sexy girl to Cape Cod.

Richard disappears. I'm numb now and I don't care. He's staying at his friend's place, sleeping with the girls there. It's sad. He doesn't even come to see Amantha. I start looking at other men, but most of them seem stupid and callous.

Sometimes he shows up at home to paint. Painting saves him. He is always able to get up early and work. Without creating, Richard is finished.

I write poems, play guitar and hug my daughter, but I am starting to become crazy. He, too, is becoming crazy and it is one insanity against the other, creating an unbelievable nightmare. There is no will to get out of bed in the morning. If it were not for Amantha I would stay in bed and wither away.

Not only does Richard reject me, but he rejects Amantha too. He won't look us in the eye when he speaks. There is shame there. I ask him why he acts as he does and I receive no answer. All he says is "You annoy me."

One afternoon we are walking in the street and he beats me. He can get very violent. He's falling apart. Here is a boy who was so soft, so kind, becoming a monster.

Later in the cafe, a young man from Minnesota comes in and smiles and I smile back. His hair is a bit long but he has a healthy clean-cut look... blonde, blue eyes, sturdy... the opposite of Richard. Mark is a sculptor and I wonder if he is not another crazy artist, but when he smiles he seems so calm, so sane, so warm. It is a slow night in the Four Winds and when he invites me to come back to his place "to see my large etchings" I take off early and go with him.

He has an apartment on Hudson Street, not far from the White Horse, where he hangs out. Part of me is nervous, but part of me feels that this is right. I need a defense against Richard; I need someone to love me before I am destroyed.

His sculptures are sturdy like he is and I can sense that he is a little nervous too, which I like. His hands are all over me and we are falling onto the bed, and I just hold him and feel his hardness and I cry and I come and I...

Richard has gone to Brooklyn to the home of a Lubavitch rabbi to become a religious Jew. He writes me a letter. "I beg your forgiveness for all the evil I've done to you. If you wish, we could live in peace, harmony and love, following the laws of God and the Torah. We will go to Israel, the three of us and begin anew. Richard." I cry when I read the letter, but it is too late. I had met Mark. Richard had destroyed the love I had for him. It could not come back.

Because I do not Hope to Turn/ Repentance

RICHARD 1969

Sometimes I want to get on my hands and knees and crawl home to Kelly. But I cannot. My soul must do what God requires. I'm a Jew. I must obey the commandments of the Torah, no matter what my heart wishes. And a Jew cannot be married to a goy and produce non-Jewish children. This is against God's law. I love her, I love her. I love her. I love her and Amantha. I cry when I think of Amantha's sweet, pouting, loving face. But I can never see them again. If I see them, my resolve will be broken: I will go back to them and suffer the torments of a soul taking the wrong path.

I am living in Brooklyn in a small room in the house of a Lubavitch rabbi, *Rav* Weinberg. Three times a day I go to a *minyan* in shul, sometimes at 770 and sometimes in a small *shtiebel*. The rest of the time I learn—classes in Torah, Talmud, Tanya, *Halachas*. I try to concentrate on the classes, but too often my thoughts stray to Kelly and Amantha. Will I ever be able to break the hold that Kelly has on me so I can marry again? Will I meet a pretty, Orthodox Jewish girl? I know myself too well. My heart struggles with the head. If I marry a plain, wonderful soulful, but not pretty, religious girl, the heart will yearn. If I go back to Kelly or marry another beautiful goy or non-religious Jew I will be unhappy. The head will know that I am living a lie.

Coming back from Israel this August I sat down next to the most beautiful girl I have ever seen. She told me that she was engaged to a Frenchman in Washington D.C. and was on her way to see him. Sitting next to her I longed for her, her facial and sexual perfection. Yet even if I could have won her I would suffer the torments of disobeying God and His Torah.

We are taught that the nine months in the womb is a preparation for our 80 years on earth. Similarly, these eighty years are a preparation for the infinitely longer world to come. What we do on this earth determines how we will spend that time. There is perfect justice. If punishment or reward do not come in this life it will come in the next.

I have completely stopped looking at women. I sleep, eat, pray, learn and never leave the streets of Crown Heights. This is my second attempt to become a religious Jew, my second sojourn at *Rav* Weinberg's.

Six months ago, I left Kelly, both of us screaming at each other. I felt only blackness. My chest and stomach tight with unbelievable anxiety. Where would the strength come from to leave what I loved more than anything in the world... my wife and child. I could no longer go on. Only drugs kept the anxiety and the conflicts from destroying me, but the drugs, in turn, were destroying my body.

I wanted to be a Jew, to follow the laws of God, yet my heart wanted to be with Kelly and Amantha. I was split in two until it all burst and I collapsed in the street unable to go on anymore. I made it to *Rav* Weinberg, who took me in, but I was restless, not yet committed to a life of full devotion to Torah. My eyes still looked at the women, but not only with lust. I had become obsessed with the idea of finding a Jewish wife and making a Jewish family. The first mitzvah in the Torah is "Be fruitful and multiply." A Jewish man fulfills that mitzvah when he has a Jewish son and daughter.

I started dating, but all the women I met were either beautiful without souls, or soulful and religious without beauty. Dating made me more and more depressed and I missed Kelly and Amantha.

One day I was coming back from Manhattan on the subway when a tall girl with incredible legs walks onto the train ahead of me. I stare at her and she gives me a friendly look, the trace of a smile and an invitation with her eyes. I speak to her... something banal. She replies. Her name is Laura. She's Italian, but she knows everything about Judaism. She'd lived with an Israeli. There isn't a *shiksa* in New York who hasn't lived with a Jew.

Her smile is warm, friendly. She gives me her phone number. Back in Brooklyn I think only of her. Thoughts of her body possess me; all my Torah learning is distant. This is why one mustn't make the first step, not with the eyes, not with the feet. I see her the next day after she finishes her job. The second she appears I am lost. Her body is so powerful, so beautiful, that I have no resistance.

She is afraid… a Jew and a goy… a religious Jew, a relationship that can lead nowhere. She says that she always falls for men like me and it always turns out badly. I pretend that she can become Jewish. Maybe she will convert. After meeting so many unattractive girls, here is a beauty, a body and, perhaps a soul.

Deep down I know it is no good, but I am no longer in control.

We end up in her apartment on the upper West Side. Her body is even better than I imagined—perfect legs, ass, muscular, athletic. We finish with me coming on top of her and she unsatisfied. I am afraid to enter her but after a year of celibacy I have reached my limits. Laura says that she has been five months without sex and is going crazy. She must have me. Next time there will be no holding back. There is no more talk about Judaism or conversion. It is all sex.

A few days later I take the subway to her apartment like a man condemned to death. She opens the door. I enter; she sits on the couch. I can only fall against her; my desire is so overwhelming. So are my fears and my guilt. An observant Jew in the home of a goy about to have intercourse. There is also the fear of sickness… gonorrhea, syphilis.

We are in her bedroom where she gives me a condom. In spite of my incredible desire I can hardly function. Nerves and fear are preventing it from growing, but eventually I enter her and come immediately.

I sense an awesome emptiness, a dislocation. I am no longer me. I am fear. I have sinned. There is no me, only a sense of doom. In a bed in a strange apartment with a strange girl. *Yamulkah* and *tzitzis* discarded. I am unreal.

I get up from the bed and walk into the bathroom. The condom is off. Did it fall off inside her? Could I have gotten a disease? Fear grips me. I had no pleasure; she had no pleasure. She will search for someone else, while I try to grope my way back.

She has gotten out of bed, and her magnificent legs and ass walk towards the bathroom. We pass each other and say nothing. I dress, uncomfortable, embarrassed, guilty. She comes out of the bathroom wrapped in a robe. "Goodbye," I say sheepishly, and leave.

In the street I feel dirty. I must go to a *mikveh*. Maybe I can wash away my stain. Scarlet shall turn to white, as it says in the Yom Kippur prayers. In the subway I shut my eyes, feeling only the urgent need to get to the *mikveh*.

The *mikveh* is in the basement of a Yeshiva. A long row of old, worn, silver aluminum wash basins with containers for the ritual washing of hands. Outside of a door a boy in black *yamulkah* and long *payus* is collecting one dollar from each person entering. Inside are rows of wooden benches with hooks on the wall to hang clothing. There are about a dozen men in various stages of undress, most with beards, some with *payus*, a few clean shaven. They are all pot-bellied or skinny. No athletes sitting in the Yeshiva or kollels.

I take a towel, undress, go into a shower and then walk down the steps into the pool. The water is surprisingly very hot. I stand with the water up to my chest, shut my eyes and whisper to God, "Please forgive me my sins and purify my soul." I duck seven times under the water and leave the bath. I wonder if my soul has been cleansed. I don't feel any different. I lack that faith, which can accept that everything comes from God. No matter what happens, it is good. Instead I am only thinking of venereal disease.

And so begins two months of torture. Burning in my penis, swollen lymph glands, burning eyes, arthritic-like symptoms. Two months living in a nightmare of fear and guilt. Visiting the doctor and being tested for every disease known to man. I wait for the results but am afraid to call the doctor and learn my fate. I'm allergic to antibiotics and if I've caught anything I'm lost. My punishment.

I can't take being alone anymore, and one day on the verge of cracking up I tell Rabbi Weinberg the whole story. He calmly calls the doctor and hangs up. "All the tests are negative," he says. I cry from relief.

I vow never to sleep with a woman outside of marriage again. During the following weeks my desires disappear. I have conquered them. I am free.

Although there is no desire there is guilt and fear of God. The pressure in my chest is unbearable and it doesn't go away for weeks. I feel that my soul is scarred. I have deliberately sinned, opposed the Torah, and the anguish and anxiety are intolerable.

I pray and tell God that my soul, which had been in the mud, is becoming pure. I want only God's light, to be taken to the light. Over and over I repeat, "I am purified. I have a pure soul. I am a sinner, but I repent... I repent. I want the angels to take me to the light. My soul is now purified." The pressure in my chest diminishes.

There is no running away from God's law. Every mitzvah brings you nearer to God, especially when done with joy while for every sin there is punishment or suffering. In Judaism, the word for sin, "avera", means "off the mark." As you break the laws, the soul goes further away from God, from its source, from true happiness, from its purpose for being in the physical body, which is nearness to God. After all, God breathed his essence into us. The punishment is alienation. So God makes corrections in this life or the next. We suffer, so that soul can return to the correct path. But, too often, we are lost and don't know which is the right way to act. We make bad choices.

There is a need within us for perfection, for purification. But we are frail. David tried to emulate Ramakrishna and become an instant saint. It drove him to the brink of insanity. In Judaism we learn to do one mitzvah at a time. Too many returnees try to do things too fast. I fit into this category.

I need God. I need Kelly. But I can only have one. You can't be in two places at the same time... an observant Jew deliberately breaking Jewish law. Decide. Kelly is pleasure, sexual pleasure, female pleasure, comfort. But I cannot defy God. I knew I had to leave Kelly, but I kept hoping against hope that she would become Jewish. I dreamed up all kinds of supernatural events... A voice from Heaven, a burning bush. You can change a person's appearance, but not the soul.

During my last days with Kelly I remember leaving the apartment and joining David at the Caffe Reggio, the little cafe on MacDougal Street. A short-haired Italian waitress wearing black tights and a black sweater takes our orders, a cappuccino for David, tea for me. Half the tables in the cafe are filled, most of the customers with drawn looks, winter sniffles, hoping the coffee or tea will revive them, add some life, some interest, some hoped-for meeting. The winter light illuminates the dark Renaissance paintings on the wall. David is leafing through a small volume of T.S. Eliot's poems. There is more of David's writing on each page than there is print.

"It's interesting," says David, "Eliot became a Catholic. Look, in 'Ash Wednesday' he writes,

> *'Because I do not hope to turn again,*
> *Because I do not hope*
> *Because I do not hope to turn*
> *Desiring this man's gift and that man's scope*

I no longer strive to strive towards such things.'"

The words strike too close to home.

When I come back to the apartment and see Kelly, lovely Kelly, I know I am living a lie and I decide I must overcome my weakness, my lust for Kelly, my love for Amantha—and do what my soul was destined for—and become a Jew. But I don't have the strength. I am afraid that instead of finding God I will only find loneliness and emptiness. My soul feels empty.

It is a second meeting which triggers the final break.

At a friend's home—he has an interesting visitor. A man about 30, black skullcap, stocky, clear blue eyes. An Israeli named Dov. His story is fascinating. He was an officer in the Israeli army in 1965. Inadvertently, he entered a room where some of his men were holding a séance, communicating with dead spirits even though this is forbidden in Jewish law. A glass was in the center of the table and the 22 letters of the Hebrew alphabet were placed in a circle around the glass. The glass moved, unaided, to the different letters, writing a message. At first, he didn't believe it, because he was not religious and didn't believe in life after death. He asked the people to move away from the table to prove they weren't manipulating it. The glass continued to spell out words. The first spirit was a soldier who had been killed in the Sinai campaign of 1956. He said that he was being punished and had to wander from place to place, back and forth without rest for 240 years.

One of the soldiers was surprised because he knew that the law stated, if one died fighting for the Jewish people then the evil judgment of the Heavenly Court was removed. The spirit said that he was being punished for sleeping with another man's wife and for not keeping Shabbat.

A second spirit came and spelled out his name. Dov was shocked. It was his best friend, Motti, who had been killed in a cross border anti-terrorist raid about a year earlier. Dov asked Motti when the next war would break out. Motti said in June 1967. And what would happen to the 12 men in the room? Motti said they would all die in the war.

Dov was very skeptical since he knew he would be out of the army in March of that year. He did, in fact, leave the army in March, but when the Six-Day War broke out in June he was called up again into the same squadron. During the war, nine of the people from the séance group were killed. He and the other two were riding in a jeep in the Sinai when an artillery shell struck them. His two companions died and he died, too.

He was floating above his body and was being drawn into a bright, white light, an incredible luminescence. As he watched his body below, he had a feeling of being pulled irresistibly towards this white light, a sensation of relief, of love, of joy. But Dov had recently married and had a baby daughter and he didn't want to die. He asked this wonderful force out there to return him to his body so he could be with his wife and daughter. Then his grandfather—who had been a great *Tzaddik*, a great rabbi—appeared and told him that everything would be all right.

He returned to his body, the medics picked him up, drove him to a mobile hospital where an operation was performed and he lived. After the war he went to a rabbi and spent all day and night talking to him. The next day he bought *tefillin, tallit, tzitzit,* and *mezzuzas* and became an observant Jew. He has come to Brooklyn to have an audience with the Lubavitch Rebbe.

His story shakes me up—the glow of the afterlife, the beautiful light, but also the punishment for not obeying commandments. The idea of a spirit wandering for a specific amount of years was strange. Doesn't the spirit world live outside of time?

The Kabbalah explains that there are four worlds, the world of action, transformation, creation and the upper world. The upper world is beyond time and space. In the world of action, our physical world, there is no place for spirits. However, in the other two worlds, spirits exist, and they can still be bound to time.

When I heard his story I was seized with fear of God, with a fear for the punishment of my soul. I could no longer hide it from myself. That night I left home.

In the book, *Out of the Night*, Jan Valtin, a leading Communist agitator in the 1920's and 30's, describes his agony as he realizes that the communist and Stalinist ideal, for which he had dedicated his life, was phony, and he was really working for brutal and power- hungry men. Thousands of his comrades had died for the cause, and he has sacrificed his own beloved wife and five-year-old son for the Comintern and Stalin's Soviet Union. Trying to hold on to his belief, he quotes Lenin, Marx, Engels, Hegel and elegies to Stalin, yet he realizes that he has been living a lie and he has given up his wife and child for nothing, for emptiness. I am giving up my wife and child for Judaism, for an ideal. What is the difference between Jan Valtin and me? Only that his ideal was man-centered while mine is God-centered. God rules the universe with perfect justice and perfection. Any man-created 'ism' has got to be flawed; it is not something one sacrifices one's family for. But for God and the sake of the soul it must be done.

Then why Judaism? Why not Vedanta, Buddhism, Theosophy, Christianity, etc? With all these religions I could stay with Kelly and Amantha. I know the answer. I am a Jew and the Jewish soul can only be elevated and fulfill its destiny through the path of Torah. I have no choice.

A few days later I am talking to Rabbi Sharabi who tells me a story about his rebbe from Morocco who would walk up to a tree and put his hand out. A bird would jump on his hand and the rebbe would put the bird in his pocket. He saw this happen several times before he asked the rebbe why he was doing this. The rebbe said the bird asked to be taken home and killed with a kosher knife and prepared for a kosher meal in order to free the soul which had entered the bird for the purpose of correction.

Nachman of Breslov believed that the only authentic religious life is produced by the most desperate struggle with the self. He believed that one needs to talk to God, pour out one's soul to God because, as it is written in the Psalms, "God is close to all those who call upon Him, to all those who call upon Him in truth."

He writes that *Tzaddikim* constantly talk to God, and their conversations allow them to soar higher and higher from one level to the next. This appeals to me. I start conversations with God. I cry. I tell Him of my pain, my conflicts, of Kelly and Amantha. I want to feel enveloped, safe. The Torah tells us that we are a holy people, a separate people, a nation of priests, and our path is different from the other nations.

I am crying in my cellar room; my tears fall. Does God hear? Instead of going to learn, I take a train to Manhattan. The women there are so beautiful, feminine and available. Again, I'm torn between the holy, the *halacha*, and the desires of the flesh. I must move one way or the other. Staying in the middle is a nightmare. Either have one's mind on Torah and never look at women with lust, or sleep with someone. But I can't seem to move off center. I'm pulled in two opposite directions and like a man tied to two horses I'm about to be ripped apart.

I meet Sarah at a Lubavitch lecture. She's a convert, blonde, sexy, a dancer. We end up in a room together and we do not comport ourselves as religious Jews. Nor do we have sex, but I come on top of her. And as I do, the words of Nachman haunt me, "Through the loss of seed, the murder of countless souls takes place. Souls who might otherwise develop into precious children. This also delays our long-awaited redemption."

But what do we do if we can't find the right wife? Never have sex?

I don't think Sarah would make a good marriage partner. There's a coolness in her. I need warmth, loving, a pure soul. When she leaves, I feel empty and guilty. I've plunged again.

In the home of the Lubavitch Hasidim one finds only religious books and pictures. No radio, TV, novels... as little as possible to bring in the outside world and its temptations. How much of my past should I cut away because of my return to Judaism? Does one throw away every picture, every letter and cut off communications with all non-Jews, with all women, artists, with Kelly and Amantha, my non-Jewish child?

I want to marry a religious Jewish girl, have Jewish children, lead a Jewish life but I am also drawn to who I was. I cannot eradicate my past, my personality. Or can I?

I know if I even look at Kelly, I will fail and give up the Torah path. I am too weak. Her beauty, smile, personality will overwhelm me. I'm afraid to call Amantha in case Kelly answers the phone. We'll talk and then become linked again. Ten words from her mouth can bring me to my knees. So I must keep away.

SHABBAT. A small Lubavitch shul. I am called up for an *Aliyah*. As I step down I see the faces of young men with *payus* and black *kippahs*, bearded rabbis leaning over the Torah scroll—faces linked to God. Suddenly my whole body starts to burn, to become warm from the top of my head to my toes. I experience an incredible peace, as if God is touching me. This is the first time in my life I've ever had this sensation.

I stay rooted to the spot. I can't move. My body continues burning, tingling with a warmth and a feeling of joy, of peace, of being one with God. It is like a taste of the world to come. Total tranquility; a taste of eternity.

The feeling lasts for hours. I'm part of the world but not really here.

Shabbat lunch with a Lubavitch family. I make conversation, but I am in a different world. Such a feeling of happiness. The beautiful deep-eyed, pale children at the table stare at me, the "Ba'al Teshuva," the repentant.

I leave the family but cannot go back to my room. Instead I walk the streets with this unusual feeling of other-worldliness. My soul is somewhere else—on a higher plane.

This feeling lasts for hours, and then a beautiful girl with an incredible ass walks by and the bubble bursts and I am on earth again.

Today my teacher quoted from the Alter Rebbe, the founder of Lubavitch Hasidim. The Rebbe said we are so small and God is so great, so how can we relate to such awesome power? In his mercy, God gave us the Torah and mitzvahs which tell us what to do, what He wants of us. God and Torah are inseparable.

Moshe Chaim Luzzatto, the Italian Kabbalist, said that men cling to evil ways because they see evil as if it were goodness, and good as if it were evil. They find all kinds of rationalizations for evil, which brings them to the point of destruction.

I started to paint and. I drew the deep beautiful eyes of one of the boys in the synagogue. Then another face and another... The Torah scroll, the candles, the *bima*, the old men with long gray beards. After two hours of drawing I wondered how I could have cared for anything else.

So why do we suffer? Luzzatto explains that man does many evil acts and continually breaks the law, encouraging God to destroy the world. Instead, in his mercy, he takes the souls which are predominantly good but have committed bad acts and he punishes the person. This saves these souls, so that in the next life they can reap their reward. Evil people, who have done a few good deeds, He rewards in this world in proportion to their good deeds and then destroys their souls. Of course, there is also merit from parents, grandparents, past lives, etc. The final outcome is balanced and just.

We cannot understand God's ways. A story comes to mind. Chaim is a poor struggling tailor living in country A. Country A goes to war against country B, and because Chaim has a friend in the war ministry he gets the contract to make the uniforms for the now enlarged army. When the war ends, Chaim is a millionaire. We look at it like this: country A went to war against country B and Chaim became a millionaire. In God's view it may be different: God wanted to reward Chaim and make him a millionaire, so He made country A go to war against country B.

There is also a Hasidic tale about a man Yankel, who had a terrible life of suffering. His wife was a vixen, his children misbehaved; He was unable to make money and feed his family and was continually ill. Yankel had reached the end, and so he went to the rebbe and said he wanted to kill himself because of all the suffering. The rebbe shuts his eyes to think about the problem and while the rebbe is meditating Yankel falls asleep. In his dream he sees himself standing before the Heavenly Court. Behind the judges is a huge scale. The chief judge says, "Yankel, to determine where you will spend eternity we will weigh your bad deeds and your good deeds." The judge signals, and a large door opens and hundreds of white angels fly out and land on one side of the scale. "Your good deeds," says the judge. Yankel smiles. He never knew he had done so many good deeds. "And now for your bad deeds," says the judge. Another huge door opens and hundreds of black angels fly out and land on the other side of the scale. The scale slowly goes down and soon the bad deeds outweigh the good deeds. Yankel is sweating with terror and fright.

Then the voice of the judge calls again, "and now for your suffering." A third door opens and gray angels fly out and alight on the scale along with good deeds. Slowly the scale starts to change its balance as the gray angels push the scale down. The scales become almost even, with the bad deeds just slightly outweighing the good ones. Yankel is sweating and sweating. He begins screaming, "More suffering, more suffering, more suffering..."

Yankel wakes up. The rebbe opens his eyes and says "So, Yankel let's discuss your problem."

"No, no, no," says Yankel, "everything's fine," and he jumps up and runs out of the house towards his home.

Our sages teach us that everything is for the good, everything comes from God and that everything is God. There is no separate existence from God. To make our lower material world God contracted his energy and the material gives us the illusion of separation. It is not what happens to us that is important, but how we handle it. This idea is similar to other religions and positive thinking approaches. But we Jews have the additional task of doing mitzvahs, Torah commandments. This is our special closeness, our special holiness, our special burden.

It seems impossible. Try to grasp the idea that the world of pleasures, of the senses is here *only* to enable us to fulfill the aim of learning Torah and doing mitzvahs. Life upside down.

The nights are lonely. Images of Kelly's body control my thoughts. The impurities from all my past lusts for women are like an anchor preventing me from climbing spiritually.

I try to replace the images of Kelly with holy images. There is Rabbi M., his eyes on fire, his face glowing, walking with his children on Shabbat. There is the Western Wall in Jerusalem with *tallis*-clad men praying.

And then there is Kelly's face and body and I am lost. But I will not crawl home. A 14th-Century rabbi in Spain wrote "a little light casts out much darkness." Destroy the evil impulse just a little bit, that terrible space between the head and the heart and it will allow the holy point in every Jewish heart to expand. A little progress can go a long way.

Tonight, I am again reading Rabbi Luzzatto:

> *Our sages of blessed memory have taught us that man was created for the sole purpose of rejoicing in God and deriving pleasure from the splendor of His Presence; for this is true joy and the greatest pleasure that can be found. The place where this joy may be truly derived is the World to Come, which was expressly created to provide for it; but the path to the object of our desires is this world, as our Sages of blessed memory have said (Avoth 4:21), 'This world is like a corridor to the World to Come'. The means which lead a man to this goal are the mitzvahs...*

In the subway waiting for a train to Brooklyn I see a very sexy girl leaning against a post. I stare at her even though I know I shouldn't. Just beyond her is a Hasid with *payus* and beard, composed. I look at him, then at the girl. The two parts of myself symbolized in stark contrast. Who am I?

At a lecture today, the rabbi said "we were created to have pleasure in God." I walk the streets repeating the phrase, "created to have pleasure in God." There is no other way to find happiness or fulfillment. Judaism is a religion of joy. Why can't I attain it?

Back in my room I take out my paints and start to paint holy faces, the faces of Shabbat. Deep-eyed, gray-bearded men in prayer shawls... young, soft, sweet looking pale faces of boys with *payus*.

After I finish painting I put some music on the record player. Joan Baez's "Plaisir d'Amour" followed by the Stanley Brothers and Flatt and

Scruggs bluegrass, some Leadbelly blues... Mississippi John Hurt's "Ain't nobody's dirty business how I treat my baby, nobody's business but mine," and finally Hair—"This is the dawning of the Age of Aquarius." While the folk music lifted me up, Hair makes me feel uneasy. Too many memories of drugs and orgies and near insanity. I stop the record and replace it with a Mozart horn concerto, lie down and fall asleep.

In *shul* I meet a kindred spirit, an interesting young man with dark piercing eyes. Jeremy has a beard, payus, large white Yamulkah, huge *tallis*, brown robe, a Breslov Hasid, thinking about God, Nachman of Breslov and California blondes. He tells me he grew up in California on the beach, watching the perfectly shaped blonde girls and lusting after them. Now that he has become a religious Jew it is difficult for him to marry; he still is attracted to that California beach girl type, but he also wants a spiritual Jewish religious girl. In L.A. he was being driven crazy by loneliness and conflict, until he finally went to a small Breslov community in New Mexico.

"Only there do I find peace. There are no temptations—only stark, beautiful nature and holy people. But when I come to the city, like now, desire reasserts itself. Everyone in the New Mexico community is an artist, a writer, a musician, a hippy. All finding our way back to truth, to Torah. You must come—take your paints, your *siddur* and join us." Nachman appeals to people with passion and artistic qualities. He understands the dark side of our nature, but also shows us how to get close to God. "It's the ultimate high," says Jeremy.

I ask Jeremy how he became religious. "It had to do with my grandfather and a *minyan*" he tells me. "We lived in New York before we moved to California. I was very young and my grandfather suffered a heart attack. It was in January, a freezing, cold January. The doctor came and told him to stay in bed and that they would take him to the hospital the next morning. He lay in bed that night and he could hardly breathe. The next morning, he hears a voice from the street, 'Yisrael, we need one more for the *minyan*... Yisrael, we need one more for the *minyan*.' My grandfather never missed a *minyan*. He got out of his bed, a man who had just had a heart attack... My mother and father tried to stop him. But he went out the door, and as soon as he hit the freezing cold weather, he died. We went to California. I hung out on the beaches, hungered after the beautiful girls, but I never forgot his story... and when I met a Breslover Hasid in Los Angeles—he had come from Israel—I knew what I had to do and who I was."

He is returning to the Breslov community in two days and says I should come with him. But I need to get married. I can't take the loneliness. In New York I have a much better chance of meeting an attractive Orthodox Jewish girl than I would in New Mexico.

Jeremy agrees and disagrees. "Your future wife and you were part of the same spiritual entity and were separated at conception. That's why we have this natural urge to look for our soul mates, and all the problems, distractions, frustrations impeding this search are what causes so much of our confusions, and sexual and psychological problems. If it's your destiny, you'll meet your wife in the middle of the Sahara Desert."

To get away from the distractions and the ugliness of New York is tempting. I could grow better spiritually in New Mexico. I decide to ask the Rebbe. He will tell me what to do about New Mexico, Kelly, Amantha, marriage, painting, Chabad, Breslov. Whatever advice he gives me I will follow. We are in a maze trying to find our way out, but we cannot. A Rebbe sees the twists and the pathways. Unlike most psychics, he is imbued with holiness in all aspects of his life. Thus, his advice comes from a pure source, a Torah source, a God source.

I leave Jeremy and his deep burning brown eyes. It is evening. The Brooklyn streets are busy with people coming home from work and going shopping. Tomorrow I will call the Rebbe's secretary and make an appointment. When the millions of assembled children of Israel received the Torah at Mount Sinai, they agreed to obey and listen. I will do the same.

Twilight is fading into night. I start to walk to my room, but my feet turn towards the shul at 770 Eastern Parkway. The night air is crisp as my steps tap out a rhythm. I'm a Jew. I have no choice except Torah. Inside 770 there are scattered groups of men. I step inside having made an irrevocable decision, because I do not hope to turn again.

Home at Last

KELLY 1969

I am a dirty bandage
Wrapped around screams
Of a too dull knife.

Pale rags pass
a shattered mirror
on a road called
"old"
and, God, how can
the reflecting Tired
be me, for last week
I was young.

Richard is living in Brooklyn with a rabbi and I'm living on pills. Uppers and downers. I'm addicted, but I can't stop the pain. I can barely take care of myself and here I am with a baby. There is no money, no hope, no future. The welfare check I receive is pitiful. Yeah, Kelly took that morning train, and all the mornings are gray.

Sometimes I think of going home to Alabama, but I'm sure I couldn't make 24 hours with my parents, and they'd probably take Amantha away from me like they took Tommy and Jane. At least there's Amantha, dark like Richard. If it wasn't for her I'd commit suicide and this time I'd do it right. I haven't slit my wrists in six years, a record.

Amantha is usually with me, but sometimes I leave her with an old woman in the building who likes her. I'm afraid to get involved with a man. Mark left me after he'd had his way with me for a few months. I guess he grew tired of fucking the same body. I, of course, fell in love with him and I still ache. Every morning I lie in bed longing for him, unable to get up. Amantha's cries force me out of bed, otherwise I know I'd never begin the day. How do normal people get out of bed, brush their teeth, eat breakfast, go to work every day? I wonder what it's like to be normal, to be sane. Not to ache so much.

Depression doesn't make friends, and I've lost all my old friends. The only person I see is a girl, Laura, whom I met a couple of months ago in a luncheonette. She's a motorcycle type, always in leather, and I think she's attracted to me, though she lives with her boyfriend in Chelsea. Once she came up to the apartment and started touching me and telling me what a great body I had. Her arms are like steel; I've never met a woman so strong. She sort of attracts me and repulses me.

I am walking up Sixth Avenue. At 23rd Street I turn left, pass the Hotel Chelsea. Make a right turn on Ninth Avenue and walk up a flight of stairs. Laura opens the door and I am struck by the sweet odor of marijuana.

"Oh, Kelly, a surprise. Come in."

Her boyfriend, Ken, is in the room smoking. He eyes me and says nothing. Both of them are in leather with cut-off arms showing their muscles. "Do you want a toke?" Laura asks me. I nod.

The pot calms my nerves. Neither of them says anything. Ken is looking at me. I don't like him. I'm uncomfortable. I need to break the silence.

"Doesn't he talk?" I say to Laura.

Laura eyes me. "Not much," she says.

"OK," I reply feebly.

They're both looking at me. I stand up. "Where's the little girls room?" I ask. Laura points.

I go into the bathroom and close the door. There is no lock. I sit down on the toilet seat. I want to get back to Amantha. As I open the door to leave the toilet, Ken and Laura are standing in the doorway blocking my exit. I try to walk past them but they push me inside with their bodies. Laura grabs me and throws me to the floor. I struggle but Ken whacks me across the face making me woozy and splitting my lip. "Keep quiet, you bitch," he says.

Laura grabs my dress and rips it off. I don't believe this is happening to me. She is kissing my breasts and moaning. My body is folded over the tub and from behind Ken pulls down my panties. While Laura and her steel arms hold me, he enters me from behind. There is terrible pain. I try to struggle but Laura smacks me in the face. My only thought is, how come two sadists live with each other? I have nowhere to retreat. Between Laura's blows and Ken's ramming me in the ass I am near fainting from pain.

I shut my eyes and I hear Ken moan in orgasmic pleasure. The next thing I know I am in the tub lying on my back, with a naked Laura kissing my cunt. I feel my blood and suddenly I no longer care about anything. I don't want to live any more, not even for Amantha. Maybe they are not going to let me live.

Laura's hands are all over my body. She's hitting me and screaming... and then silence.

They are gone. I live. I am lying naked in the tub, aching everywhere, unable to move. I never want to move again. I hope that they come back and kill me. There seems no purpose in continuing.

Laura comes into the bathroom and pulls me out of the tub. She takes a towel, which she wets, and wipes away the blood from my face and body. She then dresses me like a baby, finally handing me a torn raincoat to put over my old dress.

She leads me by the arm, takes me to the door of the apartment and gently shoves me out. Not a word has passed between us.

Out on the street it is dusk, usually the calmest time of day. I have decided to walk back to my apartment, take all the pills I have and lie down and die. I will leave Richard's number at the rabbi's next to my bed. He'll have to become a father. Kelly is really going home on that morning train.

On Seventh Avenue and Fifteenth Street there is singing coming from a storefront. I recognize the beautiful strains of "Amazing Grace". I look inside. The door is open leading into a small hall with about 20 people sitting in chairs. A preacher in the front leads them in the singing. "I was lost and now I'm found..." I stand on the threshold and watch.

A woman with a sweet smile is standing next to me. "Come in Sister," she says. I need to sit down, and the music pulls me in. The woman guides me to an empty seat. Many of the faces in the hall are Spanish, but there are also some street people and a few better-dressed people. The preacher, a nice looking man in his 40's, is saying, "Those who want to come to Jesus Christ and be saved please step forward."

The words hardly register, and anyway I am too weak to move. The woman is taking my hand. "Come Sweetie, let's be saved... don't miss the chance." She half lifts me from my seat and suddenly I am in the front of the room on my knees before the preacher. His hands are on my head and the tears start to flow. I am crying, out of control. Bawling. Crying and crying. Everything inside of me is whelming up. Warm arms enfold me. People are hugging me. My tears are flowing without end. At last, I am home.

American Exile

DAVID 1970

I'm working at this awful job. It's really impossible to describe except that it's clerking for the city in the rent control office. The place is total chaos all day. Nobody knows what he's doing and after a week at the job I still don't know what it's about. I'm the only white clerk there, and we all share the same miserably low wages. The job has something to do with searching out rent histories for landlords so they can comply with a new law about rent control. Everything went wrong from the beginning—a rent history sent to the wrong landlord, another placed in the wrong borough, the numbers filed wrong. Hell, half the people can't count and the other half are geniuses who would be better off doing something else. All day long, landlords are storming the place with lost, strayed and misfiled rent histories, trying to get the correct ones. They're met at the door by the imperturbable Dominic who just takes his time and is interested only in keeping the screaming landlords in order. They, the public, are the enemy and must be quieted. He and two other fellows are supposed to answer all the landlords' questions. They have less of an idea than I do about how the operation works, but they dish out the wrong answers with authority. One poor woman came back on eight different occasions trying to get the correct answer.

I sit at a desk writing numbers on a manila folder. I turn two pages and write a number, then turn two pages and write another number. I do this for eight hours a day, five days a week. It's worse than it sounds because stuff keeps piling up on my desk and I can't catch up with it. Half the stuff that's supposed to be for Brooklyn is mislabeled Queens or the Bronx. Some idiot who did the original arranging thought that BX was short for Brooklyn. I've got to arrange all the stuff in batches of 25, so they can be shipped out to the district rent offices in the different boroughs, where they can locate the rent histories, because our office can't find them.

An idiotic job, a horrible job. But worse than the job is getting to it; entering—voluntarily—the rush hour subway. Ashen, gray, unhappy people all squeezed together, stoically refraining from screaming. I have to do this on the way down and the way back. But what is even worse are the circumstances that have brought me to this job. It's supposed to be therapy. I'm seeing a psychiatrist because I've been in bad shape for the past two years. I'm suffering from anxiety hysteria which takes awful forms and has completely controlled my life, breaking up my marriage, separating me from my son, and generally making life miserable for me.

I'm swallowing Thorazine and Stelazine by the bottleful, which would keep me tranquil if it weren't for my restless mind. My mind which fights the eternal fight. Part of me wants to return to the ashram where I spent the summer, to lead the spiritual life as a monk. Another part would like to be with my wife and child again. Bit by bit I am being reduced to nothing. As the battle rages, all thought becomes unsafe: God, sex, even films and the world around me are unsafe topics. So, I close my mind until it becomes like nothing... and I become like nothing and I go to my job, return home and eat, sleep, subway, job, eat, sleep, subway, etc., afraid to think, afraid to be, hoping that the symptoms won't appear, two 45-minute sessions a week with the shrink... on and on and on to nowhere.

Sitting at my desk thinking of Serge, my beautiful son whom I haven't seen for months and don't know when I will see him again. Serge, whom everybody loves because of his special 3-year-old charm. Serge walking down the street saying "hello" to everybody and when someone doesn't reply, "fucking man not say hello." Serge playing pinball machines and slot machines in cafés in France and Denmark. Tears fill my eyes as I write this, and whenever I see a child or a mother and a child, tears automatically come. Serge and his Daddy, so close and loving, hugging each other, wrestling, kissing his stomach, making him laugh. Oh, God, I want so much to be with him and in my lonely gray exile here in America I am so far away.

I'm thinking of the time we went to the soccer game in Copenhagen, Serge, Austin and myself... Naestved was playing Bronshøj. It was raining but we went anyhow. We had to find a way to fill all the empty days, days on end with nothing to do except the *Tribune* crossword puzzle. Five of us were living in a huge farmhouse 60 miles south of Copenhagen: Kerstin, Austin, Francine, Serge and myself. Kerstin and Austin got married eventually. It started as a joke when they were living in our place in Maisons-Laffitte in France. But more of that later. We went to Copenhagen, and in a police station I got directions to the Bronshøj playing field. I drove our beat-up 1956 Opel to the field and squeezed into a parking place. Serge wasn't very happy with the rain and he complained during the whole game. Everybody guzzling beer, and from that day on, whenever one mentions a football game to Serge he would say, "and watch everybody get drunk."

Serge the comedian exaggerating his looking left and right after being told to be careful crossing streets. He turns the motions into a sort of Indian Rain Dance, which makes us all laugh, if only there were something to laugh about. I am suffering so much from my problem that I have forgotten how to laugh. Our marriage is just misery upon misery, yet we love each other and love Serge.

And so when I came back from America after unsuccessfully looking for money for a film and Francine said it was all over I cracked up and clung to her, desperately wanting her, whom I had so often wanted to be rid of before. Serge and I finally going to Majorca together on a package tour, but I am haunted by dreams of Francine and am declared mentally unstable by the Spanish government and given permission to return early. We stay, however, and Serge makes friends with a little Danish girl, while I have good days and bad. The best moments are when we take our bath together and he puts his head on my stomach.

We return to Copenhagen and I try desperately to patch up my marriage, but it is too late and I am too sick and so with my last effort I leave for the Ramakrishna Ashram in France.

A word about Kerstin and Austin: We met Austin when Bob brought him into our hotel room on Rue de Tournon in Paris. Serge was four months old and we were always looking for baby-sitters. Austin was 17 at the time and Bob had met him in Greece. He would baby-sit for Metro tickets and some canned couscous which I cooked in the room. Austin was to stay with us for almost four years until our breakup. He became my assistant on the film, a sort of general assistant specializing in finding extras, many of whom he laid, it turned out.

Well, long after the film had been made and my sickness had begun, Austin was living in our apartment along with Kerstin. Kerstin was going out with Lazlo who had also been an assistant on the film. Austin and Lazlo were big rivals. So, to get back at Lazlo, Austin asked Kerstin if she would marry him. Kerstin agreed, and that's how their affair and eventual marriage began. Austin was a fresh-mouthed 19-year-old at the time while Kerstin was three years older. They got married in the Mayor's office in Naestved. Serge cried during the short ceremony and I had to take him out.

Now they are living in England, Kerstin having had an affair with a black American while Austin was with me in America. We returned from that unsuccessful trip with me losing my wife and Austin's in love with someone else.

Austin adores Serge and vice versa. Everyone adores Serge. The greatest happiness of my life was being able to watch Serge's face while I pushed him in his carriage along the roads of Maisons-Laffitte. Days spent taking care of Serge; I was up with him in the morning while Francine, always weak, slept. Serge refusing to play soccer because he couldn't kick well enough. Walking together in the Forêt St. Germain, and when he wouldn't walk pushing him in his carriage through the woods. On the other side of the road are chickens, which we would watch hour after hour.

Thinking of badminton and spiritual conflicts. Badminton out on the lawn of the farmhouse. I was the best player, followed by Austin. We had some gruesome battles. Badminton was the great time-killer that summer. The house was always filled with guests as well as Mildred, our *au pair* girl. There was Freddie and Gerard, Kerstin, Michael, Tony and

Kyoko. The latter two causing Francine to leave home and flee to her parents—another bone of contention. Tony, shoulder length hair and beard, became the center of a furor that summer when John Lennon and Yoko Ono came to visit him in Denmark. Tony was Yoko's first husband and father of Kyoko. Francine couldn't stand him and felt he was taking over the house, so she left home saying she wouldn't return until Tony left the house. Serge and Kyoko would fight instead of play.

Part of me always wants to leave the world and enter a monastery. The ashram in France beckons. This clouds all of my waking moments and some of my sleeping ones. I am a man divided against himself. And I don't know how to stop it. At various points, the conflict comes out into the open and destroys me. It happened in Holland where Francine, Serge and I had gone to visit Leonika who baby-sat for us back in the beginning of our Paris days. Leonika lived in The Hague with her mother and sister.

Her mother ran a tobacco shop, a strange forceful woman who was later to contribute to one of the horrors of our marriage, the abortion.

Bob had introduced Leonika to us. He had seen her putting up posters for her acting group and couldn't resist her legs, so he picked her up, slept with her and then brought her to our hotel to baby-sit for us. Serge has a long list of baby-sitters and they're all a bit in love with him.

Now that I've at long last rid myself of sexual desire, I think of how much of my marriage was involved in desiring other women and how this fact lies at the root of the disaster. Of course, Francine's jealousy was excessive, which strained our relationship. Finally, the day came when she was no longer jealous and then she lost all feeling for me.

Thinking of Francine, watching her ass swaying on the steps as we walk up to our apartment in Maisons-Laffitte. Thinking of the "old Lady," Mme Foch Nielsen, a French woman married to a Dane, a member of the resistance who had been killed during the war... She was a wonderful woman, but always complaining about some ailment or another... Her house was filled with homeopathic remedies. Serge liked to visit her because he could get cookies and candy and play the piano... She would tell us about her friends, her past, her children, not suspecting that our marriage and lives were being destroyed by my sickness...

The tears again as I think of Serge—barely a year old—on the carrousel on the Boulevard Rochechouart near our apartment. He could never get enough... and two years later in Tivoli, Serge and I going from ride to ride, from animals, to airplanes, to cars, and more cars... and more cars. Serge in his paradise.

More memories of Serge sitting at the table pontificating as to the relative goodness of people. "Janet no good," he would always say about our au pair girl, Janet. "Mama OK" etc. I'd usually be OK though sometimes I'd get a "no good." If one got a "no good" one would attack Serge by saying "Serge no good." Serge would always retaliate with a "Serge OK."

Food and Serge were anathema. He just didn't like to eat. But he grew sturdy enough on milk. Until he was almost three he used a bottle which had to be refilled several times a night. One night, after being woken up once too often, I threw away his bottle. He screamed for two days but then got used to taking his milk in a glass before going to bed. That was in Maisons-Laffitte.

"Until ye turn again and become as children you cannot enter the kingdom of heaven." One day I tried to act just like Serge on the train from Naestved to Copenhagen. Francine got very embarrassed.

Francine had a favorite restaurant on Vesterbrogade where she could have some kind of chicken and watch the people go by.

I recall the train from Naestved, which I used to take so often. A Saturday trip to Tivoli with Serge, a trip to Nordisk films, a trip to see Jorgen Hansen, a shopping trip with Francine.

One day I ride the train to Copenhagen and enter a bar. On the TV screen are pictures of men landing on the moon. I am indifferent. My own pain is too great to care about even the most major events happening outside. I order a beer to dull the pain as Neil Armstrong takes the first step on the moon.

In the summer, riding the bike from Maglebjerggaard (our farm) to Naestved. Our farm was located in a small one-store town called Stenstrup. The only person we ever met was a drunken sailor named Kurt. One night at 3 am he arrived at the house with a bucketful of eels. Francine couldn't stand him, though Austin and I found him amusing. He would often come by with beer and we'd have to sneak him into the house. Since he spoke only Danish our conversation was limited.

I try not to think of those horrible nights we spent on the verge of divorce. Up all night, always going to the brink and then pulling back. Once Serge got wind of what was happening and came in to make us dry our tears. The next night he lay in bed refusing to go to sleep until we did. He was only three.

I bought Serge a large poster of Pippi Långstrumpa, the Swedish child heroine. One night, Serge is talking in his room. I listen; he is saying, "Good night Pippi Långstrumpa, Good night Pippi Långstrumpa, good night." He then puts his comic books away and goes to sleep. The next day I say to him, "You were saying good night to Pippi last night, weren't you?" Serge replies: "I not say good night Pippi Långstrumpa, I say fuck you, Pippi Långstrumpa, fuck you."

The happiest time we had together was when I was editing the film. I would go to work every day on a creative project and then come home to my wife at night. I worked daily with Claude and we did well together.

The first hotel we stayed at in Paris was filled with bed bugs. We were at Agnes Varda's when I discovered how badly bitten we were. We couldn't go back to that hotel so Agnes found us a room in a hotel near where she lived and we moved in there. Our next stop was the spare room of a French-Polish architect where we stayed a week. Then Bob found us a room in his hotel on Rue de Tournon and we stayed there for three months.

It was in this hotel where I first met Lazlo. I had advertised in the *Herald Tribune* for an actor and Lazlo came to answer the ad, not so much to act but to meet me because he had seen and liked my first film. This started a long friendship, and later when I made the film he was assistant director.

It took another two years before the film was made but Lazlo would come and eat some of Francine's great meals. I would usually lie down after eating and fall asleep for the night. We went to Holland together where we almost got the money to do the film in Amsterdam and shared the disappointment of being turned down. That was also the occasion of the first time I was unfaithful to Francine. How stupid I was. It was on Francine's birthday, or the day after.

Once I went with Colin Stewart's 17-year-old virgin friend and took him to Copenhagen so he could get laid. He was dressed in an old suit and a bowler hat and had hair down to his shoulders. We went to a couple of places in Nyhavn before arriving at "Revolution" and scoring a Swedish girl for him. He took her back to the farm and got laid for the first time. He was obsessed with sex, his virginity and the New Testament, but said he would forget about sex when he lost his virginity.

The last time I saw him was two days after the event waiting for a train in the Central Station in Copenhagen, hungering after girls.

Colin Stewart stayed with us twice. Colin is a huge red-head poet from London, a member of the Exploding Galaxy. One day we cycled the 15 kilometers to the beach and back. He was with a girl, Tove. They got undressed at the beach, went into the water and made love. Nobody batted an eye. That's Denmark.

The second time he appeared, we were in the process of almost starting a jazz night club/café in Naestved. It never came off, however. It was sort of a last gasp to get something to do in Denmark. The guy we were associated with was a violent pacifist, a former sailor named Gert. He was going to buy the house and we were to run it. Francine couldn't stand him and wasn't sure he was authentic. He never did get the money to buy the house, though he wheeled and dealed. Finally, I decided to take off on a trip to Germany and try to find money for a film. I said I wouldn't come back unless I found the money. I didn't get the money, but I came back. A hopeless search. Lonely and sick. With Tatyana in Freidberg. Up to a mountain inn to hear the local jazz band and celebrate Tatyana's engagement. Lots of beer and wurst. Strange evening. Alone in a hotel near the Railroad Station in Frankfurt... suffering.

Once the Exploding Galaxy came to France and we went down to Orléans to put on a performance. I played an astrologer in a sort of happening-dance-drama, and then showed my film. The English liked it, the French didn't.

Before we went down to Orléans, the waiter in Le Buci wouldn't let Colin and Carlos into the café. When they didn't leave he pulled a huge knife and threatened them. I felt good with the Galaxy. More like my true self.

When I think of Francine I see flaming red hair halfway down her back, a blue dress and a super figure... Chain-smoking cigarettes, fluctuating weight, hardness and understanding, softness and complaining... a contradiction. She is good and evil together, angel and devil, lover, mistress, friend, wife, enemy, mother, chick and mother again. Mother of the beauteous man-child, he of the lovely smile and the dazzling eyes.

He calls for his 'be-bye,' which is what he called his bottle.

Kenneth was another friend who visited us at Rue de Rochechouart. Kenneth was always filled with ideas for scenarios. Once we wrote a war-spy film together, an elaborate sort of James Bond affair. One day Kenneth borrowed my camera and went to America. I haven't seen him since. Francine didn't like Kenneth very much. Of all my friends she liked only Lazlo and Colin, but thought Lazlo to be a bit of a fool in his relations with women. There was some truth in this, as Lazlo became a changed character whenever he had a girlfriend. His independence and nobility would disappear, and he would kind of be led by the nose by whomever he was with. One of his girlfriends, a Swede, landed him in jail on a marijuana charge. He spent two and a half weeks in La Santé prison. The police followed this girl to his apartment and then raided. She had been connected with drugs before. At his trial he received a suspended sentence and is forbidden to enter France for five years.

Lazlo's first girlfriend was named Henrietta, a Dutch girl he found on our trip to Amsterdam for the film.

Henrietta had a lovely figure and sort of led Lazlo around, changing him completely. He ceased being fun to be with. All of his friends told him to get rid of her, but he thought he was in love. Finally, they broke up and he was his old self, until he fell for Katerina, the Swede. Now he lives in Sweden and has become very independent.

Today is a day off from work and nervous tension has gotten hold of me. It is a question of whether to live in the world and continue to fight the un-winnable and continual battles or to go to the Ashram.

In Amsterdam I bought a painting from an American painter. It depicted a prostitute, the wife, and a young man torn between the two... It was a beautiful painting and I brought it back to Francine. But naturally she didn't like it; too close to home. I would always do stupid things like that, thinking we were getting at truth.

A happy moment in the darkness. A Sunday dinner in Vordingborg with Francine and Serge. We felt like a family that afternoon. Francine drove back, scraped a car, while Serge was impossible in the back seat and I had to hit him, something I didn't like to do.

Every Saturday during the winter there would be telecasts of English soccer on Danish TV. We could see Leeds United, Wolverhampton, Chelsea, Manchester, Sunderland. Now I look at the standings in the *Times* and see the names, and it all comes back. During the fall we would see Naestved play on Sundays. Every game Austin and I attended, Naestved won. When we didn't go, they lost.

Thoughts of Serge with his hands held out to his side as if to say, "Who me?"

And Francine preparing supper with a smile on her face.

A smile.

Today there is such pain in memory: Francine and Serge. In Denmark we took the car one day with Kerstin and Austin and rode around the countryside looking at old farm houses. It was enjoyable. Serge and I holding hands walking past a farmhouse. Austin walked with us while Kerstin and Francine stayed in the car. We climb back into the car and drive on.

On the bus in Copenhagen going to a scientology session, thinking about how I would like to become an observer and not a participant in life.

Passing the jewelry stands on Boulevard St. Germain near Rue Bonaparte with Francine. Should we buy something for her?

With Serge at the zoo, wandering from animal to animal. When I broke up with Francine, Serge and I went alone to the zoo in Copenhagen. Before that, the three of us used to go together in Paris's Bois de Boulogne. Serge fed the goats and enjoyed himself a lot. There was also an airplane merry-go-round on which he could ride.

In London, shopping on Kings Road with Francine. The memory pierces me today. We buy a pair of pants for her in a men's store. Later on we buy some boots, short ones with laces. They look sexy.

After a month I quit the real estate job and go to a Vedanta monastery near Chicago. On the train I read, hoping to subdue my fears and uncertainties:

> *Man is born in this world with two tendencies—Vidya, the tendency to pursue the path of liberation, and Avidya, the leaning towards worldliness and bondage. At his birth both these tendencies are, as it were, in equilibrium like the two scales of a balance. The world soon places its enjoyments and pleasures on one scale, and the spirit, its attractions, on the other. If the mind chooses the world, the scale of Avidya becomes heavy and man gravitates towards the earth; but if it chooses the spirit, the scale of Vidya becomes heavier and pulls him towards God.*

> *People engaged in worldly activities are like a fish in a trap. They can come out of it by the way they entered, but they prefer to sport inside the trap with other fish, hear the sweet sound of murmuring water and forget everything else. They don't make an effort to free themselves from the trap. The lisping of children is the murmur of water and the other fish are relatives and friends. Only one or two make their escape by swimming away. They are liberated souls.*

I want to be a liberated soul. What other reason are we born for? Why else are we here on earth? Entering the monastery is the only logical choice.

But after two days in the monastery I realize that I'm not ready to be a monk. Everything is foreign to me, the Sanskrit terminology, the Indian dress and customs. It is all strange and I don't feel at home.

I also miss Serge so much. I think of his little face rubbing against mine. I am kissing his belly, his cheeks. I love him so much. This is an attachment I am unable to break. I think only of him, my beautiful son.

Ramakrishna says that yearning for God must be so great that you should be able to shed tears for Him. I can shed tears for my son, but not for God. The seed is not yet ripe. Perhaps later, perhaps in another life. I have too many attachments to the world. I'm a monk with my intellect, but not with my heart. I ask to see the Swami. As always, he is kind and understanding.

"I'm ready to renounce everything," I tell him, "women, fame, my work, the small pleasures of the world, but I cannot renounce my son. I love him too much."

He looks at me kindly. "You must be strong. Attachment to your son leads to other attachments. You will marry again, have two or three more children and then go through all kinds of suffering."

"I am too weak, then. I must leave. I suffer too much from missing him. Perhaps I can get over it. I will write to you."

"Go then," he says, "and when you have conquered it come back. I know you are a sincere person."

I leave the monastery and return to New York, to my indecision and fears. Perhaps I should go to Israel, after all, I'm a Jew. I try to project myself in Israel, but soon thoughts of Francine and Serge overwhelm me.

Memories of Denmark. Visiting Francine's parents who go crazy over Serge. Taking a Valium to keep calm. Both of Francine's parents are nice. Meat, boiled potatoes, gravy and a cooked vegetable for dinner. *Smørbrød* for lunch. Lots of television and walks.

Speaking of walks, I remember the beauty of Fredriksberg Park, lovely trees, ducks on the water. Read Krishnamurti the day I took off for the ashram. Kerstin was in the apartment when I got back, Francine and Serge having gone to Aarhus. We talked. It was like twilight. The end of an era.

ABOUT THE AUTHOR

A graduate of Brown University, Peter Emanuel Goldman was an award-winning filmmaker in New York and Paris in the 1960s. His films include the prize-winning *Echoes of Silence, Wheel of Ashes, The Sensualists* and *Pestilent City.* He was considered to be the only link between the American Underground and the French New Wave.

Later he became a foreign policy consultant for private organizations, think tanks, and governments.

PHOTO BY
VERA MICHAL GOLDMAN

www.ingramcontent.com/pod-product-compliance
Lightning Source LLC
Chambersburg PA
CBHW070427120726
47910CB00003B/674